SECRET OF THE RED PLANET

A NOVEL FOR TEENAGERS

BY CHRIS HAWLEY

Mirador Publishing
http://www.miradorpublishing.co.uk

FOREWORD

One evening in mid-2007 I was invited out to dinner at Pepper's Restaurant in Nairobi by my daughter and her family and friends.

I cannot remember how the conversation led to the topic but during the meal I was talking to my granddaughters, Sofia and Annamaria about the planet Mars. Their school friend Michelle said jokingly that she herself was from Mars and I said that one day I would go there to see her. That is how the story was born.

The storyteller is an ordinary English teenager, living in an unnamed but typical small town, with a dream to fly to Mars. I am not Bill and I should not be identified with him. The story takes place during July and August 2007. Events occurring in the World during this time have been brought into the story to add reality to it.

The story is of course fictional. However, the scientific and astronomical data is as accurate as I am able to make it. Information given about Mars, Earth and the Moon and their relationship and positions in the Solar System are factual. Mars has been near to opposition during the period the action takes place. I have presented the phases of the Moon and Earth as accurately as possible.

The geographical features of Mars are as faithfully described as possible. I am sure the Monuments of Cydonia actually exist. There is still heated debate about whether they are natural or they were constructed by living beings, maybe even beings from outer space. Perhaps the pyramids of Egypt and America were also built by the same beings or by humans with incredible spiritual powers.

I have drawn attention to the environmental degradation taking place on our beautiful planet and we have been painfully slow in waking up to the damage we are doing and even slower in trying to deal with it as a World community.

Perhaps there *are* extraterrestrials on Earth giving us a helping hand.

I am sure you often wonder if other inhabited worlds exist out there in the depths of space. It would not be strange if creatures similar, or perhaps entirely different from human beings, exist among the countless solar systems in our Universe. You may also wonder how it was that the ancestors of the Similarians and other human Martians living on Mars in the story came to be exiled from Earth in 11,994 BC and what kind of world they left behind. And who are these Zoggs, who threaten to invade our solar system? These questions may be answered in a sequel to Secret of the Red Planet.

As for the 'unbelievable' elements of the story, notably the Uninet, telepathic communication over immense distances, time travel and huge, Earth-crossing asteroids, I would say that anything is possible. Telepathy *was* practiced by so called 'uncivilised' peoples and I believe there are particles as yet undiscovered by humanity that exceed the speed of light. In reality there is no such thing as time, (it is a creation of the mind) and therefore in theory travelling through time is possible and may one day become a reality. And the bubbles? As Bill says in the story, there are some things in life you just do not understand and have to accept.

CHRIS HAWLEY
LAMU, KENYA
December 2010

To my four grandchildren, Ben, Sofia, Tim and
Annamaria.

PART ONE

Mars Here I Come

CHAPTER ONE
THE DREAM

I have always wanted to build a space ship and fly off into space. What a thrill to experience the 'G' force that presses you back in your seat as you hurtle up into the sky! What a thrill to see the Earth from up there, getting smaller and smaller as you penetrate deeper and deeper into the blackness! What a thrill to float around inside the spaceship, free from the effects of gravity!

Our Science teacher at school told us that it costs millions of dollars to build a space ship and millions more to sent it out into space and bring it safely back again. I was afraid what he said was true, but…….

'Only rich countries can afford to do it,' he explained to us. 'You need very strong materials to withstand the pressure and heat, and astronauts have to be trained for years to be able to man spacecraft.'

'But Sir,' I said. 'I don't have millions of dollars and I don't have the time to spend years training. I want to go to Mars now!' I had this very strange feeling that it was my destiny to go to Mars, and why wait for Destiny to make up its mind. I didn't want to go when I was a pensioner!

'Mars, is it? Well, boy,' he said, laughing. 'If you think you can build a spacecraft and go off to Mars and be back before the beginning of next term, you are welcome to try and we all wish you the best of luck, don't we boys and girls?' He looked around at the class. There was some tittering and some whispering from the rest of the class. Although I was popular at school, I had a reputation for being clever. I excelled in my exams and was always at the top of the class. For that reason I was often ragged.

'Thank you, Sir,' I said. 'If I don't make it back in time, I'll send you a message.'

He laughed again. 'From Mars? Don't forget your mobile phone. Anyway, you do that.' He was mocking me: that was obvious.

I will show him!

Now that I had the doubtful blessing of our Science teacher, my next problem was to find a place to build my space ship. In the end I decided on the wooden shed at the bottom of the garden. Dad had recently bought another shed and had erected it nearer the house. It was here that he stored his tools and other gardening equipment. Dad is a bit of a do-it-yourself fiend, which is useful because I was going to need some tools with which to make my spaceship.

What materials was I to use? Titanium was light and strong but much too expensive for a sixteen year old boy, (almost seventeen actually) on a two pounds a week pocket money. Aluminium foil was a good substitute, I decided. Mum uses a lot of the stuff and she would not miss a few rolls here and there. Dad's extra-strong glue would hold it together. Yes and those old window frames he threw out in the Spring would make an excellent frame, a bit on the heavy side though. I was beginning to get really excited. I wonder what the people on Mars will say when they see me coming!

The rocket motor was the trickiest part. To escape from the Earth's atmosphere needs a powerful thrust, and reliability was important. I couldn't afford to break downhalfway to Mars, could I? What could I use? In the end it was to be the old lawnmower motor that was going to propel me on my journey of a lifetime.

Mum was marvellous. Every time I said to her, 'Don't forget the tinfoil!' she would add it to her shopping list. I asked Dad if I could borrow his extra-strong glue and use some of the old window frames and the old lawnmower motor and he didn't even ask me what I wanted them for. But of course he had a pretty good idea.

I had a fair amount of clearing out to do in the old shed. Dad was so pleased with me for doing a job that he had been putting off for months, he even helped me with the Ford van to dispose of some unwanted things. At last I had collected all my materials together and was ready to start building my spaceship.

CHAPTER TWO
THE GOOD SHIP 'SILVER STREAK'

The long holidays had arrived. Mum and Dad were never very keen on beach holidays. Both of them always found something to do. Most of my friends were going away and it would give me time and privacy to concentrate on my dream project.

I worked like a lunatic, putting in all the hours I could. I had to help my parents sometimes but I knew that was my duty and I didn't mind. The days were long and the weather warm.

The spaceship took shape. Sometimes Dad would put his head round the door of the shed and enquire what I was doing, as if he didn't know. I would say that I was building something, which was quite obvious to anyone with eyes in their head. He was happy that I had found something interesting to do during the holidays.

After two weeks of hard work, the spaceship itself was ready. It hardly looked as good as those American ones I had seen on the television but I had made it all by myself. The inside was fitted out for maximum comfort, with a padded bucket seat that could be adjusted. Even the floor was carpeted from a piece of old carpet I found in the loft. Nor had I neglected fuel for my body. I had carefully selected all the food with maximum nutritional value. All these were stored carefully so that they would not float about once we were outside the Earth's atmosphere. I was satisfied that I would not lack any material comfort on my long journey. Our science teacher had told us that Mars was many millions of miles away from the Earth so I calculated the journey would take weeks and I doubted I would be in time for the beginning of term. Well, my experiences in space would be worth more than dry old school lessons.

The control panel was made out of several old computer keyboards, connected to the controls by metres of copper wire, which had been left behind by the electricians when they rewired the house.

All that remained was to fit the motor. I must admit that this was the hardest part of all. The motor had to be really well fixed to avoid it coming loose during the stress of blast off and re-entry into the atmosphere. I thought my steering invention was very neat. The engine was mounted on a swivel, operated from the control panel in front of me. I decided that the petrol tank was not sufficiently big to hold enough fuel for the journey to Mars, so I modified an old water container, hoping it would not be too heavy during liftoff.

I turned my attention to my space suit. I went to the library and read about what it was like on Mars. No water, the book said, and cold too. So a warm space suit was important. There was a picture in the book of an astronaut, wearing a globe on his head that looked like a fish bowl. I thought of the one standing on the shelf in the shed. I felt guilty every time I saw it and remembered killing the goldfish by overfeeding them. Why don't I wear it on my way to Mars: their old home would have a purpose in life again and they would not have died in vain? I chuckled to myself at the idea of wearing a fish bowl on my head. I might even frighten some Martians!

What to do about water? I was already taking a lot of petrol, which weighed a lot. But, I thought, all those Martians who lived there must have learned a long time ago how to make water. I would ask someone as soon as I arrived. They are very kind people, I was sure of that. Just take water for the journey and hope for the best, said the optimist in me. The pessimist in me was defeated and so that was what I decided.

Finally, the great day was upon me. The spaceship was complete and ready for testing. I used all the money I had saved from my pocket money over the past six months to buy petrol, new sparkplugs and a secondhand safety belt.

One final thing: what to call the spaceship? I pondered for an hour before coming up with a name I liked. 'Silver Streak,' that's what she'll be called! So 'Silver Streak' she became. I painted the name carefully, but not very neatly, on her side and held an emotional naming ceremony, in which I broke a bottle of sparkling mineral water against the side, as I had seen done when ships are launched. And she is a ship of sorts, I thought. 'May God protect her and all who sail in her!'

CHAPTER THREE
LAST MINUTE PREPARATIONS

'Er Dad!' I said the next morning. 'I'm off to Mars tomorrow.'

'Are you, son? Well, have a good trip!' He winked at me and gave a chuckle.

'You don't believe me, do you Dad?'

'Of course I do, son.' He smiled a knowing smile. 'Have you told your mum?'

'Not yet. Dad, do you think the people on Mars are friendly?'

'Sure to be. I bet they are more friendly than the people in this street.' My father was always critical of the neighbours. He said they were stuck-up, about what he couldn't say, because they didn't have anything to be stuck-up about. He was never afraid to express his opinion and it was not always greeted with enthusiasm by the hearer.

Anyway, his opinion of Martians really pleased me. I couldn't wait to be off.

'Don't forget to bring me a stick of rock from Mars,' was his final comment as he went out of the door. Dad was a large man in his early forties, with thinning brown hair. He often suffered with his back, and as he disappeared down the hall I could see he was having one of his bad days.

He still doesn't believe that I'm going to Mars tomorrow. But when my spaceship lifts off at 5 o'clock in the morning, he will know I was not joking. I smiled as I saw the vision of my parents at the bedroom window, open-mouthed with surprise as a spaceship disappears into the sky, trailing a stream of vapour.

I hardly slept that night; I was so excited. Well, wouldn't you be? It's not every day you set off on a journey into space.

At 4 o'clock in the morning it was getting light. I got up and, as quietly as I could, I washed and dressed. I had to laugh when I looked in the mirror at the bundle of sweaters standing there. The comedy would be complete with a fishbowl on the top!

I tiptoed down the stairs, being careful to avoid the creaky floorboards. I wrote a note and left it on the kitchen table.

HAVE GONE TO MARS. BACK IN ABOUT SIX WEEKS.
DON'T WORRY ABOUT ME. I'LL BE FINE. LOVE, BILL

As I entered the shed, I looked back at the house. There was no sign of life. I must admit I had a few misgivings about going at that moment. Would I ever return? Would I die a lonely death in the far reaches of the Universe? Would I find a beautiful Martian girl and settle down on Mars, have a dozen half-half children and live happily ever after? In that case, I would send a message to my parents and invite them to Mars for the wedding. I wonder if they would let me roam with my mobile phone as far as Mars. With that interesting thought, I set about preparing for takeoff. But wait! I forgot one thing, my digital camera. Nobody is going to believe my story unless I produce some photos. I crept back into the house and returned with the camera, which I stowed in a pocket next to the control panel.

I opened the roof of the shed and climbed into Silver Streak, buckling myself tightly into the seat. I turned on the ignition and saw the red light appear. So far, so good! I held my breath and pressed the starter button. A whirring noise and then..............the engine burst into life. The spacecraft started to vibrate and I was afraid the engine was going to come off. But the next moment there was a loud whoosh and...........Silver Streak was airborne. I gave a shout of joy. I am on my way at last! Mars, here I come!

CHAPTER FOUR
RESCUE

As soon as I had recovered from the initial thrill of liftoff, I looked out of one of the small portholes in the side of the spacecraft. I had time to focus on the little garden shed, the small back garden and the house in which I had been born and brought up. But within seconds these objects were like toys. The streets of our neighbourhood criss-crossed below me. The few vehicles making up the early morning traffic filed along like matchbox toys and I could have picked up ten of them in each hand. Soon the small town that I knew so well was just a patch of brown and gray in a sea of green. Some clouds passed me by, little fluffy summer clouds. The sun was a ball of orange in the early morning sky.

Up and up we went, Silver Streak and I. A bout of fear crept into me, like the onset of a dose of flu, but I shook it off and an undercurrent of intense excitement took its place.

The horizon took on a curved effect and looking down I could make out the coastline of England, the channel and France over to the right. To the left of me, the Atlantic Ocean lay in darkness. Still higher we rose. Above me, the sky became darker. We were leaving the atmosphere behind. The horizon was more rounded now. I could see the whole of Europe, just like the photographs taken from space that our teacher had put up on the walls of the classrooms. Dawn had not reached the coast of Portugal or the extreme West of Ireland, but as I looked North, I could just see the polar ice cap, pure white. I knew that in July at the pole the sun didn't set and it was light all night.

All of a sudden I realised that I was cold, very cold, in spite of the two sweaters and anorak that I had on. And I was short of breath, dangerously so. But Silver Streak continued on its upward journey, the engine rattling away behind me. It was then that it happened, or should I say, everything happened at once. I began to doubt the ability of my faithful craft to make it to Mars. For the first time since that science lesson, it occurred to me that the teacher may have been right after all. Maybe I was unprepared. I hadn't even had one lesson on how to fly to the planets, let alone the years of training that our teacher said we needed. Perhaps the materials I had chosen were not ideal for the task. Kitchen foil is thin, I had to admit. Was it possible that I had made a miscalculation in the choice of engine and the amount of fuel needed? Lawnmower motors were designed for cutting grass, not for propelling crazy boys into space. And which way was it to Mars? Was it up, down or sideways? Our Earth is spinning and one moment Mars is on one side of the Earth and the next moment it is on the other. All these thoughts ran through my mind. And in the middle of this jumble of thoughts, the engine spluttered and died. What was to become of me now?

At that same moment a curious thing happened. Through the porthole I saw approaching an enormous bubble, reflecting all the colours of the rainbow, just like a great soap bubble of the kind children like to blow. As Silver Streak began to falter, the bubble wrapped itself around us, so that we were entirely enclosed. And do you know what? From that moment, it was as if we were floating on a cushion of air. I no longer felt cold and I began to breathe normally. Where did this bubble come from? I did not understand it but I was grateful to be rescued in the nick of time.

I looked up at the sky again. It was completely black. The stars were incredibly clear, and there were what seemed millions of them. I could make out the planet Jupiter, larger and more distinct than the stars, the sun shining on one side of it. Mars was nowhere to be seen but I knew it was out there somewhere. The sun was a fiery ball but it did not shine like it does on Earth. I knew that it was because there was no atmosphere to reflect the light rays.

I began to feel light headed and I was surprised to find how easy it was to lift my arms and legs. Weightlessness! I loosened my seat belt and as I did so I floated out of the seat. I was careful to hold onto the belt, but I let myself float around, first up to the roof of Silver Streak and then, with the slightest push with my hand, upside down. This is fun! But don't overdo it, I told myself. Soon I was back in my seat.

Looking back, I could now see the Earth as a distinct ball, blue and brown and white. The yellowish-brown of the land stood in sharp contrast to the blue of the ocean and patches of white cloud spread out around the globe. It was the most beautiful sight that I had ever seen in my life. That is the home of the human race, I thought and how fortunate we are to have such a wonderful world! I understood why astronauts become emotional when they view the Earth from space. Was there another planet like it in all the Universe? At that moment I shed a few tears, tears of joy mixed with tears of homesickness. Would I ever see it again? Of course I would. Where had these fears come from? I had been rescued by a bubble, how and why, I had no idea. This was an adventure like no schoolboy has ever had.

We were moving away from Earth very fast now. As I watched we seemed to fly faster and faster and the planet Earth became smaller and smaller. What was propelling us? The engine was dead. What strange force was taking us further and further away from home? And where was the bubble taking me? To Mars, surely. Whatever it was and whatever the force behind it, I had complete confidence in it. There was no question; it was looking after me.

I relaxed and settled down to enjoy the ride, confident now that I was in safe hands. Time passed. I scanned the heavens, trying to identify some of the brighter stars.

It was then I saw Mars for the first time. The red planet! And red it certainly was. Way off to the side, Jupiter appeared as a misty ball. I could hardly contain my excitement as I looked spellbound at the two planets. And as I watched, Mars grew gradually larger and larger. We were heading straight for it, the bubble, Silver Streak and I.

One edge of Mars was in shadow, so that the planet seemed to have its edge trimmed off. We were approaching it at an angle, heading towards the dark side. But before we reached the line between night and day, we dropped quickly down.

Just as I was thinking that we were going to crash at great speed into the surface of Mars, I could feel us slowing down. I glanced back over my shoulder and was amazed to see how small the planet Earth looked, just a tiny ball. We must have been travelling very fast indeed. I had always believed it takes months to reach the red planet. We must have taken no more than a few hours. I tried unsuccessfully to work out in my head how fast we had been going. But now, there was no time to practice mental arithmetic. We were approaching the ground.

The landscape was carved up by ravines and there were a few small craters dotted around. The soil was red, with patches of browner colours. There was no sign of any life, just a great expanse of bare ground. It struck me as being very inhospitable, not a bit like the soft green of the English countryside. I will admit that I felt a bit homesick. Bill, stop it, I told myself. You are having the most fantastic adventure that anyone has ever had. Enjoy it!

The bubble was certainly in control. It brought us very slowly down, no parachute, nothing. Our landing was so soft, I hardly felt a thing. We were down on the ground. Now what? I sat for some moments, wondering whether I should get out of the spaceship or just sit tight and wait for the first Martians to appear, as I was sure they would. I decided to stay where I was. After all, the temperature and atmosphere inside the bubble was perfectly comfortable; outside I was not so sure. I had read that it was much colder than on Earth. The sun was low down on the horizon. Was it rising or setting? After a while I decided it was morning. The sun, softer than on Earth, was rising higher in the sky.

I had not been waiting more than fifteen minutes when I saw three bubbles approaching, seeming to float along the ground. They were smaller than the one that still enclosed Silver Streak. They had suddenly appeared from nowhere. How strange! Two of them stopped about a hundred metres from me, while the third bubble came up to our big bubble. I could make out a figure inside. At that moment I was afraid. My heart thumped hard. What was it like? Was it aggressive? What was it going to do to me? I was about to find out. The bubble appeared to merge with the one enclosing my spacecraft and the figure stepped inside.

I was about to meet my first Martian!

CHAPTER FIVE
I MEET MY FIRST MARTIAN

'Hello Bill! My name is Michu. That is my Martian name but if you like you can call me Michelle. That is the nearest I can think of in your language.'

I was too stunned to speak. I sat with my mouth open, while a million questions raced through my mind.

How is it she looks just like a human? Martians were supposed to be small and green, with antenna sticking out of their heads and to speak with strange, hollow voices.

How does she know my name? It is as if she were expecting me.

How is it she knows how to speak in English?

Those were only some of the questions that perplexed me.

'I know you are confused, Bill,' she said, smiling. 'Aliens are when they come for the first time. You wonder why I am not green and speak in a strange hollow voice. And you are surprised that I know your name, and that I speak perfect English. Yes, you are quite right. I can read your mind too.'

I smiled weakly but I wasn't ready to speak.

'Come, let me help you out of your seat.' With that, she undid my seatbelt and held my hand as I climbed out of Silver Streak and stood beside her, still inside the big bubble.

Michu was small, at least thirty centimetres shorter than I, but with lovely pale, translucent skin, dark eyes and short curly hair. She had a warm smile, which showed a set of beautiful white teeth. She was dressed in a simple tunic in two pieces, top and leggings, made of a course grey material.

'You can take off those thick sweaters now,' she said. 'You'll not need them on Mars. You will be travelling inside a bubble.'

I was grateful to discard those uncomfortable clothes. I peeled off the two heavy sweaters as Michu continued.

'On Mars we travel around in bubbles that automatically adjust to the perfect temperature for the body and not only that, oxygen and atmospheric pressure too, though not quite the pressure you are used to!'

I could hardly believe what I was hearing.

'Of course, you know that the atmosphere here is only one hundredth of that found on Earth,' she went on. 'Therefore outside, there is very little air to breathe. But don't worry! We discovered a long time ago how to extract oxygen from water. Our homes are supplied with it. The air outside is mostly carbon dioxide: not very suitable for Earth people!

'But trees depend on carbon dioxide, don't they?' I had overcome my shyness at coming face to face with an unexpectedly pretty Martian.

'It is true. But trees give us away.' She smiled.

'Give you away how? I asked.

'Orbiting spacecraft have cameras, so our trees have to grow in bubbles too,' she replied. 'Otherwise they would be seen.'

'You grow trees on Mars?' I was shocked. 'How do you get the bubble round the roots?'

'No, the bubble doesn't go round the roots. You will see, soon enough. We have an orchard and a tree nursery near here to increase the supply of oxygen and to provide the fruit that is very important in our diet. In fact there are many small orchards on Mars.' Then she added proudly, 'Of course they are not all as well managed as ours. Are you surprised?' Michu looked intently at me.

'Amazed! Earth scientists are still trying to decide if there is life on Mars. They would be very surprised to see you and hear about fruit and orchards and making oxygen and all that,' I said.

'We keep a low profile for a good reason. It is not that we are afraid but the truth is we are not ready to be invaded by an army of clumsy Earth people. Sorry to be blunt, but they don't always have much respect for others, even if we look the same. And when they find we can live here comfortably, they will all want to come. And then they will destroy our planet, like they are destroying theirs.'

'Mmmm! But Michelle, Michu,' I said. 'There is something I don't understand. We have sent several spaceships to Mars, with powerful cameras and everything. How come they haven't seen you?'

'Ah!' Michu threw back her head and laughed. 'It's quite simple, Bill. In the bubbles we are invisible.'

'But I saw you coming.'

'That's because we wanted you to see us. We didn't want to frighten you.'

'Do you mean to say you can make yourselves visible or invisible at will?'

'Exactly! Our bubbles have an important feature. As a precaution we materialise an extra skin all round that we can see out of but doesn't allow those outside to see in. What do you think of that?'

I nodded. 'Cool!' But now I had a hundred and one questions in my head.

'I know you have a hundred and one questions in your head,' she said and gave me a knowing wink. We both laughed.

'I think I am going to enjoy my visit to Mars,' I said.

'You can be sure of that, Bill. Now no more questions for the moment. There will be plenty of time. I have been given the pleasant task of acting as your guide during your stay on Mars and there are many things I want to show you.'

CHAPTER SIX
THE BUBBLE MIRACLE

Looking through the skin of the bubble was almost like looking through spotlessly clean glass: it was as if it was not there at all. I put out my hand and touched the surface. It gave ever so slightly in response to my touch. Michu watched me, sensing my curiosity.

I looked out at the vast expanse of red desert that surrounded us. As far as I could see there was nothing but desert and more desert. There was no way of knowing if it was hot or cold outside. Of course I knew it was bitterly cold, colder than the Antarctic in winter. But inside the bubble I was perfectly comfortable. Incredible!

What happened next came as just another surprise in a day of surprises. Michu appeared to give the wall of the bubble the slightest push. She guided me forward and before I knew what had happened, I found myself in a bubble of my own. I looked round to see another bubble forming and a moment later Michu was inside it.

Then she began to tell me a little about her home. 'Mars is only half the size of your Earth and therefore the gravity is less, only forty percent of the gravity on Earth actually. Inside the bubble you don't have to walk because it flies above the ground, but if you did, you would bounce up into the air.' She touched the floor of the bubble with her foot and gave a little jump, rising at least a metre into the air, taking her bubble with her. She laughed as she landed back on her feet.

'I can hear you just as well as if there were no bubble walls between us,' I remarked.

'Of course! But you will be surprised to know that they are extremely strong. As Mars has hardly any atmosphere, the greatest danger is from meteorites.'

'Why is there no atmosphere?'

'Not enough gravity,' said Michu. 'I was telling you about meteorites. On Earth all small meteorites burn up before reaching the ground. You call them shooting stars.

Here on Mars there is little atmosphere to burn them up, so many of them hit the ground. Our bubbles are strong enough to protect us from small meteorites.'

'What do you mean by small?'

'Well, most are no bigger than grains of sand. They don't reach us. Some are as big as marbles. And we have been studying comets and asteroids for centuries so we know when to expect them. The odds against a meteorite hitting a Martian have been calculated at millions to one. Of course it does occasionally happen. I remember my mother telling me. Before I was born someone was struck by a little piece of rock from outer space. That was the last Martian, as far as I we know, to have died an unnatural death. But during periods of heavy meteorite showers and when an asteroid is due, we make sure we are safely out of the firing line.' She shrugged her shoulders and smiled.

We started walking away from Silver Streak. I looked back at the spaceship I had built and which had nearly abandoned me to freeze to death. Once again, Michu read my thoughts.

'You won't be needing that anymore,' she said lightly.

'Do you mean to keep me here for ever?' I asked anxiously.

'She laughed. 'No! That is, unless you really want to. No-one has ever stayed permanently, although one or two aliens have settled here for a while. Most are dying to go back home after a short time. You will find that Mars is not at all like Earth.'

'And do you mind telling me how I will get back home to Earth?' I asked her.

'The way you came,' she replied. 'Do you think you would have made it here in that old contraption of yours?'

I laughed. I knew she was right. If the bubble had not rescued me, I would have died a lonely death in the depths of space. I shuddered to think of it.

'You mean I'll go back in a bubble?' I asked, excitedly. I could just see the expression on my parents' faces when they see a bubble landing in their garden with their son inside. I had to smile at this. Then I remembered the camera and the food I had brought with me that were still in Silver Streak. In the excitement of meeting my first Martian, I had completely forgotten them.

'Leave them behind, Bill. The food you will not need and the camera; that you will not be allowed to use here.'

'No photos to show my friends at school?' I was surprised at this.

'You will understand why.'

'But I don't want to lose it,' I said.

'It is safe where it is for now. Someone will inspect your landing craft later, as a matter of routine and will bring it to you at that time.'

Michu had turned and was gliding off in the direction of the other two bubbles that were still standing in the place where she had left them. I cruised along behind her. My bubble seemed to know where it was going.

We came up to the other bubbles. I could now see that there was a girl inside each bubble. Michu introduced us.

'This is Sofu and this is Anamaru,' she said. 'They are sisters. I think you can tell. And girls, you know who this is.'

'Welcome to Mars, Bill,' said Sofu and Anamaru at the same time.

'So you know all about me!' I said.

'We have been expecting you,' said Sofu, smiling.

Both girls were small, had long blonde hair and blue eyes, very different from Michu, but with the same soft, pale skin. I guessed they were in their early teens and were obviously sisters. They both wore the same grey tunic that Michu was wearing.

'Let me explain,' said Michu. 'You see, as soon as anyone on another world directs his or her intense thoughts towards Mars, we pick up the thought waves. We then know all about that person and his intentions. Some aliens, excuse the term, no offence meant, some non-Martians who try to come here encounter some technical problem or other and we have to go out there and rescue them, like we did for you. We consider it our duty to bring them safely down to Mars and return them to their home planet when they have had enough of being here. But we reserve the right to refuse someone if we detect that their motives are not good. To the American astronauts we do not exist and we like to keep it that way. Honest amateurs like yourself we help.

'So you get many visitors from other planets then?'

'No, very few actually,' said Michu.

The three girls were obviously enjoying the experience of showing a poor dumb alien how clever Martian people are.

'Incredible!' I breathed.

'You have seen nothing yet,' said Anamaru. You Earth people think you are so advanced but actually, compared to us, you still haven't got to the Stone Age.

'Nothing at all will surprise me,' I said and we all laughed.

CHAPTER SEVEN
SIMILARIA

The four of us set off across the desert. The three girls chatted and laughed among themselves as we sped along, each in our own bubble. I didn't understand a word of what they were saying. I guessed it was a Martian dialect. Strange! I wonder what other Earth languages they speak. I'll add that question to my long list of questions.

After some time Michu turned to me and smiled. 'It's not much further now. We are nearly there. Are you tired? You must be hungry too.'

'Not tired at all,' I said. 'But I must admit I feel a bit hungry, and thirsty.' I realised that, in my excitement I had left home without even a thought about breakfast. And here I was, millions of kilometers from home and not a bite to eat.

'Don't worry, lunch is waiting for us,' said Michu.

I wondered what Martians eat for lunch. Soup? Salad? Cheese and pickles? This thought made my tummy rumble and my mouth water.

The girls were laughing. 'Those are Earth foods,' said Sofu disdainfully. 'You will soon see,'

I had better learn to control my thoughts. Martians know exactly what you are thinking!

After another few minutes we reached the crest of a hill. We stopped to look down.

'There is home,' said Michu, pointing down into the valley.

I strained my eyes. 'Where? I can't see anything but red soil and rocks.'

'Come on, Bill!'

Finally we reached the floor of the valley. A short ride brought us to the foot of a huge, grey-brown cliff face, where we paused, our bubbles almost touching. Michu appeared to concentrate hard for half a minute. Then as if by magic a doorway appeared in the cliff face and a large bubble filled the whole space. The girls beckoned me forward and I followed them. My heart was beating against my ribs with excitement. Where was I being led?

The next moment I found myself inside a small chamber, enclosed by grey rock on three sides while the fourth side consisted of a black hole, Michu approached the dark space and called to me to follow her. Then she slid forward into the opening and the next moment she had disappeared downwards into the blackness. I stepped back in surprise but Sofu, who was just behind me, gave me the slightest nudge and I found myself falling into nothingness. But it was a gentle experience with the friendly bubble enveloping me. After what seemed like a few moments, during which I lost all sense of time and space, I suddenly found myself in an enormous cavern. It must have been more than a hundred metres high. It was decorated with thousands of crystals, which reflected soft lighting of different colours, blues, purples, oranges and greens. It was so incredibly beautiful, it completely took my breath away. I stood for some moments, just peering up into the heights, unable to speak.

A moment later Anamaru was standing beside me. 'Do you like our home?' she asked.

'It's fantastic! It's amazing!'

'It's all natural,' she said, proudly.

'Really? And how many people live here?'

'Ninety nine.' She paused. 'You will make it one hundred.'

'And how many people live on Mars, altogether?' I asked.

'Around a hundred thousand,' added Sofu, who had come to join us.

'Is that all? On Earth there are more than six billion.'

'Something like that, I have heard,' she said.

'Yes, but look what a disaster your planet is,' said Michu. 'Most of your people live in poverty. You are destroying your forests that give you rain and supply your oxygen. You are polluting your rivers and your seas. Your famous United Nations keeps saying that everyone on Earth will soon have access to clean drinking water and this disease and that disease will be eradicated. The truth is, more and more viruses are emerging and in a hundred years, if you go on the way you have been going, water will be as precious as gold. At the rate at which you are destroying your ozone layer and pumping carbon dioxide into the atmosphere, you will soon poison yourselves into extinction.

'Unless you do something about it very, very soon,' put in Anamaru.

'Of course we are doing what we can to help you,' said Michu.

I looked at her in surprise. 'How are you helping?'

'Just now there are about five hundred Martians living on Earth. They are working with your environmentalists to counteract the damage being done. Of course you don't know they are Martians. They look just like you; they just have a lot more understanding of environmental matters than your people.'

'Do you think they will succeed in averting disaster?' I asked.

'That is for your people to decide, Bill. But do you know what?

'What?' I asked.

'Your mission will be to help them,' said Michu. You will become a scientist one day and you will work on saving the environment. That is why you have come to Mars.'

'Come to Mars for that?' I said in astonishment.

'Yes. You have come here to learn from us and to get inspiration. We have managed to live in harmony with our environment for thousands of years. We understand very clearly that we are an integral part of our environment and our survival depends on preserving it. Our use of natural resources is very carefully controlled. We also control our population because we know that Mars cannot support too many people. There is much for you to learn from us.'

'I see,' I said. 'Martians living on Earth! That's really cool!'

We all laughed.

'Anamaru and I have other duties,' explained Sofu. 'So we'll leave you. We'll see you at lunch.' The two girls walked off, leaving Michu and me alone.

I realised for the first time since entering the cavern that I no longer had the bubble. I had not noticed when it left me. I was surprised to feel neither cold nor hot and I could breathe perfectly.

'This cavern is controlled for temperature, pressure and air content,' explained Michu. 'You may find going up and down more tiring because you are not used to the mixture of gases in the air. There is very slightly less oxygen than you are used to. We have had thousands of years to adapt. Tell me if you have any discomfort. Now, follow me. First you must wash and then eat.'

Michu led the way along a steeply descending pathway deeper into the cavern. I stared up at the beauty of the roof as we walked. After a few minutes we came to a wall of rock, in which there was a rough opening. Passing through, we came across a small pool on the left-hand side of the path. It was about twenty metres long and fifteen metres wide. It looked quite deep and was lined entirely with rock. Soft blue and green lights shone from under the water, giving it a magical look. The ceiling was lower here, about thirty metres high. Like the roof of the cavern, it was a mass of crystals, which sparkled in the soft lights. It felt warmer here than in the main cavern.

'Bathe in there; you will find the water agreeably warm.' Michu said brightly. 'Take your time, there is really no hurry,' I looked round for further instructions but Michu had already gone.

I bent down and touched the water. It was warm. I studied my reflection in the crystal clear liquid. Is that really you or am I dreaming? I asked my reflection. The rippling face just looked back at me but said nothing. I looked round to see that no-one was watching then I quickly took off my clothes and slipped gently into the pool. Not only was the water warm but it was softer than any water I had ever felt. I swam around slowly, relaxing every part of my body. Then

I lay on my back and floated easily, without having to move a muscle. The beauty of the ceiling above me lulled me into a half sleep. If there is a heaven, this is it, I thought.

CHAPTER EIGHT
AN UNUSUAL LUNCH

Voices outside the chamber brought me back to my senses. I swam easily to the side, climbed quickly out of the water and reached for my clothes. Beside them were a small towel and a two-piece suit. I had not noticed them before. They were made of the same course material, and similar to the suits worn by the three girls. I quickly dried myself on the towel and put on the suit. It fitted me perfectly. I rolled my own clothes into a bundle and, putting them under my arm, I went out through the gap in the rock into the main cavern. There, Michu was standing waiting for me, talking to a boy of about my age. Michu called out to me.

'Did you enjoy the bathe? She asked.

'Wonderful!' I replied.

'Bill, meet Manu. He is 16 years old, Martian years, that is. He also lives here in Similaria.'

Manu was about Michu's height, with dark, curly hair and dark eyes. He bowed. I also attempted a bow, not a very elegant one. I took note of the fact that Martians don't shake hands.

'It is not our custom to shake hands,' explained Michu. Once again she had read my thoughts.

'Welcome to Similaria,' Manu said to me, spreading his arms wide.

'What does the name mean?' I asked.

'Similaria? You don't have a word like it in English but it means, roughly translated, a place underground where the water comes to meet you in a special welcome. There is nowhere on Mars where the water actually reaches the surface of the planet. But your astronomers have observed the dry river beds that convince them that there was once water on Mars. What they don't know for sure is that there still *is* water, but only underground. And we are very determined to preserve it, to keep it hidden and prevent it from becoming polluted.'

'It was the best bath I ever had in my life,' I said. 'How on Earth do you get it like that?'

'Perhaps you should say 'how on Mars do you get it like that?'' Manu said and we both laughed. 'Let me explain briefly…..'

Michu interrupted. 'Let it wait for later, Manu. Bill is starving. Let's not make him wait a moment longer. By the way, give me your clothes; we'll get them destroyed.'

I hesitated for a moment, wondering what I would wear on the way home. I remembered that my mobile phone was still in the pocket of my trousers. I took it out and handed over the clothes. Michu indicated that I should also give her the mobile, so I handed that over too, deciding it was not really important enough to argue about. I was convinced that it would not work on Mars anyway.

Michu led the way back along the path by which we had come. After a few minutes we took a turn to the right and up a long flight of steep stone steps, which led to a kind of platform half way up the cavern wall. I was breathless by the time we reached the top and had to stop to rest. From the platform we could see right across to the far side of the cavern in the soft light. The place seemed deserted. Apart from the four I had already met, where were the other ninety-five?

Manu read my mind and immediately supplied the answer.

'It is easy to lose a hundred people in this place. But some are on an expedition to some volcanoes with a group of visitors from another clan. We keep an eye on them for safety reasons. Besides that, they will enjoy the outing. They will be back later today.'

The floor of the platform was covered by rough matting and dotted here and there were cushions of different colours. Manu pulled five cushions into a circle and we sat down. Michu told me that Sofu and Anamaru would soon be joining us.

At that moment, an older woman appeared from a rough opening in the cavern wall. She was short like the others and had grey hair. Michu said the woman was her great-grandmother. To me she didn't look old enough, her skin was so smooth. She was carrying a tray with five plates, which she set down on the matting in the middle of the circle. The contents of each plate were identical, seven dark purple fruits the size of plums, a pile of small, red berries and three dark green leaves. Is this going to satisfy me? I could tuck into one of Mum's steak and kidney pies just now. I thought to myself.

Manu and Michu laughed at my thoughts. It was Michu who explained.

'These few things will supply all the goodness you need for the rest of the day. And you will feel quite satisfied. Most of the food you eat on Earth is lacking in nutrients and just causes ill health. On Mars we never cook our food: it only destroys the nutrients. Of course we don't have fire, due to the shortage of oxygen, so there is no means of cooking, but even if we did… We eat to live long lives, like my great-grandmother. She is over a hundred years old, Martian years, not Earth years. She will probably live another hundred! But here come Sofu and Anamaru. We can start, but first, a prayer. We never eat without thanking the Almighty for sustaining us.'

After the prayer, we ate in silence. I noticed they all ate slowly and with great concentration, enjoying every morsel. I tried to do the same but it was very hard and I was the first to finish. But I was surprised how filling the food was. Michu was quite right: I felt very satisfied.

'Thank you,' I said. 'The purple fruits were delicious. Where do you grow them?'

'If you like, we'll visit the orchard tomorrow and you can see for yourself,' said Michu.

'Yes, that would be fun,' I said, yawning. 'Sorry, I feel a bit sleepy.'

'Good, because we always rest for ten minutes after eating,'

Everyone lay back on the matting and closed their eyes, but in no more than ten minutes they were all wide awake.

Sofu and Anamaru both got up and excused themselves, saying they had urgent duties to attend to.

'Do you have any questions before we visit the library?' Michu asked.

'Wow! I have so many questions I don't know where to start,' I replied. I thought for a moment. 'How is it you know English so well?

'It is important to us to study all the major languages of the planets we have contacts with.'

'How many planets do you know, apart from Earth?' I asked in amazement.

'Oh many!' said Michu, 'but only a few have intelligible life with which we can communicate, and none of those is in our solar system.'

I thought of all our nine planets. I couldn't imagine any of them supporting life.

'That's right, Bill,' Said Manu. 'Starting from those nearest the sun, Mercury is very hot and has no atmosphere. Venus is shrouded in poisonous gases. Jupiter, Saturn, Uranus and Neptune are just enormous balls of gas and Pluto is very, very cold and again it has no atmosphere. Only Earth and Mars are somehow hospitable.'

'Not many people on Earth would think Mars very hospitable,' I said with a laugh. 'But you are used to it.'

'We came here prepared.....' Michu stopped suddenly.

I was stunned. 'So you came from another planet?'

'Er... yes.' She looked uncomfortable.

'Which one?' I asked, excitedly. I waited for an answer, but none came.

Michu and Manu looked at each other. I sensed they didn't want to tell me.

'The other planets where we have friends are in other solar systems,' continued Michu, changing the subject.

I was intrigued. 'Very far away?'

'Yes, several light years,' said Michu, in a matter of fact tone.

I had learnt that light travels at about 300,000 kilometres per second and a light year is the distance that light travels in one year; a very, very long way!

'Have you been to these planets?' I asked.

'Heavens no!' said Michu. 'I am too young. Very few Martians have, actually. It takes so long to get there, even at the speed of light. But we don't need to physically go there: we can communicate very well with them.'

'Can your bubbles travel at the speed of light?'

'Faster than you could imagine but well below the speed of light,' said Manu.

'Wow! That is fantastic! And another thing, what do these beings look like?'

'None look like you and me,' said Manu laughing.

'And some are invisible,' added Michu.

'Invisible?' I cried.

'Yes Bill, invisible,' Michu said, unable to hide her amusement at my lack of understanding. 'Let me explain. Some forms of life have gone beyond the need for a material body; instead, they exist in spirit form. In this way they are not bound by the restrictions that we have to accept. They can literally be anywhere in the universe just by wishing it. They are beyond time and space entirely. You may be surprised to know that these spirit entities live side by side with us on Mars.'

'Wow! I would love to meet such beings,' I said.

'It is doubtful you ever will,' said Michu. 'You have to be fairly evolved yourself before you can detect their existence.'

'Can Martians detect them then?

'Certainly!' replied Michu. 'We know they are there but communicate, no. But there are evolved people on your planet who can also detect them.'

'Like the yogis of India?'

'Let us just say a very few beings.'

'I can see you have evolved a lot further than most of Earth people have.'

'Yes,' said Michu, 'Now, for the library!'

I imagined rows and rows of books. What a surprise was in store for me!

CHAPTER NINE
A LIBRARY WITHOUT BOOKS

As we stepped through the doorway of the library, I saw no books whatsoever. But of course, a civilization as advanced as theirs, they had certainly found a more economical way of storing books than that. But I could see no hardware of any kind either.

Michu and I had reached the library along a narrow path that wound steadily upwards along the side of the cavern, leaving the dining area immediately below. As we were near the roof of the cavern, I had had an opportunity to examine more closely the brilliant crystals that reflected the soft lights so beautifully. They were of varying sizes, from small ones of five centimetres to large ones measuring almost twenty centimetres. I had not been able to count their faces exactly but I had estimated that each one had around fifty.

'Each crystal has exactly eighty one faces,' Michu told me. 'But not all of them are visible.'

It had crossed my mind to ask her what was the source of the light but we had now reached the opening to the library. Inside, I scanned the enclosure. It was about thirty metres long and fifteen metres wide. A low parapet wall of rough stone extended the length of the room facing the cavern. On the other side the rock face was flat and had a sheen, a bit like marble but not shiny. The arched roof was only a few metres above the floor. The only furnishings in the long room were a rough carpet in a natural colour and a few cushions similar to the ones in the dining room. There was nothing whatsoever to show that it was a library.

Michu turned to me and smiled. 'Like you we have the internet, you might call it the Uninet, because it is truly universal,' she said. 'The difference is, we don't use hardware. We communicate to it with our minds.' The smile broadened to show her fine white teeth.

'You talk to your Uninet?'

'We don't talk to it but we communicate through thoughts, subconscious communication. Not only the Uninet, but we communicate with your internet too.'

'So how do you access the information?' I asked.

'I was coming to that.' Michu then closed her eyes and stretched out her arms with the palms of her hands facing forwards. I watched her face in fascination. After a few moments an orange glow appeared in the centre of her forehead and a beam of light shone onto the rock face in front of her. It was like being in the cinema. As yet the large screen was blank.

'What would you like to see?' she asked, still keeping her eyes closed and her head facing the wall.

I thought for a moment. 'Some sports news, the football results, how Man. United got on in their first game of the season against Chelsea.' I was not sure if they had finished playing. I had left on Saturday morning but couldn't work out in my mind how long ago that was.

Michu again closed her eyes and her lips moved slightly. On the screen there appeared a webpage, which gave a summary of the principal sporting events of the day.

One of the items was the match I was interested in. She concentrated and another page appeared, giving an up to date account of the match.

'So they won 4-0, that's fantastic!' I said. But how strange! I am on the planet Mars, having the experience of my life and I am so stupid as to be worried about a ball game halfway across the Universe.

'You Earth people take your sport very seriously, don't you?'

'Much too much, I am beginning to think, Michu.'

'Would you like to see something on the Uninet?

'Sure.'

Michu thought for a moment and then her face brightened up. 'I know something that will interest you,' she said. 'It's a website placed by the Global Ministry of Tourism on the planet Sonam.

'Never heard of it!' I said.

'I know you haven't. It cannot possibly be seen from Earth, even with the most powerful telescopes. But you know the star called Rigel.'

'I've heard of it, yes, but I've no idea where it is.'

'Sonam is the largest of several planets in the solar system of Rigel. Your astronomers have not yet discovered them. Rigel is one of the brightest stars visible from our solar system. It appears in the constellation of Orion. But it is incredibly far away, some 900 light years.

'Phew!' I paused. 'But, Michu, this tourism website you are showing me must have been created more than 900 years ago for us to be able to see it, because light takes that time to reach us.'

'You are quite right,' she said, nodding her head. 'But the beings living on Sonam and the other nearby planets are their potential customers. It is just that we can pick up the signal.......900 years later!

'The people, or beings, or whatever, that made the website are not alive any more, are they?'

'There's a good chance they still are. Beings on Sonam live to be well over a thousand years old. There is not one that dies before his or her old age, because there is no disease. Can you image life without disease, Bill?

'No! It is hard to imagine. So the people living on the nearby planets take their holidays on Sonam.'

'So would you, if you could reach there. It is apparently one of the most beautiful places within ten thousand light years from here. But it is hard to describe in words what it is like. Let's see the website.'

Michu went into what I can only describe as a trance. With eyes closed, she became very still. Her face froze. Suddenly the beam of light shone onto the wall and it came alive, colour, movement and sound. I immediately understood what Michu had just said about it being hard to describe. There before my eyes was a view taken from a few hundred metres from the ground, looking down a beautiful valley towards the deep blue sea. The whole area was a mass of flowering plants and trees and I swear I could smell them. The air was thronged with birds of all shapes, sizes and colours, wheeling and swooping, singing and whistling. I could see animals too, most of them looking like nothing we have on Earth, but elegant and colourful. A being appeared on the screen and started to talk in a language that I could not understand but it sounded sweet, like a bubbling stream. The being wore no clothes but I could not decide whether it was male or female. It had arms and legs and a head, with two eyes and a mouth but other than that it didn't resemble a human being. What struck me most about it was the soft colour of its skin and the way it shone with a special kind of lustre. I turned to Michu. She smiled a faint smile without moving.

'Would you like to go there for your holiday? She asked me.

'Where's the nearest travel agency. How can I book?' I grinned.

'Unfortunately, until we have discovered how to travel faster than the speed of light we are doomed,' she replied.

'Do you think we will ever manage to do that?'

'Nothing is impossible, but with a body to carry along with you, it is better to forget your holiday on Sonam for the time being.'

'It looks idyllic,' I said. 'Look at the wildlife!'

'You know, Bill. Let me tell you something. Sonam people are pretty advanced. They have understood better than anyone the importance of preserving their environment. All beings on the planet live in harmony with all others. The balance is maintained perfectly. And they have a very stable society, little changed for the last hundred thousand years. You will learn a lot from this website. Another day we shall spend more time. Oh, and another thing, Sonam people are hermaphrodites, as are all the life forms in their solar system. They reproduce independently.'

'Without male and female? I cried.

'Yes, they have both male and female organs inside their bodies. There are even some life forms on your planet that are like that.

'I have heard of that,' I said. 'But people!'

'It's hard for you to understand, I know.'

'I know I must be dreaming,' I said.

Michu tossed back her head and laughed and I laughed with her. The screen went blank.

'Now,' she said more seriously. 'I know you are wondering why we call it a library.'

'That's exactly what I was thinking.'

'Well, it's not exactly a library in the strict sense of the word. But every book that has ever been printed on Earth is stored on the Uninet, and we can show it on our screen. Three times every *surama* we have reading sessions here and most members of our Similaria clan meet here to read a few of the latest books that have made an impact on your society.'

'You say a few, Michu.'

'Yes. In one evening we normally read five or six books. We have learnt to read quickly. It is the only way we can keep up to date with what is going on your planet.'

'That's really cool! But, Michu, what is a *surama*?'

'A *surama* is an arbitrary period of time, Bill. It takes nearly seven hundred Martian days for our planet to make its journey round the sun, one complete circuit making one Martian year, so we divide our year into eighteen *suramas* for convenience. Each *surama* is 38 Martian days, except for one *suramas* containing three more days. You will understand this because on Earth some months are shorter than others, because your year is not an exact number of days.'

'Yes, February has 28 days and 29 in each leap year. But I'll have to think a bit more about that one,' I said. 'It's a bit complicated for me to understand. But I will remember that one surama is 38 days.'

'Never mind. I know it is confusing. Our two moons are small and close by and therefore they don't take long to go round Mars. Phobos goes round three times in a day, so we don't have a lunar month like you do on Earth. Like your Earth week, our *surama* is an artificial division.'

'How is our Earth week artificial?' I asked.

'Well, a year is the time it takes for the Earth to go round the sun; a lunar month is the period between one full moon and the next; a day is the time it takes for the Earth to spin once on its axis. A week is made up of seven days, but it has no real meaning.'

'We Christians say that God made the Earth in six days and rested on the seventh,' I pointed out.

'All civilisations have their legends, Bill.'

I must have looked puzzled because Michu laughed and then said, 'let us get back to what we were talking about, books, I think.'

I nodded. Martian years and *suramas* left my head and I switched back to the subject of libraries.

'We ourselves have never printed a book. We keep a lot of knowledge in our heads and what is not there, well, the Uninet provides.'

'So you don't need printers or any kind of machinery.'

'None whatsoever!'

'And weapons?' I asked. 'What about security?'

'We have never had the need for it. We have no police force because we have no crime.'

'And no enemies?'

At that moment, Michu's face clouded over and she did not immediately reply. I could see that something was distressing her. But what? Did they have enemies? Was there a threat of invasion from another planet?

'I am not supposed to talk about it, you see,' said Michu, thoughtfully. Her face brightened up suddenly and her eyes shone. 'Don't lets be morbid, Bill. We want you to enjoy your holiday on Mars.'

'I don't see how it is possible not to,' I said.

As we left the library and started the descent along the pathway back to the dining area, I couldn't help feeling something was troubling Michu, something she was obviously not supposed to tell me. These people were so wonderful and I found it hard to imagine that others could want to do them harm. Throughout the rest of the day I had the unpleasant feeling something was dreadfully wrong in Similaria, or maybe the whole of Mars.

CHAPTER TEN
A MEETING OF THE COUNCIL OF ELDERS

I learnt that the Council of Elders of the Similaria clan met twice every *surama*, about every eighteen days, in the Grand Hall. It was an important occasion, as it was the only time when all the ninety-nine members of the clan got together. Everyone who could was expected to be there. It was the meeting where they discussed important things that affected them and anyone, whatever their position in the clan, was free to speak their mind. No agenda was prepared in advance and nothing was written down. I got to know that, in fact, Similarians didn't record anything in written or printed form. Normally, no-one outside the clan was allowed to attend so I was excited when Michu told me that I was to be invited to the next meeting, to be held that evening. I was curious to know why I was so honoured.

'Is there anything special I need to wear?' I asked.

'Everyone here wears the same,' she replied. 'Simple, isn't it?'

'Not even the elders wear special clothes?'

'No person is considered more important than any others. The elders show their importance in the clan only by their dignity.'

'Our teacher told us it was the ideal of Communism,' I said, 'a society where everyone is equal.'

Michu laughed. 'But in the end some became more equal than others, didn't they? The problem was greed. Leaders were not prepared to serve the people: they only wanted to serve themselves, to amass power.'

'And the people suffered terribly, didn't they?'

'Yes, the ordinary people were downtrodden and stripped of their dignity. Even now the majority of the world's people live in inhuman conditions. Similaria, like most clans on Mars, runs on the hard work of all members. No-one gets paid for what they do; they do it for the good of all. We all eat enough and we are all fully occupied. If we as a clan are lacking something, there is always a neighbouring clan that would help out, just as we would help another clan if it needed it. We are a very close community but we never forget the needs of others around us.'

I shook my head. 'If only we could live like that on Earth.'

'Perhaps you will one day,' said Michu. 'You will be one of those who will bring about change on your planet.'

What she had said occupied my mind as we made our way to the Grand Hall for the meeting that evening. Was my visit to Mars planned by others for the sake of the future of our world? What part was I destined to play in the rescue of our environment? I was excited and at the same time scared.

The Grand Hall was reached by a series of ascending pathways and stairs, leading upwards to the end of the cavern furthest from the entrance. As Michu and I climbed higher and higher, turning first this way and then that, at times a winding stairway appearing to be suspended in midair, at other times a narrow ledge that seemed to be hollowed out from the rock face, I looked down from time to time. I could make out figures coming up behind us, shadowy in their grey suits in the dim light. As we climbed, the roof of the cavern rose before us and then suddenly opened out, revealing an enormous dome, which towered above us. At the same time the final stretch of path levelled out and we entered the magnificent hall, several times larger than the largest cathedral I had ever seen. It certainly deserves its name, I thought, and I wondered how many Martians could fit in such a place, many more than ninety-nine, I was sure.

'It is used for many purposes,' explained Michu, as we began to cross the hall, our footsteps echoing on the stone floor, 'As well as clan meetings, we hold regional get-togethers, where many other clans from hundreds of kilometres around meet to discuss matters of mutual interest. We also hold indoor sports meetings here.'

'Which sports do you have here?' I asked.

'Our favourite sport is the game of *Sombrillo*.' Michu stopped to greet a group of Similarians, who were chatting together. I was introduced as an Earth friend. 'Will I get a chance to see a game?' I asked, as we continued on past the group towards the middle of the hall.

'I hope so, Bill,' said Michu. 'I will explain the rules of the game later. It is very exciting to watch. Players can jump many metres into the air to head the *sombro* and the skill is in judging its course and making contact with it without touching another player. The pitch is very large, at least twice as big as your football pitch.'

'Wow!' I could image why it is so popular on Mars.

'We have other games. There is no reward for the winners of any of the games. We play for the enjoyment and the exercise, not for competition.'

I thought of how much our top sportsmen earn and because of the rewards how much importance is placed on winning. Our sports on Earth have become so commercialised the enjoyment of the game is often spoilt. I couldn't wait to see my first game of *Sombrillo*. Would I get the chance to play?

'You could attend a practice session and if you like it you might get a chance,' Michu said encouragingly.

By now we had crossed the hall and were heading in the direction of a smaller area on the right hand side, enclosed by natural rough stone walls, where there were already about thirty people standing in groups. They must be preparing themselves to speak at the meeting, I thought. Or perhaps those who went on the expedition were telling the others about it. No more was said about the game but the excitement of the idea was to stay with me.

When everyone had assembled and had sat down on the cushions provided, the hall went quiet. Michu and I sat down in the third row from the front. Before us, against the wall of the cavern, there was a raised platform, a kind of stage. It was empty and I realised that it was where the elders would sit. I studied the ceiling of the enclosure. It was lit by the same soft light and the crystals reflected the

light to all parts of the chamber. I counted the seated
figures. There were ninety-two, and some of them were
children. I saw Sofu, Anamaru and Manu and we exchanged
greetings across the room. I did my arithmetic and decided,
if there were ninety-nine Similarians, there must be seven
elders. We waited in silence for the elders to appear.

During that time my mind wandered off. It went back to
the morning, (I suppose it was the morning), and my
landing on the Red Planet. Such a long time ago, it seems to
me. Yet it could only be a few hours. I wonder how many
hours there are in a Martian day and in a Martian night. But
maybe they don't have days and nights like we do. But now
I remember seeing some of Mars in shadow as we landed,
so there must be some darkness. I will have to ask Michu.
And another strange thing; living under the ground like they
do, how do they tell if it is day or night? I haven't seen a
clock since I arrived and yet everyone seems to know what
time to come to the meeting. How do they know when it is
time to eat and time to go to bed?

After what seemed like hours, but was probably only
twenty minutes, all heads turned towards the right and I
craned my neck to see what was the cause of this. Out of an
opening in the wall on the right of the platform appeared a
man dressed in the standard Martian tunic. He had long
white hair and a long white beard. Behind him walked a
woman, similarly dressed, who I guessed was younger
because her hair was just beginning to go grey. She was
followed by three other small figures of varying heights,
one woman and two men. What struck me most was that not
one was fat and they all walked very straight. I then
understood what Michu had said about their dignity.

The five elders look their positions on the cushions
provided. Why only five? I said to myself. That means two
Similarians are not here. A prayer was said, after which a
short silence followed. Then the white-haired man got to his
feet, bowed and spoke in a clear booming voice, in a
language I could not understand. After speaking for five or

six minutes he paused and then continued in perfect English.

'For the benefit of our special guest, who does not speak our tongue, *Kisoro*, I will repeat what I have already said to you, dear brothers and sisters.'

He looked straight at me and smiled. No-one else looked round at me, and that surprised me. They all knew who I was, where I came from and my reason for being there. I was touched by the friendliness of my welcome and the politeness shown by not staring at me.

'Welcome all of you to our first meeting of the year 7445. This is an important occasion and I an extremely grateful for your one hundred percent attendance. Our sister you will meet later. We thank the Almighty for allowing us to be together and for its blessing for the continued health of our dear community.'

The white-haired elder went on to give, in English, a short summary of the main events of the year 7444, with its successes and difficulties. He then spoke again in their language for another ten minutes, before continuing in English.

'Similaria faces challenges in the year ahead. All of these are surmountable with the cooperation and ingenuity of our people, save one.' Here he paused and looked round at the audience.

I turned and looked at Michu, who gave me a quick glance and a nervous smile. My mind went back to earlier in the day, when I had asked her if their clan had any enemies and she had not wanted to tell me.

'You all know, with the exception of our visitor, to what I am referring. It is so important that we elders have decided to dedicate a special meeting to this one issue that threatens the very existence of Similaria and indeed the existence of life on our planet. The meeting will take place tomorrow at this time. All of you are urged to attend.'

My heart began to beat faster. I could feel my hands shaking. What was this issue that threatened life on Mars? Would I be allowed to go to that meeting?

The elder turned to the woman sitting on his right and they exchanged a few words. He spoke to us briefly in *Kisoro* and then sat down. The woman got up, bowed and addressed the clan. At one point Michu got excited and I wondered why, but when the woman translated her talk into English, I understood. There was to be a *Sombrillo* practice in two days. I was specifically invited to be there and to join in if I wanted.

The rest of the meeting was taken up with discussion on various subjects. Several clan members got up to give their comments or to ask questions. One woman stood up to give a report on the volcano they had just been to visit. The volcano was not expected to erupt in the near future, even though some tremors had been felt during recent *suramas*. At the end of each topic, someone would give a summary in English just for me. I was especially interested in one particular subject.

'Is it true that we are to expect an unmanned spacecraft from Earth soon?' asked a thin man sitting close to me. He spoke in very clear English, obviously knowing that I would be interested.

'Yes, it is true, Huron, in less than seven *suramas* from now,' replied another elder, rising to his feet and bowing. 'According to the NASA website, the unmanned probe that was launched in 7444 is due to soft land on 21st March next year (Earth reckoning), that is the 1st day of *Surama* 7. Of course the exact location of the landing site is kept strictly confidential, but we have an idea that it could be only a few kilometres from here. We do not know the precise purpose of the mission but it will no doubt be collecting soil and rock samples for analysis. You know that Earth people are desperate to know for sure if there is life on Mars. It is for us to prevent them from doing so. We all know the importance of keeping away from the area while the probe is active. If it threatens to reveal any of our activities, we have a standing procedure to deactivate its instruments and put it out of action.'

Shortly before the meeting ended a young woman entered the enclosure carrying something wrapped in a grey cloth. She climbed onto the stage and approached the elders. All of them got up and surrounded her. They all looked very pleased. Then one of the women elders, with her arm round the young woman's shoulder, came up to the edge of the stage and faced the audience. The bundle was unwrapped to reveal a small baby. The elder spoke in *Kisoro* and the crowd clapped enthusiastically. Then she spoke in English.

'May I welcome the newest member of our clan, born today? May he live to be three hundred years! His name by the way is Kim. I joined in the clapping. It was then that I understood why two Similarians had been missing from the meeting.

The white-haired elder closed the meeting and the audience began to disperse quietly. Sofu, Anamaru and Manu came up to join us. The five of us began to cross the hall. All of us were a bit subdued. The news of a serious threat had been received with concern by all Similarians and their concern was infectious. I felt for them. Judging by the elder's warning, the situation was serious. What part was I to play in the drama ahead?

CHAPTER ELEVEN
A GOOD NIGHT'S SLEEP

'Manu, you will show Bill where he is to sleep,' said
Michu, as soon as we had finished eating.

'Yes, Michu, we shall be sleeping in the same chamber.'
Manu turned and looked up at me. 'Are you tired, Bill?'

'Now you come to mention it, yes. But believe it or not
it is the first time I have even thought about it. Days on
Mars are very different from Earth's. It is hard to know
when you are supposed to sleep.'

'Mm. You will not find it difficult to adjust. Martian
days are only very slightly longer than Earth days. Mars and
Earth take about the same time to turn on their axis. On
Earth you divide your day into twenty-four hours, a man-
made division of time. We don't have hours. Our day is
divided into 18 *somos*, which would be about one and a
third of your Earth hours. But we don't use them much in
practice. We don't have clocks so we have grown up to
know almost precisely how much of the day has elapsed,
even though much of the time we are underground.'

'You have your clocks built in,' I suggested.

'Correct, Bill. You noticed that the whole clan was
present in the Grand Hall at the proper time. All the day's
activities run smoothly because everyone knows what to do,
where to go and at what time.'

'Simple, isn't it?' said Anamaru.

'Well, I think it will take some getting used to,' I replied.

'So, Bill, time to get some rest,' said Michu, putting her
hand on my arm and squeezing it gently. 'We all have a
busy day tomorrow and there is so much for you to see.
Manu, see that Bill is comfortable.'

'You don't have to remind me, Michu.'

Manu and I said goodnight to the girls and headed off in
the direction of the sleeping accommodation, which was on
the far side of the cavern. On the way we chatted and I was
able to get some answers to questions that were puzzling
me.

'When we came inside Similaria,' I began, 'we dropped down a kind of shaft. It was like going down in a lift of a tall building, except that it was completely dark and it went down very fast.'

'Faster than you think, Bill.' Manu stopped for a moment and made a sharp downward movement with one arm. 'In the time it takes for you to count up to one hundred you have descended more than five thousand metres from the surface.'

'Five kilometres! So we must have moved very quickly indeed!' I said incredulously.

Manu moved on up a sharp incline. When we reached the top, he stopped and turned to face me. I was panting noticeably. 'For several reasons we live far below the surface of Mars. Firstly it is far too cold to live up there. There are many metres of permanent frost. Water cannot exist on the surface because the atmospheric pressure and gravity are too weak. Down here it is much warmer and there is plenty of water.'

I remembered the warm bathe I enjoyed earlier in the day. 'And the water is so soft!

'Yes! Compared to your water on Earth; at least the water I tried when I was there.

'You have been to Earth!?' I almost shouted the question, I was so surprised.

Manu laughed. 'What is so strange about that? You came to Mars in a rickety old bundle of scrap iron. Surely you must know that in our bubbles we can pop back and forth as easily as you ride to town in a bus.'

I wasn't too pleased at his description of Silver Streak that I had slaved weeks to build. But in the end it had not served the purpose and I knew it was a bubble that had saved me.

'I suppose so,' I said. 'But even so, the idea of it... it's quite funny really, you going to Earth I mean.' I imagined Manu walking down our road in his grey tunic and with no shoes.

'No, we wear the same clothes are you, uncomfortable as they are. Suits and ties are not made for maximum comfort.'

Manu moved on and I followed. After a while I said to him, 'and what was it like for you?'

'On Earth? Well, I had a good time and met some wonderful people.'

'Earth people or Martians?'

'Oh! Both of course. But I'll tell you about my trip another time. We are nearly there.'

Indeed, we had reached a small, dimly lit enclosure, where there were several flat stone platforms arranged against the wall of the cavern, all of them identical. These, I figured out were the beds. One end of each platform was raised to form a pillow and the beds sloped gently upwards towards the bottom, so that the feet of the sleeper would be at the same level as the head.

'They are designed that way,' explained Manu, reading my thoughts. 'Here, take this sleeping cover.' He handed me a blanket made of the same material as the tunics that everyone was wearing.

Manu pointed to one of the beds. 'That's yours, Bill. I am right next to you. First, you will need to visit the toilet. It's through there. You will find a container with some green coloured water; that's to wash your mouth out.'

Returning to my bed, I noticed that Manu was already asleep. I lay down, covering myself with the blanket. The bed was very hard. I lay on my back and began to go through the events of the day. And what an exciting day it had been! It seemed hardly possible that I had got up at 4am that morning, travelled millions of kilometres through space, met many Martians, attended a clan meeting; all in one day! Then I thought of my parents and wondered how they had reacted to my message and sudden disappearance. Would they be worried? Would they have called the police and reported me missing? I decided to ask Manu in the morning if there was a way I could get a message to them. That was my last thought before I drifted off into a deep, dreamless sleep.

CHAPTER TWELVE
A VISIT TO THE FRUIT FARM

'Time to get up, Bill,' came a voice from a long way off. At first I couldn't place the voice and I was not even sure where I was. I opened my eyes, expecting to see my mother's face and to hear her harsh voice, wanting to know whether I was going to sleep all day, or what. Instead it was the face of Manu smiling down at me.

'The day has begun. Did you sleep well?'

'Like a log,' I replied, stretching my arms and legs and yawning.

'You didn't find the bed too hard?'

'At first, yes. How long have I slept?

'Exactly eight hours; that is if you went off at the same time as I did.'

'More or less.'

'Well, Bill, today I believe Michu promised you a trip to the farm. But first we shall bathe and have breakfast.'

'Sounds good to me,' I said, eagerly.

After visiting the toilet and folding my blanket, which I left on my bed, I followed Manu back down the way we had come the night before. Then we branched off and I recognised the pool where I had bathed before. Manu and I stripped off and we both plunged into the warm but refreshing water. We swam around for a while, before resting at the edge of the pool, holding onto the side.

'How do you heat the water?' I asked Manu.

He chuckled. 'We don't. Have you never been in a hot spring?'

'No.'

'The water comes from very deep down underground. It passes through fissures in the hot rock and that is what heats it. There are hot pools and some that are cooler, like this one. Convenient, isn't it?'

'Brilliant!' I had to admit these Martians knew how to live simply and in harmony with nature. No burning of fossil fuels, no machinery, no pollution!

'We use natural energy sources here. We know we are part of Nature and we know it is wrong to try to control Nature. Your people will one day come to the same understanding.'

'And I am to be part of the game.'

'That's about the size of it, Bill! That is an expression you use, isn't it?'

I was quiet for a bit, while I tried to digest this momentous idea, which kept coming up.

'Manu.' I said finally.

'I'm all ears! Another expression from your country!'

'It's amazing; you know more English than the English!' We both laughed.

'But seriously, Manu, I am a bit worried about my parents. They must be frantic with worry. Suppose they call the police and make all sorts of announcements on radio and TV. Is there some way I can contact them? Just to let them know I am alright?'

'Of course, there are ways. But I will have to get clearance from the elders. It is absolutely forbidden to make contact with other planets without their permission. Leave it to me. I'll speak to someone today.'

'Thanks, Manu.'

We climbed out of the water and dressed in clean tunics. Then we made our way to the dining area for breakfast. There were several people already seated on cushions when we entered the dining area. Some were eating. I spotted Michu, Sofu and Anamaru sitting together at the far side. As we crossed to where they were sitting, everyone greeted us warmly. As we came up to our friends, I noticed another girl with them. She was smaller than Anamaru, about 1.25 metres, had black hair and large dark eyes and the same smooth, pale skin.

'Good morning boys. This is Diana; she is Manu's sister,' said Sofu, getting up. Diana bowed and I did the same.

'I hope you slept well, Bill,' said Michu.

'Perfectly, thanks!' I replied, sitting down between Diana and Anamaru.

Almost immediately, an elderly lady came from the kitchen carrying stone plates and a stone dish, containing a grey mixture that I was not able to identify immediately. She put down the dish and I saw what I thought were mushrooms.

'That is exactly what they are,' said Michu. 'They are highly nutritious; much more than your mushrooms. We grow them in special caves. We eat them everyday....raw.'

I must have looked very doubtful because they all had a good laugh at my expense. However, once I had tried them, I had to admit they tasted better than they looked.

We all ate in silence. Once again everyone concentrated on the food. Only when everyone had finished did we start chatting, mostly about the trip we were to make that day. Michu told me I would not be allowed to attend the special meeting to be held in the evening, because of the very secret subject that would be discussed, though she did say that the elders would be giving me a special audience later, to tell me a bit of Similaria history and some other interesting information about Mars. I felt very important when I heard that. Imagine, the elders giving me a special audience!

The party to the fruit farm was to include Michu, Manu and the manager of the farm himself. We met at the foot of the tube that was to take us to the surface. Michu stood in front of the entrance and as soon as a bubble appeared, she stepped into it and was gone. Next it was my turn. I was a little bit nervous, having a clear memory of coming down the day before. I need not have worried because the bubble began very slowly, gradually increasing speed so that the effect was not too noticeable. It was pitch dark inside the bubble and it seemed to take ages. Just as I was beginning to wonder if I was moving at all, the bubble started to slow down and within another minute we were at the surface and I stepped out of the bubble into the chamber, where Michu was waiting for me. She smiled. A minute or so later, the manager appeared and then Manu. Michu then stood still and seemed to command the wall to open. I thought of 'Aladdin and the forty thieves' story. A hole appeared carrying a large bubble, which we all crowded into. On the other side of the wall we transferred to a larger, long-distance bubble, which hovered for some time in the soft light of the Martian morning.

'The journey will take about half a *somo*, that's about thirty-five Earth minutes,' said Michu. 'Similaria is some degrees north of the Martian equator in an area that your astronomers call Chryse Planitia. Incidentally we are not so far from the landing site of Viking I, the first unmanned craft to land on Mars back in 7428. We will be travelling south towards what you call Valles Marineris, a deep canyon, in some places more than 200 kilometres wide and clearly visible from Earth with a powerful telescope. The terrain is not too rough until you get near the canyon but by then we shall be there. There will not be time to see the canyon itself but maybe another day we shall do a tour and you can also see some of the largest volcanoes in our solar system.'

'It seems a long way to have a farm,' I ventured.

'It's true, but conditions are just right in that area, plus the mountainous scenery gives us good cover and NASA avoids that kind of terrain when choosing landing sites for its probes.' Those machines cost a fortune to build. Why risk them landing on the edge of a big boulder and overturning?

'I see. How far are these volcanoes?'

'Around 2000 kilometres, but our flying bubbles soon cover the distance.'

'Are the volcanoes likely to erupt?' I asked.

'It hasn't happened for many thousands of years, so I wouldn't worry too much,' said Michu, laughing. 'Now let's be off.'

The sun was still low on the horizon as we set off across the red, barren desert. The sun was smaller than it appears from Earth. I mentioned this to Manuel and he told me it was because Mars is almost 80 million kilometres further away from the Sun than the Earth. No wonder Mars is so cold! He told me also that it appears much less bright than on Earth, due to the thinner atmosphere and the distance from the Sun. But I was very comfortable inside our bubble and I was thankful for that.

A few large boulders cast long, pale shadows. Other things of interest in the landscape were a series of deep, wide valleys that looked as though they were dry river beds and the odd impact crater, caused by meteorites hitting the ground. Manuel told me that the valleys were actually created at a time when Mars had seas and rivers. I wonder what happened. Imagine, seas and rivers! And now Mars is nothing but desert. Manuel said the history of Mars would be explained to me another time. I thought to myself at that moment that I was the luckiest boy ever to have existed. What a story I would have to tell the boys at school!

'You will have to swear to keep all this a secret before you leave Mars, Bill,' Manu warned, frowning. If you go shouting about your trip to Mars, they will either come looking for us or they will put you in a mental home! One or the other, and neither would be good for you or us here.'

'I understand, Manu,' I said. 'I am so sorry! I would never want you Martians to suffer at all.' I was cross with myself for ever having mentioned it, even in thought. When you think something, it is as good as saying it because everyone knows what you are thinking.

Soon the scenery became more mountainous. We must be getting near that canyon Manu talked about. Our bubble negotiated the steep, rocky hills with no difficulty. Another few minutes and the bubble came to a halt. We were hovering half a metre above the ground at the top of a rocky hill. Looking down into a valley, the farm manager pointed ahead and told me that was the farm. I couldn't make out anything definite, although I could see that the area was less red and slightly browner. We descended into the valley, the bubble moving slowly now.

Suddenly we came to a wall of what looked like an enormous bubble, twenty or more metres in height. The bubbles in which we were sitting merged into the wall and the next moment we were inside the enormous bubble. The scene that met my eyes made me gasp. Nothing could be seen from outside but inside was an orchard stretching away up the valley. The trees were of different kinds and all seemed to be loaded with fruit of varying sizes and colours. We came up to a nearby tree and I recognised the fruit we had eaten for lunch the day before. The farm manager picked one from the tree and handed it to me. I remembered to thank the almighty for the gift and then enjoyed it. The others also ate one.

When we had finished eating, the farm manager, whose name was Zigal, invited us to sit on some stones that were arranged in the form of a circle.

'I wish to explain what we do here,' he said in a deep voice. He was a small man with dark hair and curiously green-yellow eyes that fixed on me as he talked. He sometimes glanced at the others but mainly his talk was directed to me. I noticed his hands were unusually rough, typical gardener's hands.

'Apart from the fungus that is grown inside, all the food we eat in Similaria comes from here. We grow twenty-five different types of fruit. They provide all the vitamins and minerals the body needs. You may have a chance to taste all of them while you're here in Similaria.'

He looked at Michu and she nodded, smiling at me. Then he went on.

'The soil here is good and there is an abundance of water deep beneath the surface. Inside the greenhouse bubble the moisture and temperature is controlled by means of the warm water and air that is forced up to the surface. It is a self-sustaining ecosystem.'

I interrupted him. 'What do you mean by self-sustaining system?'

'I'm sorry for being too technical but I am what you would call a scientist, you know. A self-sustaining ecosystem is a system where the living things, in this case the trees, interact with the environment, the water, gases in the air and also the decaying vegetation, which is recycled in the soil and provides the nutrients for the trees, and so on. We don't need to do anything. But what we do is important for us. You know that the Martian atmosphere is mainly carbon dioxide. The tees love it. And they give us the gift of oxygen. We don't allow any of that precious oxygen to escape into the atmosphere. If we did that, it would drift off into space and be lost. We store oxygen and water vapour for use in Similaria. ' He smiled, obviously proud of his valuable contribution to the clan's welfare.

'Zigal has worked here for eighty years,' said Michu. 'His father worked here and his grandfather before him. Now his daughter is being trained to take over from him in twenty years or so. She will show that girls can be good scientists too.'

'Zigal laughed, his green eyes flashing. 'My daughter may turn out to be the best in a long line of family fruit farmers. We are all the time developing news strains of fruit. That is my main job here. We cannot eat all that we produce. We barter our surplus harvest to neighbouring clans,' said Zigal. 'One clan supplies us with the tunics we wear and sleeping covers, another with stone containers.'

'Where does the cloth come from to make the tunics?' I asked.

'It is imported from Zuron,' said Michu.

'Where's that?'

'Zuron is a planet in the solar system of Rigil Kent,' explained Michu.

'Another solar system?' I cried.

'Rigil Kent, or Proxima Centauri, as it is more commonly called on Earth, is the nearest star to our solar system, only 4.3 light years away.'

'Wow, that's fantastic!'

All three of them were amused at my ignorance.

Michu went on, 'It is a civilisation that has specialised in cloth production. Their cloth is produced from plants that only grow there. The material is extremely hardwearing. It lasts as long as we do, or longer. We order only once every hundred years or so.'

'More like two hundred,' said Zigal.

I could hardly believe that something could last so long.

'How do they transport it from there to here?' I asked.

'By spaceship, of course!' said Zigal.

'Sorry to be so ignorant,' I apologised. 'It must take a long time to get here.'

'Yes, about thirty years,' said Michu.

'Thirty years!'

'The spaceships are unmanned. The people on Zuron load them and sends them off. As the ship approaches Mars the supplier, the Martian clan that holds the franchise, receives a signal and they meet it with a transport bubble. Then they send the spaceship back to Zuron.'

'Just like that!' I said, shrugging my shoulders. 'But how do they pay Zuron for the material?'

'They don't, actually' said Michu.

'They do it for nothing?'

'Well, the Mars global council has a kind of agreement with Zuron. If ever they need help and we can, we have agreed to help them.'

'What kind of help would that be?' I wanted to know.

'Anything. Nothing is specified. Maybe they will never need our help. It doesn't matter. On Earth it is hard to find those who will do things for no immediate gain. Not all living beings think that way......fortunately.'

I could say no more. I was learning so much, and it was humbling.

We had a good tour of the fruit farm. At the far end was a field in which green vegetables were growing. These were the ones we had eaten the day before. Two Martians were picking leaves and tying them into bundles, for transport to Similaria, I was told.

At last our tour of the fruit farm was over and we made the journey back, after a meal of another kind of fruit, yellow and juicy. The sun was high in the sky. It must be midday, I thought.

At last we arrived at Similaria and made the descent into the cavern. As is the custom we all rested for some time. The rest of the day was spent meeting other Martians and getting to know the layout of the cavern. When it was time for the special council meeting, everyone made their way to the grand hall. Before she went, Michu took me back to the library and accessed the Earth Internet and I got up to date with the BBC news from home. Nothing much had happened, the usual politics and fighting in the Middle East and in Afghanistan. I half thought there may have been a news item about a missing schoolboy but there was nothing. But I enjoyed seeing the news of my favourite football and cricket teams. South Africa was thrashing Pakistan. Only a miracle could save them. In football, Manchester United was second in the League behind Arsenal, having beaten Chelsea 4-0 in the Saturday game.

It was late into the night when Michu returned to collect me. She looked strained. She didn't want to say anything about the meeting but I could tell there was something very serious going on. She shed a few tears and I did my best to comfort her. I began to feel some deep attachment to her. At that moment she drew away from me.

'No Bill,' she said gently. 'I am older than you and we cannot get too attached to each other. Soon you will go back to Earth and you may never see me again.'

'I can stay here,' I said quickly, and then I realised she was right. 'What you say is true, Michu, but I will love you anyway.'

She held my head in her hands and kissed me on the forehead. She turned quickly away. Then we left the library and went our separate ways.

'I *could* stay though,' I said to nobody in particular.

'Could you?' said a voice behind me.

I turned to find Manu walking towards me.

'Remember your mission on Earth, Bill,' he said.

I said no more but I thought about Michu for a long time before falling asleep that night.

CHAPTER THIRTEEN
SOMBRILLO

When you go to sleep thinking of something, that something is often the first thought when you awake the next morning. So it happened to me on my third morning on Mars. My first thought was about Michu. My next thought was that Manu had said nothing more about getting in touch with my parents. I sat up and looked towards his bed but it was empty. I sprang out of bed, thinking I may have overslept. As I did so, Manu came out of the toilet.

'Don't worry, we're not late,' he said cheerfully, taking hold of his blanket and folding it. 'And I know you're still concerned about your parents. Don't worry about that either. I have spoken to one of the elders and she has a plan for you. When you meet with the elders they will explain to you what you need to do. Until then there really is no need to concern yourself. It will come out better than you expect.'

'That sounds funny! How do they know what I expect?'

Manu looked at me and I understood immediately. It seemed that nothing I thought escaped the notice of these Martians.

'Thoughts don't stay in the head, Bill,' said Manu. 'They zoom off into the Universe, to be intercepted by anyone able to do so. Think of thoughts as being the same as light or radio waves. You should not see your mind as a closed box, available to you only. There is really only one universal mind, yours only being a small part. Do you understand?'

'I can understand what you are saying but it is such a crazy idea, I don't think I can believe it, not just yet, anyway.'

'Believe it, Bill. It's true,' said Manu. 'In time, you will understand.'

I was not to see Michu that morning. Manu and I bathed in the pool and breakfasted. Later he took me to see the caves where the mushrooms were grown. We descended much further underground. The more we dropped down, the warmer and more humid it became. My main impression of the trip was the strong smell, which after a time became unbearable and we had to return to the comfort of the main cavern. But I was glad that I had seen them. I was impressed with the ingenuity of the Similarians.

On the way back from the caves I reminded Manu that he had promised to tell me about his trip to Earth.

'Well, it was an official visit, so there was not much time for sightseeing,' he began. 'My job was to accompany school inspectors around schools to assess to what extent environmental issues were built into the syllabus in European Union countries. I posed as a senior schoolboy from Spain. I speak Spanish fluently, as well as English and French and Russian. It was interesting. The EU has become very conscious of the importance of developing environmental awareness at an early age. I think I made an important contribution.'

'What did you think of Europe?'

'Stimulating! I loved it!'

'Did you visit England?'

'No time, unfortunately. Maybe the chance will come.'

The *Sombrillo* practice was to take place in the afternoon in the Grand Hall. Today it was the men's turn. We were to wear our normal costume but with a coloured headband. Manu had brought one for me.

Manu was one of the brightest hopes among the youngsters of the clan. I learnt that he had already played for Similaria against some of the neighbouring clans, even though he was still young and inexperienced.

As we made our way towards the Grand Hall, Manu explained the game to me.

'*Sombrillo* is a team game. We use a small bubble, called a *sombro*, about four times the size of your football. It is weighted so that it does not float away too far. The players are only allowed to touch the ball with their heads. The goals are rings made out of the branches of fruit trees, about a metre across suspended about ten metres above the floor at each end of the pitch and the team that scores the most goals wins the match. There are eighteen players on each team. No player should barge another.'

'Cool! Michu told me it needs a lot of skill to judge the path of the ball and not to hit another player. I can't wait to see it!'

Manu laughed. 'We have a lot of good players here, men and women. There are not enough boys to make up a full team of eighteen players but boys are allowed to play in the practice sessions and they sometimes play in informal games of nine or twelve players. It's a great honour to play for your clan. I have played several times.'

'I know, I was told. I hear you are a budding superstar! A Martian Ronaldo!'

'Well, I don't know,' he said, humbly.

We had reached the Grand Hall. Many Martians had gathered for the entertainment and were standing around expectantly. Some of those who were to take part in the practice were standing in a group and they greeted us as we approached. One of the players was holding the sombro. He tossed it to me and I caught it with two hands. It was much bigger than a football, slightly soft and I could see through it. But what was most interesting was its luminous turquoise colour. I threw it into the air. It sailed up several metres and I was afraid I would lose control. The others had a good laugh as I ran to catch it. There was clapping of hands and I felt a bit embarrassed. I was no David Beckham with a football and a sombro was much more difficult to control.

The coach, an elderly man, but still looking amazingly fit, came over to speak to me. 'Don't fret if you're not too involved at the start,' he said. 'Just watch the others and you'll soon get the feel of the game. Remember, heads only.'

He divided the men into two roughly equal teams, so that no-one was left out. One team wore red headbands and the other, blue. I adjusted my red headband and grinned at Manu, who was poised ready for the signal.

My heart beat faster with excitement as we waited for the coach to start the game. He stood still and it was so quiet you could have heard a pin drop. Then he suddenly dropped his hand and from then on it was all movement. Players darted here and there. Sometimes a player would nod the sombro too hard and it would sail high towards the dome of the hall and the coach would tell him that was not the way to play, that the sombro should be kept close to the head and controlled. Then one player from each team would position himself to head it to another player on his team. It was not often that players collided with one another.

At one point Manu got hold of the sombro and I got the impression that it was somehow stuck to his head, he controlled it so well. He beat two opposing players and with the slightest flick of his head, he sent it sailing up above the goal and down it came, into the cloth basket. There was applause from all around, Reds, Blues and the spectators. I could see why Manu was in the team, young though he was.

But goals were difficult to score and by the end of the game the Reds had scored two goals and the Blues only one.

The sombro was passed to me only twice during the game. The first time I misjudged it completely and ended up in a heap on the floor. Manu picked me up and gave me a word of encouragement. The second time I managed to position my head neatly to give the sombro a push towards another player, who was, unfortunately, wearing a blue headband. So much for my first Sombrillo practice!

All in all it was wonderful fun and I was thankful for the opportunity of playing. I doubted if I would be picked to play in a proper match. I could hardly have played more hopelessly.

As we left the hall, I saw Michu approaching.

'How did you enjoy your first game?' she asked, as she came up to me.

'First and *last*, I should think, judging by the way I played!' was my reply.

Michu threw back her pretty curly head and laughed. 'You should see *me* play!'

'I'd love to,' I said. I pictured her playing. When I saw her frown, I blushed.

Michu held my arm and took me aside. 'Bill, the elders will take me off the job of being your guide if they see you getting too attached to me.' She looked me straight in the eyes. I thought at that moment how beautiful she looked.

'I can't help the way I feel, Michu,' I said. 'But I promise to behave. I would not want another guide.'

'Good! Now, about the programme for the next two days. Tomorrow we are going to visit the greatest volcano in the solar system and the Valles Marineris, you know, the canyon I told you about. It is also the largest in the solar system. The following day we shall go to see the Monuments of Cydonia.'

'You mean the famous face and the ancient city?
'Exactly!'

'Cool! There is a lot of argument back home about them. Some say they are made by beings from outer space and some say they are natural. What is the truth, Michu?'

'Wait till you see them and you can make up your own mind.'

No amount of questioning would make her tell me more. I couldn't wait to see them with my own eyes!

CHAPTER FOURTEEN
HIGH VOLCANOS AND DEEP CANYONS

A large bubble was parked by the cliff face as Michu and I passed through the entrance way into the soft grey light of early morning, each in our own personal bubble. The sun had still not risen above the horizon. High above us in the sky, one of the two Martian moons reflected the sun's rays.

'That's Phobos,' Michu explained. 'It is the larger of our two satellites but very small compared to your moon. It is only about nine thousand kilometres away.'

I could just make out that it was not round like our own moon.

'It is elongated,' Michu continued. Actually it was not formed at the same time as Mars, like your moon was. It is a captured asteroid.'

'How do you mean 'captured', Michu?'

'It was one of the larger bodies in the asteroid belt, between here and Jupiter. It had an elliptical orbit round the sun, which sometimes brought it close to Mars. On one of its trips round the sun it came too near Mars and the gravity would not let it escape. Fortunately it managed to settle down into a stable orbit.'

'Why was it fortunate?' I was fascinated by this information.

'It could have crashed into the surface of Mars and, you know, an asteroid of fourteen kilometres long can make a very big hole in the planet, with devastating consequences.'

'Amazing!' I said. 'What would happen?'

'Imagine the dust for one thing, and the earthquakes and volcanoes.'

'Yes. It happened once on Earth, I remember reading. An enormous meteorite hit the Earth and wiped out the dinosaurs.'

'And most of the other species living on your planet at the time,' said Michu. 'The thing was over ten kilometres across. The sun was not seen for years. That was sixty-five million Earth years ago. And there have been many others.'

'Really?'

'Yes. Luckily, large asteroids are less common in these times, but millions of years ago both Mars and Earth suffered many major collisions. But it is still possible, even now.'

I shuddered to think of a huge lump of rock hitting my home town.

'Tell me more.' I was impressed at her knowledge of our Earth's history.

'Another time, Bill, we have a lot to see today.

I looked up again at Phobos and noticed that it had already moved Eastward in the direction of the sunrise. By the end of the day it would already be back in the sky above us.

Michu and I entered the large bubble and took our seats on cushions. I noticed there were several other cushions. Just then five other Martians came in from behind and, after greeting us, sat on the vacant cushions. I was told they were visitors from another clan living East of Cydonia, who were on a tour of our region. They were an assortment of types, brown or fair, like the Similaria clan, but they wore a greenish tunic. Like all Martians I had seen, they were small and wore no shoes.

We sat for some moments and I guessed they were praying silently to themselves. I did the same. Then suddenly the bubble began to move, slowly at first. It rose some few metres above the ground and then before I knew it, we were climbing swiftly into the air. In no time the ground was far below and we were moving forward. The red desert stretched out all around. A large dry river bed passed below us as we sped on. The sun was shining over to our left. Before long, the landscape grew more rugged. Long shadows marked the mountains. Then, as we rose still higher, I could begin to see the Valles Marineris stretching from far in the West for what looked like hundreds of kilometres towards the East. I wonder what could have caused such an enormous gash in the Martian crust.

'Asteroids, Bill,' was Michu's reply to my thought.

'Phew!' I whistled. 'That was a mighty big one to cause that!'

'If only you knew how big.'

'How big was it then?'

'Well, there were three big ones actually, remains of a gigantic comet. One was more than ninety kilometres across. The smallest was about thirty kilometres, but still a monster.'

'And one of them tore a chasm that big?' I was utterly fascinated.

'Not exactly 'tore' but the impact of the biggest asteroid way over to the South East caused Mars to literally burst its seem, and there, you see one of the results in that chasm.'

'Incredible!' I cried. Heads of the other passengers turned to look at me.

'Yes, you may say incredible.' Michu shook her head and continued. 'And that is not all that happened. The force of the asteroid ploughing its way deep into the centre of Mars, followed by two more, blew away millions of square kilometres of the crust of the northern hemisphere of Mars. It was literally blown away into space. That gigantic explosion also caused four enormous volcanoes to erupt. We shall see them later.'

'Were there any Martians living at that time?' I asked.

'No. That was many hundreds of thousands of years ago. But there were creatures living on Mars then.'

'What kind of creatures?'

'Mostly minute amphibians and tiny fish-like creatures in the oceans.'

'I knew there was water on Mars, but oceans as well!'

'Oh, yes. Those must have been wonderful days on Mars, 'said Michu wistfully.'

'So what happened to the living things?' I asked.

'Nothing could survive such a calamity, Bill. All life was wiped out. The energy created by the combined impact of those asteroids caused the seas to evaporate and most of the atmosphere drifted off into space. Mars, over a period of only a few years, became uninhabitable. Only the spirit beings remained.'

I added, 'because they have no body, they can't be harmed.'

'Correct.'

'But you can survive,' I put in, hopefully.

'We were prepared. The life at that time did not have the intelligence.'

My mind went back to a previous conversation and I wondered again where these Martians, that looked so much like us, came from. Michu gave me a look, as much as to say, 'I know what you're thinking. Forget it.'

I looked down at the canyon. We seemed to be going down. After a pause, Michu continued.

'There were other effects of those mighty impacts, too. For a start, Mars is much smaller than the Earth and its rate of spin should be much quicker, but it is not. The impact had the effect of eventually slowing down the rate at which Mars turns on its axis.'

'Now twenty-four and a half Earth hours.' I was pleased to show of my newly acquired knowledge.

'Exactly! And you know that Mars has an unusually elliptical orbit, which takes it quite near to the Earth every so many years. At the moment it is relatively far from you but sometimes it is much brighter in your night sky. Of course Earth will also look correspondingly bigger to us on Mars.'

'I know. Mars came close to us just four years ago. It was bright red.'

Michu went on, 'and over long periods of time the north-south tilt fluctuates.'

I interrupted. 'I'm lost, Michu. Can you explain what you mean?'

She laughed and her dark eyes shone. 'You know, of course that the Earth tilts back and forth on its axis once every time it goes round the sun.'

'That is what causes our seasons,' I said.

'The Earth tilts to the South and you enjoy your summer in England.'

'When we get a summer at all,' I quipped.

'Well, Mars has seasons in much the same way because Mars also tilts, strange as you may think, almost exactly the same amount as the Earth. The difference is that the degree of tilt varies over long periods of time and then the seasons also change.'

'Mars and the Earth are so alike in many ways though,' I said.

'Seasons on Mars are much longer than yours. But the polar ice caps do grow and recede as yours do, in time with the tilting.'

'What are the ice caps made of, Michu?'

'The North polar cap is made of frozen carbon dioxide and water ice. The South Pole has only frozen carbon dioxide. The water ice never melts because it is too cold, and therefore it has not followed all the other water into space.'

'But why is it that water cannot exist on the surface of Mars?' I wanted to know.

'The ground pressure is too low, less than ten millibars, compared to one thousand on Earth. But we are lucky to have as much water as we want underground.'

Michu gave me one of her charming smiles. Martians, I knew, would never forget the gift of water, the sustainer of life. How many people on Earth really appreciate that wonderful gift?

I had been right, the bubble was descending and soon we were below the rim of the canyon, which stretched as far as I could see in each direction. The walls soared up on each side. At the bottom, far below, there were signs that a torrent of water once swept along its length and the sides were heavily eroded by steep streams.

A sudden thought struck me. I was surprised that I it had not occurred to me before. Who was in control of this bubble?

Michu laughed. 'Who is flying this thing? Is that what you are wondering?'

'Mmm,' I nodded, a little crossly.

'Remote control.'

'Remote control?'

'Yes, from Similaria. Our entire trip is programmed in advance.'

'Like my rescue in the depths of space, I suppose,' I volunteered.

'Like your rescue, in the nick of time,' laughed Michu.

'Alright, you win.' I had to admit I was out of my depth.

The bubble continued along the canyon, controlled by someone in Similaria.

'How deep is this canyon?' I asked.

'Seven kilometres, several times deeper than your Grand Canyon.'

'And the Americans think everything over there is the biggest.' I could not resist the temptation to poke a little fun at our brothers from across the Atlantic.

'I might add that their foreign policy of late has produced some of the very biggest blunders of all time,' said Michu. 'And they are the biggest producers of greenhouse gases.'

I had to agree with her on that one.

After what seemed like hours we reached the end of the Western end of the Valles Marineris and climbed out onto level ground. The bubble increased speed. After some time I noticed ahead of us what looked like three big boils in a line.

'Those are the Tharsis Montes, gigantic volcanoes, created at the same time as the Valles Marineris. Aren't they impressive?'

'Fantastic!' I agreed.

'But you wait!' said Michu.

'What must I wait for?'

'The biggest volcano of all, Olympus Mons!' she announced dramatically.

It was not long before it appeared over the horizon. It was majestic, to be sure.

'Twenty-five kilometres tall, the highest volcano in the solar system,' said Michu. 'And over seven hundred kilometres across.'

'Wow! One of the seven wonders of the solar system,' I said.

We passed directly over the crater at a height of only about five thousand metres.

'The caldera is over sixty kilometres wide,' Michu told me.

'The crater? And is it active?'

'Not any more, Bill. It burst out as a result of the huge asteroids we talked about earlier. Imagine the heat! The whole of Mars must have rocked.'

I tried to imagine what it must have been like to be a poor creature alive at the time of the disaster.

'And shall I tell you something, Bill? If the asteroids had been much bigger, Mars would not exist today.'

'You mean it would have been blown to bits?' I cried.

'You've got it!' No Mars! Just thousands of bits going round the sun in a belt between Venus and Jupiter.'

'You mean Earth and Jupiter, surely.'

'No, I mean Venus and Jupiter, Bill.'

My mind was racing. What does she mean? Mercury, Venus, Earth, Mars and Jupiter in that order. Then I knew her meaning. Earth would also not exist today.

'You've got it Bill. The chances are that some of that material that once made up the planet Mars, going around in all sorts of peculiar orbits, would at some point collide with the Earth. Maybe the Earth would have survived, but barren like Mars is today, with no life at all. It is more likely that an asteroid, many hundreds of kilometres wide, would have blown the Earth to bits. But of course it was not meant to be.'

I was quiet for the rest of the way back to Similaria.

CHAPTER FIFTEEN
CYDONIA

Cydonia lay several hundred kilometres to the North-East of Similaria. We started off in a bubble similar to the one that had taken us to Olympus Mons, and perhaps it was the same one. The bubbles seemed to come in all sizes, almost as if they were made to suit each particular journey. Nothing was going to surprise me, even if Tony Blair suddenly came in saying he was really a Martian and he had been tricking us all these years!

Accompanying Michu and me on this trip was an elderly woman called Zeena, who had studied the monuments for many years. She was short, like most Martians, strong looking, with gray hair and brown eyes. She bowed low at our meeting and smiled broadly, showing a set of uneven teeth. She introduced herself as Zeeeena, pronouncing it as if it had an extra couple of e's.

The sun was before us in the salmon pink sky as we sped off in the direction of Cydonia. All around us lay the same red desert, littered with rocks and boulders of varying sizes and shapes. We passed several dry river beds and a few impact craters, mostly small.

We had not gone far when the bubble started to lose height and at the same time reduced speed. Michu pointed to something on the ground over to the right. At first I could not see what she was pointing at. Then I saw a small metal thing on thin legs, with arms sticking out in all directions. I realised I was looking at a landing craft. I looked enquiringly at Michu.

'Something of yours that was left behind,' she said jokingly.

'Viking?'

'Viking I, your first successful landing on Mars.'

'Since then there have been several more, haven't there?'

'Pathfinder, which landed over to the South-East of here about five years ago. A remote controlled rover on wheels. It surveyed the area, sending back film.'

'I was still small but I remember reading about it later. American Spirit was a more recent rover.'

'You know, Earth people should not litter someone else's home with junk. Why don't you take it back with you, Bill?'

I knew she was joking. 'You could make use of it, Michu. Make it into knives and forks. Eating with your hands is not civilised.' We laughed and Zeena joined in.

As we left Viking I behind, I continued to look at its remains, a sad corpse that was likely to remain there long after those who celebrated its success are no more, until finally it is lost beneath layers of Martian red dust.

Our bubble climbed higher and increased speed once more. Nothing relieved the monotony of the desert stretched out below.

For some time my mind dwelt on the possibility that before long a manned flight to Mars would become a reality. I could not imagine the Martians would be pleased to have Earth people nosing around on their doorstep. Just imagine the day an American astronaut comes face to face with his double. He will think the Russians have beaten him to it. The cold war would begin again, even colder this time, on the cold surface of Mars. I smiled to myself.

'It's no joke, Bill!' said Michu. She had been studying me for a while and was reading my thoughts.

Suddenly, Zeena called across to me. 'We are reaching Cydonia. Look ahead!'

I peered out of the bubble in the direction she was pointing. I could see in the distance a group of pyramid shaped objects, and many small mounds. As we drew nearer and the bubble lost height, the objects became clearer. Farther off to right there was a much larger pyramid, regular in shape. My first impression was one of awe. These were the monuments that had caused so much argument back on Earth for the last thirty years, since they were first discovered in photos sent back by Viking I. My second impression was that they must be artificial. I had seen nothing like those shapes since landing on Mars and here they were, all grouped together. They had to be made by someone! But whom?

Zeena was pointing out to Michu excitedly in their language all the different objects. I wondered how many times she had seen these same things and yet she was still like a child with a new toy.

'The face!' I shouted. I had spotted it further ahead. 'The face! I can see the face!'

Zeena beamed and she showed all her teeth. 'Well? Is it a face or is it just a trick of light and shadow?' she asked.

'It's a face, for sure. I have no doubt!' I said with utter conviction.

'NASA has said all along that all these things are natural formations, fashioned by wind erosion.'

'Then NASA must be blind!' was my immediate reply.

'Or maybe they wanted to hide something,' said Zeena. 'Governments on Earth like to keep things from the people. Frightened people are not easily governed. You may remember some years ago all the fuss about UFO's. The American Government squashed all debate because they feared what would happen if their people knew that aliens were visiting Earth. But many people saw those UFO's and aliens walking about. The military dealt with them. Those who said they had seen it all were labeled as insane. We shall go and have a closer look at the face,'

As if the bubble heard her words, it suddenly swooped down and came to rest on the ground. Around us the varied shapes of the monuments stood out against the sky with their short shadows all pointing to the West.

'This is the centre of the complex,' explained Zeena. 'Your researchers call it 'The City.'

'It doesn't look much like a city now,' I said.

'The pyramids of Teotihuacán don't either, do they?' she said.

'You mean the ones in Mexico?'

'Yes. Once, thousands of years ago, it was a bustling city and the Pyramids of the Sun and the Moon were religious structures, aligned to those heavenly bodies.'

'And the ones in Egypt too,' I added.

'Isn't it strange that pyramids should occur on Earth and on Mars too?'

I nodded. 'Some people on Earth say that they are connected in some way.'

'There is a lot of similarity between them,' said Zeena. 'And in Egyptian mythology, Mars is very important.'

'So who made all these pyramids, Martians or Earth people?' I asked.

'Why not beings from another galaxy?' suggested Zeena.

'You can't be serious!'

'It's possible.' She grinned.

'Do you mean you don't know who built these things?' I said. It was hard to believe that there was something these people didn't know.

'Let's leave that till later,' she said evasively. Then she went on to explain the various features of 'the City.' We moved about the central area in the bubble. Each mound was explained to me in detail. We circled the most prominent pyramid. On the South-Eastern side it appeared to have been eroded so that it looked less like a pyramid than from the other side. Then we sped off to the South-East to the biggest and most impressive of the pyramids. Zeena told me it was over one kilometre high and more than two and a half long, making it one thousand times bigger than the pyramids of Egypt. But it was not in the least like the pyramids of Egypt, which were made of thousands of blocks of stone, piled on top of each other. The pyramid before me seemed to be one solid block. How was it possible for someone to build such a massive thing?

'These monuments were built very many thousands of years ago,' explained Zeena. 'If you study them closely you will see that they *are* built of stone blocks but over the millennia erosion has worn them down, so that the blocks have lost their sharp edges.'

'And where did the stone come from?' I asked.

'From quarries not so far away. They too have been eroded by wind and are no longer very distinct.' She paused. 'And now for the face!'

We headed off to the North and soon the face came into view. We approached it at ground level. It appeared as a huge raised structure hundreds of metres long. Zeena told me it was altogether 800 metres high and about 2.5 kilometres long. As we came close to the wall the bubble lifted into the air, until we had cleared the cliff face. Another few hundred metres up and I could see the face clearly.

'Amazing!' I cried. 'It really does look like a head, complete with headdress.'

'A trick of light and shadow?' asked Michu provokingly.

'But I still don't see who could have made such an enormous thing.'

'Puzzling, isn't it?' said Zeena.

'So you don't know who made it.' It was hard to believe.

'To be honest, Bill, we don't know for sure. When our ancestors settled on Mars 7445 year ago, these things had already been here thousands of years. We have surfed the Uninet for a website that might give us a clue but there seems to be nothing. I am sorry to disappoint you.'

'Yeh, I am disappointed.' I admitted. 'But you agree that they are artificial and not natural features.'

'Absolutely, Bill. And whoever built these pyramids also built those on Earth, in Egypt and Mexico.'

'When our ancestors settled on Mars…' she had said. So these people did come from another planet. I had suspected it.

Michu gave Zeena a disapproving look, which Zeena seemed not to notice.

'The elders will put you in the picture when you meet with them tomorrow,' said Michu.

We spent some more time examining the features of the face, the eye sockets and the lines forming the headdress. More time was taken just drifting around at a higher altitude above the monuments, while Zeena tried to explain how each was aligned to the others and the sacred dimensions and angles involved. It was far too technical for me and I understood very little.

Finally we were on our way back to Similaria. It had been a wonderful day for me. How I would like to stand up in class and tell everyone that I had personally seen the famous monuments of Cydonia, something nobody on Earth had ever seen, except in pictures taken from space. I knew that I would never be able to do that. My Martian friends would never forgive me. And I could never forgive myself either. My unforgettable visit to Mars would always be a closely guarded secret.

CHAPTER SIXTEEN
BAD NEWS

My sixth day on Mars started with a bathe and breakfast as usual. I was getting to like the mushrooms we had every morning. I had tried several of the fruits grown at the farm and most of them rated well against any of the fruits at home. But when I began to conjure up in my mind some of my favourite foods, like scrambled eggs on toast or steak and kidney pie, I decided there was not much in the Universe to beat them. Then I thought it was better to wait until I had tasted all the foods in the Universe before I made such a rash judgment. Rabbits will say that carrots are the tops when it comes to eating but they don't give other exotic foods a chance. But rabbits are pretty dumb animals so maybe we can't blame them.

I was happy to see Michu that morning. She looked a little down though, not the usual winning smile. She came up to me and we greeted each other.

'I have been with the elders and they have told me to invite you to a meeting with them this afternoon, in one of the chambers off the Grand Hall, Chamber 13. I will take you there. I will not be attending the meeting; you will be there alone.'

'What did they tell you that has made you sad, Michu,' I asked.

'Nothing, Bill. It's nothing really. Well, your meeting is not until the afternoon. Perhaps you want to go to the library again and see something of interest on the Uninet.'

'That would be really cool,' I said.

We reached the library to find Sofu, Anamaru, Manu, Diana and a few other young Martians sitting in a circle, with an older person, who was obviously conducting a class of some kind. Michu apologised for the interruption, saying she had forgotten about the class. The teacher said they were about to finish, so Michu and I went to the far side of the library and sat waiting for the end of the lesson.

'Sorry about that,' she said, as we sat down on two cushions.

'You're not your normal self today, Michu,' I said with concern, looking into her face. She looked away, not wanting our eyes to meet.

Then the bombshell!

'You have to go back home tomorrow, Bill.' It was then that she looked up and our eyes met.

'So soon?' I cried in a hoarse whisper. 'I've hardly seen anything!'

We looked at each other. A lump came up in my throat. I could see a tear forming in each of her eyes. One began to trickle slowly down her cheek.

'The elders think it best, Bill.'

'Why?'

'Because…..because…. not only are you getting too attached to me but….I'm getting very fond of you too.' She managed a weak smile and brushed away the tears from her face.

I looked at her in surprise. I hadn't realised. There was no doubt in my mind that I had grown to love her in the short space of five days, but I had not dared to hope she would feel the same for me.

'I don't want to go back to Earth, Michu. Oh, Michu, I shall miss you so much!'

'And don't you think I will miss you too, Bill?'

'What can we do?'

'Nothing, you will have to go, that's all. We cannot disobey a request from the elders. It has never happened before.'

I must have looked dejected because she gave me a sympathetic look and a smile and squeezed my hand gently. I held her hand tightly, but as I did so she withdrew it quickly.

'You'll come to visit me on Earth.' It was a statement, not a question.

'Who knows? I would have to get permission from the el.....'

'.....elders, I know!' I said crossly.

She looked hurt. 'Bill, we respect the elders of Similaria. They act in the best interests of the community. Everything here works in harmony. Do you understand?'

I nodded. 'Yes, I understand, but.........'

'No 'buts'. That is the decision and we have to abide by it.'

'But you will come, no?' I persisted. 'If you don't, I will come back to Mars.'

'You can only come if a bubble is provided,' she said.

'And that will depend on the elders, right?'

'Yes.' She smiled. 'But we *will* see each other again, I have no doubt. Anyway, you will only have to think of me and I will know, and I will see your face.'

'You know how to do that but what about me? How will I contact you?'

'You can learn how to do too,' she said softly.

'How?'

'Go inside. Meditate! Imagine my face. If I am thinking of you, then in time you will see me clearly and even talk to me.'

I was skeptical but at least it cheered me up a bit.

'No photo?' I pleaded.

'No photo. I'm sorry, it's not allowed.'

I decided then that I would meditate every morning when I got back home.

'The class has finished,' Michu said and got to her feet. I followed her to the middle of the library. She accessed the Uninet and browsed through a few websites. We revisited the Sonam Tourist Authority website again and watched an interesting documentary film about the effects of tourism on the wildlife of the planet. I saw countless fascinating animals and their habits. I saw small animals being born and I was reminded of what Michu had told me, that animals there were sexless.

Michu and I sat together for a long time. It was good to be near her and I wondered when would be the next time.

Before leaving the library, we watched BBC news. England and India were playing the final Test Match at the Oval. England had won the toss and had decided to bat first. We had lost some early wickets but Pietersen was batting brilliantly and was about to reach his century. To think, I would be seeing it live on television tomorrow!

CHAPTER SEVENTEEN
ALONE WITH THE ELDERS

'We have asked you to come here because we think you should know a little more about us,' began the Chief of the Elders, stroking his white beard.

I sat on a cushion in front of three elders. On the left of the Chief Elder sat another man with greying hair and a pale face, from which peered two small grey eyes. I recognised him from the Council meeting. At that time he had not spoken. On the right sat the woman who had introduced the newborn child at that meeting.

Michu had accompanied me to Chamber 13, told me where I was to sit, and had left immediately. I had waited only a few minutes before the elders entered the chamber.

'You have spent six days here,' the Chief Elder continued slowly, measuring each word. I believe you have enjoyed your stay.' He looked straight into my eyes and held my gaze for a while. Then he smiled and his eyes sparkled.

'I certainly have, Sir,' I replied as respectfully as I could.

'Good! Michu has been diligent in her duties as your guide.' Here he looked at me again and I turned a little red.

'You have seen some of the natural wonders of our planet, and also some of the artificial ones. You have understood a little of how we live here. Isn't that so?'

'Yes Sir.' I began to sweat a bit. This man is powerful, I thought. He read my mind and smiled kindly, I think to put me more at ease.

'Everything you have seen, everything you have been told, everything that I am about to tell you, must be treated as strictly confidential. Is that quite clear?'

I nodded, unable to form the words that came to my mind.

'Say yes!'

'Yes Sir,' I managed to say.

'Good! You will understand that if anyone on Earth becomes aware of our existence, it will be the beginning of the end of our way of life.' He looked at me sternly.

I nodded again. I began to wonder why I had been brought here if the risk was so great.

'It is important for your planet that you were brought here. Not just important, *vital*.' He stressed the last word. 'And we believe that you will not say a word when you go home tomorrow. You know you are leaving tomorrow, don't you?'

'Yes Sir.'

'And you know why, don't you?'

'Yes Sir.'

'A security risk, you understand. It is better to nip it in the bud, as you say in English.'

I nodded and the knot in my throat was there again.

'You suspect that we Martians came here from another planet, isn't that so?'

'Yes Sir.'

'You don't have to keep calling me sir. My name is Zeris.'

'Yes Sir, I mean….. Zeris.' It was hard for me to call him by his name.

'And do you know which planet we came from?' he asked, leaning forward and staring into my eyes.

'No Sir.'

'Guess!'

'I don't know Sir.'

'Just have a guess.'

'No idea Sir.'

'Earth, my friend, Earth!'

'Earth?' I whispered.

'Yes, Earth. Does it surprise you?'

'Yes Sir. But it kind of adds up.'

'We look like you, we speak your languages and so on, right?'

'Yes Sir, Zeris.'

'Let me tell you how we came here and why.' He settled himself on his cushion and began.

'At school you have learnt something of the pre-history of your planet, is that right?'

'Yes Sir.'

'Your last ice-age lasted from about 100,000 years ago until about 20,000 years ago. I use Earth years when talking of Earth matters. Twenty thousand years ago the Earth was very different from what it is today. Glaciers covered most of North America and all of Northern Europe. England north of the River Thames was solid ice and where New York City now stands was beneath a thick glacier. Most people lived in equatorial regions, where it was warmer. Most of the land that was not ice-bound was covered by forests. Many prehistoric animals roamed the land and mankind was basically a hunter.' At this point Zeris paused and stroked his long beard.

'But not all. Living alongside a primitive majority there was one very advanced civilisation. In the Atlantic Ocean, I shall not say where, lay a group of islands. It was densely populated, both onshore and in the ocean itself.' He stopped to gauge my reaction. I listened intently but said nothing.

'The people making up this civilisation were a mixture of races, brought together by a common bond. Do you know what that bond was?' He waited for a reply and as there was none, he continued. 'It was scientific advancement. They had already developed advanced living conditions and used power sources that humans are even now are only beginning to use, such as wave power, wind power and of course solar energy. We had also discovered the secret of crystal power. Those who lived under water lived in structures that extracted oxygen from the water, much like fish do, with the use of artificial gills. Heat was derived from water seeping through layers of hot rock.'

I studied the face before me. What I was hearing hardly seemed credible.

Zeris went on speaking. 'For hundreds of years this society flourished. But scientific development was all very well. There had to be something else. A group of people got together and decided to find this 'something else'. Pure materialism cannot satisfy the human soul. Of the total population of half a million, a growing number joined the new movement. When the number reached about 20,000, the National Governing Council decided that it was becoming too powerful and it had become a threat to the their authority. You see, as so often happens in society, leaders become too powerful and they become jealous of any opposition. This is what happened. They decided to ban the movement altogether. Many of the less committed members drifted back into mainstream life, but a few decided to fight for what they considered were their rights. They were exiled.

I squirmed on my cushion. I could see where the story was leading.

'About five hundred souls were exiled, exiled to a place where the Council thought no-one could survive. Do you know where that was?'

'Was it Mars Sir?'

'Mars, exactly!'

'They could have executed all of you, Sir.'

'They could have, but they didn't. They sent us off to Mars in thirty bubbles. These bubbles had been in existence for many years but it is certain that the Council believed these bubbles would not serve us adequately in our new home. There was a group within the Council that wanted us to have a sporting chance at survival and they must have persuaded the hardliners. Anyway, we arrived here over 13,000 years ago….and we survived, as you can see.' He smiled.

'Of course it was not easy at first. There were many challenges. We had to find enough water and oxygen and we had to keep warm. We had our faith and that kept us going. The bubbles kept us alive but they needed further development to make them suitable for Mars conditions. We also brought with us another valuable science, crystology, the knowledge of crystal power. You have seen the crystals which light our cavern I suppose.'

I nodded. 'I wondered how they produced light. So they are not natural!'

'Crystals were used for many years by our civilisation. Unfortunately the knowledge of crystal power has been lost to Earth humans. I say unfortunately because it is a renewable source of power that is non-polluting.' Well, once established on Mars, we increased in number over the centuries and we spread out. Now there are about 100,000 souls altogether, living in scattered communities like Similaria.'

Zeris smiled and sat back on his cushion. I was not sure what to say.

'And you counted your years from the day you got here,' I ventured.

'That is right. We are now in the year 7445.'

'And, Sir, what happened to the civilisation back on Earth?'

'A good question and I am about to answer it. It survived for another few hundred years. But like all civilisations, it had to end one day. They quarrelled among themselves and eventually a civil war broke out. They destroyed themselves. Then one day hundreds of years later, a huge asteroid struck the Earth. Then after another 2000 years an even bigger one landed in the Atlantic Ocean. The devastation was so great that most of the species on Earth were wiped out. There were earthquakes and a skyscraper high tidal wave that washed over America, Europe and Africa. Volcanic activity broke out all over the planet. There was a sudden increase in temperatures and the glaciers melted at a rate never before experienced on Earth. All that water flowing into the oceans caused the sea to rise more than one hundred metres over a few thousand years and much of the low lying land was lost under the sea, including the islands from which we had come. Billions of tons of water evaporated into the atmosphere due to this very rapid rise in the temperature and for decades, torrential rain swept across the Earth. There are many legends about a devastating flood, the story of Noah's Ark being one. Nothing now remains of those islands to show where that great civilisation once flourished.'

He stopped speaking and looked up to the ceiling of the chamber. I was trying to digest the horrifying picture that he had put in my mind. At last I was able to speak.

'Human beings survived, at least some must have,' I said.

'Homo sapiens is a very resourceful race. They soon bounced back and tremendous advances were made over the next few thousand years. All other humanoid races, like homo habilis and Neanderthal man were not smart enough and became extinct. But you know what?'

'Sir?'

'Mankind is about to make the same mistake. He is putting scientific advancement above every other consideration. It is a dangerous game.' Zeris fixed me with a powerful gaze. 'And that is where you come in.'

'Sir?'

'You will be part of the solution.' You would rather be part of the solution than part of the problem. Am I correct?'

'Yes, Sir.'

'You will go to University and become well qualified. You will take your place among those on your planet who want to preserve it for future generations. We are there to help. As you know, we have several Martians working on Earth at this very moment. You will meet some of them.'

'Yes Sir, I was told, about five hundred.'

'Good, now there is one other thing I need to say to you. The other evening at the meeting it was mentioned that we face a very serious situation here in Similaria. We hope we shall not alarm you too much but to come straight to the point, our survival is threatened.' He paused and studied my face. 'We see that you are concerned and it is understandable. You have made friends here and you fear for their safety.'

I needed to say nothing. He read me like a book.

'The threat comes from another Martian community living far over to the East in a region you have called Utopia. Coincidentally we call it Zeronera, which in *Kisoro* means a perfect place. You understand the word Utopia of course. They are more numerous than we are, in fact the biggest clan on Mars, about 3,000 souls and the population is increasing, so much so that they are in urgent need of additional resources, which at present they don't have. They are in an expansionist phase. Do you see where I am leading?'

'Yes Sir, I think so. They want what you have.'

'Right! You are intelligent, Bill. They want all that we have built up over thousands of years, and they will stop at nothing to get it.'

'Have you tried diplomacy, Sir?'

'Of course yes. We have ourselves provided children for their clan and they have done so for us too. So you see we are interrelated. At this point I should explain something. The populations of our clans are small and to keep a healthy stock we do not interbreed. A Similaria girl will look for a father for the child she wants from another clan. The child stays with the mother's clan and is brought up as a child of the community rather than as a child of the parents. The father stays with his own clan. This system has worked very well for us.'

'So there is no marriage here.'

'Correct. But let's get back to what I was saying. Zeronera not only wants to throw us out of Similaria but they want to rule Mars. They have not said so in so many words but we suspect it is true. Of course we could unite with other clans that are in sympathy with us and we could fight a war against Zeronera.' Zeris frowned and put on a pained expression. 'Unfortunately Zeronera has friends, powerful friends.' Zeris stroked his white beard before continuing. 'The planet Zogg circles Altair, a star about seventeen light years away, relatively close in galactic terms and in the same arm of our spiral galaxy. Zogg is another world where science is God. They have pursued a line of research that your Earth scientists have been doing since Einstein. One of their major achievements is the discovery of a particle that travels very much faster than the speed of light. You have been taught that the speed of light cannot possibly be exceeded. Well the Zoggs have proved us all wrong. They have harnessed that particle and can now travel enormous distances in a very short time. No Martian could possibly travel to Zogg in a lifetime but the Zoggs, the Zoggs could be here in a matter of months. Imagine! Not that they are interested in Mars as such. Mars does not have anything more to offer them than they have on their planet. But it would suit them to have allies in our solar system. We suspect what they are really interested in is the Earth.' He paused and locked his grey eyes on me.

'Oh no!' I whispered. I stared back at him. 'They want to conquer Earth!'

'We have no proof of this. Don't be too alarmed. Of course Earth is a very rich and wonderful planet, possibly one of the most beautiful in our galaxy. Who would not want to own it?'

'What would become of us?'

'Perhaps I should not have said anything about it. Put it out if your mind. We do admit that we in Similaria are becoming too alarmist about these matters. Now, you see our problem. If Zogg invades Mars and helps Zeronera to rule the whole planet, we are in danger of disappearing, or at least becoming slaves of the Zeronerans.

I pictured Michu in chains, working in a gang, while a burly Martian with a whip stands over them menacingly. I didn't like the image one bit.

Zeris went on, 'Like Zeronera, we need friends. Earth would make a useful ally for us. We ourselves have no wish to involve Earth in a galactic war but we fear it could come to that anyway. Let us explain why we see it that way. As the population of Earth increases and pollution worsens, people will look to other worlds. Mars would be first, perhaps within a hundred years from now. Then, once space travel becomes routine, mankind will look further afield for cleaner worlds. The inhabitants of those worlds will not give in without a fight. We don't want that to happen. We don't want Mars polluted like the Earth. Neither do we want to see Earth deteriorate so much that it becomes uninhabitable. That is why we are helping you to solve your enormous environmental problems. It is in our interest as well as yours.'

I could see the picture very clearly now. What did he want from us? Did he want Earth to help fight the Zoggs?

'We want you to dedicate your life to saving your world. Do you see my point? We are prepared to do all we can to see that you succeed.'

'It is my mission in life. I see it clearly now,' I said.

'Good.' Zeris smiled a warm smile. 'Now, there is another thing. Earth faces another threat, one that your people have studiously ignored up to now, apart from a few enthusiasts.'

'What is that Sir?' I asked.

'Comets and the remains of comets.'

'Sir?'

'There are many huge chunks of rock orbiting the sun in highly elliptical orbits. They are the remains of enormous comets which have been slowly disintegrating for thousands of years. Many of them cross the Earth's path, and I may say also the path of Mars too. One day one of those asteroids, let's call them that, may possibly, I only say possibly, strike the Earth, with terrible consequences. It is vital that your astronomers mount a continuous watch on these asteroids and develop the technology to deflect them before they collide with the Earth.' Zeris paused and fixed his gaze on me.

'How do you know this?' I asked.

'Mars is in similar danger: it is in our interest to know. We have tried to sensitise your politicians on this issue, with little success so far.'

I sat and digested his words. The thought was frightening.

'Tomorrow you will leave. You have our blessing.'

'Thank you Zeris, Sir. But I was told you would help me explain to my parents where I have been these seven days.'

'I was coming to that. Your parents will not know you have been away.'

I looked at Zeris with a puzzled expression.

'You will arrive home only thirty minutes after you left.' He smiled.

I was not sure I understood him.

'Does that mean I will travel back in time seven days Sir?'

'I hope it will be no more than that, otherwise you will arrive home before you have even set off for Mars.' All three elders enjoyed the joke.

This was the biggest surprise of my entire trip to Mars. They actually know how to travel back in time.

'What do I have to do Sir?' I asked.

'Michu will advise you, don't worry,' he said. 'And now our meeting is ended. May the Almighty guide you and protect you. We may not meet again.'

All three elders rose and bowed. Then they filed out of the chamber, leaving me alone to digest the contents of the meeting. I must be dreaming. I'll wake up and find myself at home in bed. My mother will be standing over me, telling me it is time to get up and not be so lazy. I pinched myself but nothing happened, except that a little red mark showed on my arm. It was no dream. This was real, REAL.

CHAPTER EIGHTEEN
HOME AGAIN

The next morning I stayed extra long in the pool. I knew it was my last time to experience the soft warm water under the glittering crystals. As I floated around I knew I was going to miss Similaria.

All my young friends were at breakfast when I arrived at the dining area. Michu got up to meet me. She looked more beautiful than ever, I thought. She took me by the arm and led me to my cushion. I couldn't help squeezing her arm affectionately.

'Your last mushrooms, Bill,' said Anamaru.

'Roll on eggs and bacon!' I replied to the merriment of all.

'Earth foods!' scoffed Sofu putting another mushroom into her mouth and rolling her eyes in mock ecstasy.

'The fruit I'll definitely miss,' I said.

'We'll send you a bubble full, don't worry,' said Manu.

'We have people in my country who inspect those kinds of things. Imagine what they would say if they found Martian fruit!'

'They would sit and eat it all,' said Diana, acting the part of the official, stuffing his mouth with two hands.

'Then they would spend the next few days in the toilet,' said Michu.

The conversation moved to more serious subjects. I told them a little of what the Chief Elder had had to say at our meeting the day before. I was hesitant about going into detail, fearing that I was divulging something the others were not supposed to know. But I need not have worried because Michu assured me that all I was told about the danger to Similaria had been discussed at the special meeting that I didn't go to.

'Oh and I was told I would go back in time so that my parents would not know I had gone anywhere. That's so cool!'

'That's right, Bill,' said Michu. 'We'll go through that just before you leave this morning.'

'So why don't I stay for thirty years and then I can go back in time thirty years. My parents will still not know I've been away.'

'Wrong!' they all said in chorus.

I looked disappointed. 'Why?'

'Because your parents will see a middle-aged man, that's why,' said Michu. 'You cannot delay the aging process.'

'Foiled!' I said.

There was a lot of amusement as they all tried to guess what I would look like in thirty years.

Finally breakfast was over and we left the dining area.

'Will you all see me off?' I asked.

'Unfortunately we all have tasks to complete today,' said Manu. 'We have to say goodbye now. I believe Michu will see you on your way.'

I said my farewells to all my friends, telling them I would miss them. I invited them to come to stay.

'Perhaps, one day,' said Manu. 'Who knows?'

I had nothing to carry with me. The clothes I had come with from Earth had all been destroyed. I wore the grey tunic and nothing else.

Michu and I took the bubble lift to the entrance to Similaria and from there we entered separate bubbles for the short trip to the top of the valley and onto the plain. After a while we came to a flat area and our bubbles stopped. I looked around and saw Silver Streak, tilted and already dust-covered, sitting sadly in the flat expanse of desert.

'The two bubbles will be there as soon as you are ready,' said Michu.

'Why two?' I asked. 'The one to take me to Earth and….?'

'The time bubble,' Michu said.

Our two bubbles came together and Michu stepped into mine. I noticed she was carrying something wrapped in a grey cloth.

'Your camera and mobile,' she said, handing them to me. I put the mobile in the pocket of the tunic but kept the camera in my hands.

'So, Bill, this is where we say goodbye.'

''Au revoir,' the French say.'

''Au revoir' it is,' said Michu, 'until we meet again.'

'Michu, I'll miss you so much.'

'Me too, Bill.'

'And I'll miss Similaria, too.'

'What is so wonderful about Similaria?'

I was surprised at this question.

'Earth,' said Michu, 'is a beautiful planet. Mars was once, but not anymore. Be thankful to the Almighty for the miracle that is yours.'

'Don't you like your home, Michu?

'Of course! It is home. But you cannot compare it with Earth.'

'You are right, Michu. The Earth and everything on it is a miracle.' I paused and looked into her eyes. 'Come with me to Earth, Michu.'

She laughed. 'That is impossible.'

'Why?'

'Forget it, Bill. It cannot be.'

'I suppose so, but there was no harm in trying.'

'Well, now I need to give you some instructions. Move in your bubble to the blue one, that is the Time Bubble. Let them touch and give the side a slight push. You will find yourself inside. Walk straight through to the other side and do the same. You will then be in your space bubble. You need do nothing more. Both have been programmed. But don't delay in the time bubble. If you do, you may go back in time too far. Do you understand?'

'Yes, I follow,' I said.

'Well, go now, and safe journey.'

'Michu?'

'Yes?'

I moved towards her. I lifted the camera and pushed the button. There was a flash and I saw her for an instant on the screen before it vanished. She was taken aback but said nothing. She knew it was not permitted but I believe she wanted me to have a keepsake. I moved closer to her with the hope of a hug. She turned and as she did so, I could see tears in her eyes. Before I could do anything, she had passed into her own bubble. I stood for a moment with watery eyes. She was gone, my Michu!

For a few moments I stood there, watching her bubble move slowly away. Then I moved in my bubble up to the blue one and followed the instructions she had given me. I felt no physical sensation on passing through the blue bubble but I knew that I had just gone back to a time before the morning of my arrival on Mars. There was no sign of my contraption, as Michu had fondly called it, so I supposed that I had not actually arrived yet, if you know what I mean. Time travel is all very confusing!

Once inside the space bubble, I settled down, ready for the journey. In no time we were airborne. The red desert stretched away in all directions as we rose into the hazy Martian sky. I looked down for Michu's bubble but it had gone. I wondered then whether she had purposely become invisible or she was well out of range. Then I knew it was because I had still not arrived. It was then that I started to cry.

'You're crazy, man!' I said out loud. 'She's a Martian! There's no future in it.' I turned on the camera, clicked the small button on the back and Michu's face was there, a startled face but Michu's anyway. I put the camera safely away in my other pocket.

By now the bubble was whisking me into space and Mars was now an enormous red ball. I began to feel very light. I looked the other way, hoping to see the Earth, shining in the blackness of space. I knew it would be hard to see at this distance. Eventually, as Mars slowly receded into the distance, I peered ahead, wondering why I couldn't see the Earth as a multi-coloured ball. I had almost made up my mind we were heading for outer space when I saw the Earth ahead of me, as a thin crescent. It steadily grew bigger, mostly shadowy, with only the slim shape exhibiting its colours of blue, brown, yellow and white. After an hour or so more, when Earth hovered solidly before me, my bubble shifted into a wide orbit, so the more of the lighted side was visible. I could make out the continent of Africa, virtually clear of cloud. The western half was in darkness. I was overwhelmed by the beauty of it all over again. Finally Europe came into view. The heel of Italy's boot shone in the blue of the Mediterranean. Sunrise had still not come to parts of Western Europe. We approached fast. I could see England now, with little cloud. I remembered how fine the weather had been the day I left home. Of course, I was arriving on the very same morning. That was really neat!

I suddenly got the same feeling as I had experienced on landing on Mars. We were going to crash. But then the bubble slowed down. Now I could see my home town. The streets were still fairly empty. A few cars, the same matchbox toys I had seen the week before, were filing along slowly. Then I saw our street, the house and then….we were on the ground. Instantly the bubble dissolved and I stepped out onto the grass, wet with the dew.

The house was there and behind me the shed where I had built Silver Streak. I couldn't resist a look inside. Maybe I expected to find Silver Streak there, but it was not. Of course, it had lifted of shortly before and would soon be just another piece of junk littering the face of the Red planet. I remembered Michu's joke about it.

Was she real?

All that remained to prove that Silver Streak had been there were a few black scorch marks on the floor. Silver Streak itself was on its way to Mars, with me or without me, I could not decide which. It was all too confusing for me.

I walked towards the house, looking up at the windows. The curtains were still drawn. Suddenly, one of the curtains moved aside and I saw my father's face. He saw me and put up his hand in a sleepy way. I went in the back door into the kitchen. My note had gone from the place on the table where I had left it.

Just then my father came into the kitchen carrying my note in his hand.

'What's all this nonsense about going to Mars?' he said, yawning. Then he looked at me again. 'And what's that strange getup you're wearing, and no shoes, you'll catch your death of cold.'

I knew there was no use explaining.

PART TWO

Fight for the Secret

CHAPTER NINETEEN
CROSS EXAMINATION

I stood in the middle of the kitchen, looking down at my wet feet and then I lifted my arm and studied the grey cloth of my tunic, anything to avoid my father's eyes.

'There's something strange going on here son,' he said, waving my note in front of my face.

'Oh, what's that, Dad?' I asked with shaky innocence, still not wanting to meet his eyes.

'You tell me.'

'I don't know what you mean, Dad.

'Now then, your mother and I are lying in bed, half asleep and we hear this strange whooshing noise and a flash. I sit up in bed and I turn to her and I say, 'Doris, did you see that?' and she says, 'yes, Stan, what was it? Go look out of the window.' So I do and I see nothing, so I go back to bed. But I don't go back to sleep 'cos I'm thinking about it, and after a bit I take another look. Then I go to your room and, surprise, surprise! No Bill.' He paused for a moment and then continued.

'Now I wonder what the hell is the boy doing. I look downstairs, nothing, then I go down the garden to the shed where you've been messing about these past two weeks and I don't find anything, except…..' He paused again. 'Except there's no roof on the shed! Odd, I thought. No sign of Bill and no roof on the shed.'

'Oh yes, I took the roof off yesterday and forgot to put it back last night.' I didn't sound a bit convincing. I looked up and met his eyes.

'Well, I haven't been five minutes back in the bedroom when I happen to look out of the window again and I see you standing in the middle of the lawn like a lemon, in that ridiculous outfit and with no shoes on your feet. Tell me if it's not a very strange set of happenings for early on a Friday morning.'

I was desperately trying to think of something sensible to say, but nothing sensible came into my mind. I decided to change the subject.

'Oh, by the way, did Pietersen get his century yesterday at the Oval?'

My father looked at me with a curious expression.

'Pietersen? Century? Which century, the 19th or 20th? If you're talking about the final Test at the Oval, it doesn't start till Thursday.'

I must have turned white for he put the note on the table and put his hand on my shoulder.

'Are you alright son?' he asked.

'I'll be fine, Dad. I don't know what came over me.'

'Lie down for a bit. Here take some water.' He filled a glass from the tap and handed it to me. 'I must get ready for work.'

He left the kitchen and went upstairs. I drank the water with shaking hands, set the glass carefully on the table and went up to my bedroom. I was in turmoil. Here was I, after a week spent on Mars with people who had been exiled from Earth thousands of years ago, back in my bedroom only an hour after leaving it. And I saw the news yesterday and Pietersen was a few runs short of his century, even though the match won't start for nearly a week. It must all be a dream!

I reached for my camera and switched it on. Michu's image was there. It was no dream. It was real!

I studied Michu's face, zooming in to maximum size. Her beautiful eyes held a startled expression but it was the Michu I knew just the same. Would I see her again? I suddenly felt very confused. I switched off the camera and placed it on my bedside table. I lay down on the bed and stared at the ceiling. After some time I drifted into a fitful sleep.

I cannot have been asleep for long when I heard the voice of my mother. Michu was saying she would be going to Sonam for her holiday and would not be back for 900 years when Mum came through the wall of the bubble in which Michu and I were sitting. She asked me if I was awake, at which Michu turned to her and offered her a purple fruit.

'Bill, are you awake?'

I opened my eyes. I was relieved to find that I had been dreaming. Mum was standing inside the doorway of my bedroom. I stretched my arms over my head and yawned. She came across to the bed and sat down on the edge, pulling the lapels of her pink dressing gown tightly across her chest. She was a small woman with thin brown hair, greying at the sides. She wore a nervous look, quite unlike her usual jovial self. She looked enquiringly at me with her grey eyes and then down at her fingernails.

'Bill, your dad and I are worried about you,' she began. She picked at the thumbnail of her left hand and frowned. 'Are you in some sort of trouble?'

'No Mum. What sort of trouble would I be in?' I said nervously.

'I don't really know. You're not taking drugs, are you?'

'God no! Of course not! Why should I be taking drugs?'

'No reason really, only, well, many youngsters are these days.'

'Not me, Mum, never!'

'I am glad to hear that. But Dad said you were behaving very strangely this morning. First you were not in the house, then you came in that peculiar suit with no shoes. Dad couldn't make it out. Then there was this noise and a flash earlier. We both heard it and it came from the back garden. And the note about.....about Mars.'

'I can't imagine what that flash can have been,' I lied.

'And he says that thing you were making in the shed is not there any more. And the note, he showed it to me. I can't help thinking something odd happened this morning. Are you sure there's nothing you want to tell me?

'I got rid of the spaceship. I sold it to Ben and Tim.'

'Your friends from school? The Tai-kwon-do addicts?'

I nodded.

'And the clothes: where did you find those?'

I didn't answer immediately because I had not anticipated the question. I was at a loss for words.

'Hey Mum, so many questions!' I'll tell you later. I'm feeling a bit weak.'

'I'm not surprised, Bill. It's a long way to Mars and you must be hungry!'

I looked at her and for a moment I thought she was being serious. Then she broke into a smile and I understood. She was entering into the game. How ironical, I thought to myself. Mum, if you only knew! I had to laugh then. We laughed together.

'Yes Mum, one hell of a way to go there and back in one morning,' I said through the laughter..

She took my hand and squeezed it gently.

'Now, take those funny clothes off and we'll have breakfast. What do you fancy?'

'Scrambled eggs on toast,' I said without a moment's hesitation.

Mum smiled and patted my leg. 'Right you are, dear. Scrambled eggs it is.'

Dear Mum, I thought, as I went down the landing to the bathroom.

CHAPTER TWENTY
SONIA

After two scrambled eggs on crispy toast and butter, as only my mum can make and washed down with a cup of tea, I felt better. No more was said about the events of the morning. Mum said she had to go out for a couple of hours and would I be alright at home on my own. I said I would be fine.

Back in my room I began to think of what I would do for the rest of the holiday before going back to start a new year. First there was Michu. I had a feeling she was thinking of me and I needed to meditate and learn how to tune my mind with hers. Next there was my mission in life. If I was to be a part of the movement to save our planet I needed to start studying. There was so much I needed to understand, the ancient history of Earth and Mars, how the Universe started, astronomy, environmental protection, energy sources, the list was endless. I decided to spend the remaining four weeks of the holiday in the reference section of our local public library.

But before anything else I had to get a print of that photo of Michu in the high Street. I would have it framed and put it on the wall opposite my bed, so that I could keep myself focused on the way forward. Michu, after all, was my teacher as well as my girl. Having thought that, I felt a surge of gratitude for what she had done for me.

I dressed quickly and left the house, having left a note on the table to tell Mum I had gone to the library to study. On my way I took the camera into the photographic shop in the High Street and printed the photo as large as I could. With the blown up photo of Michu under my arm I marched off round the corner and into the grey stone building which housed the local library. There was only one person in the reference section, a thin man reading the daily newspaper. He didn't look up as I entered. I wandered round the shelves for some time, wondering where to start. A young librarian with ginger hair in pigtails, a turned up nose and round glasses came to ask me if there was anything she could do to help.

'Do you have any books on Mars?' I whispered. You are not supposed to talk loudly in the reference library.

'Come!' and she led me to a shelf of books.

She took down a large book and opened it, balancing it on her knee. There in front of me was a large photograph of the Red Planet. A shiver ran down my spine. I felt like saying to her, 'I was there this morning,' but I just smiled quietly to myself.

'What exactly do you want to know about Mars?' was her question.

'Everything under the sun,' I said softly, smiling at her.

'Is it for a thesis, or something?' she asked.

I cupped my hand to my mouth and leaned towards her. 'Actually, I'm thinking of going there and I was wondering if you would go with me.'

She looked at me with a strange expression, pursing her full lips and closing her eyes. I guessed she thought I was making a pass at her. I was only pursuing one of my favourite pastimes, flirting with pretty girls.

'It's okay. I'll find someone else,' I said, shrugging my shoulders in a careless manner. Then without thinking, I unrolled the photo of Michu and held it in front of her. She looked at the photo and then at me over the top of her glasses and then at the photo again.

'That's my girlfriend,' I said.

'She has strange skin.'

'So would you if you lived underground. What's your name?'

'Sonia. Sonia Smith. How come she lives underground?' She looked at me again. 'Your pulling my leg, aren't you?'

'My name's Bill. Hey, listen, Sonia, I need to read lots of book about all sorts of things. I have four weeks before I go back to school. I'll be coming here every day. Will you help me find the books?'

She smiled. 'That's my job. I'll be happy to help. It's a pretty boring place. Nobody comes here except that man over there and he never says a word.'

'You're a gem, Sonia.' I could see she liked me. 'I'll start with this book and you can be looking for others for me.'

I took the book from her and went over to a vacant table. I spent an hour looking at all the big colour photos of the surface of Mars. There were pictures of Olympus Mons, Tharsis Montes and the Valles Marineris. One photo showed the dry river beds of the Chryse Planitia. Somewhere there, hidden from prying eyes, was Similaria, with its hundred Martians living five kilometres below the ground. I felt a strange sense of superiority. I looked up at Sonia. She was looking across at me and we smiled at each other. I had another urge to show her the photo and tell her that there was a lot of water underground there. Again I didn't.

As I was turning the last pages of the book, Sonia brought another book about the planets of our solar system. It had a chapter on Mars. I read it carefully, comparing it with what Michu had told me. There was a section on the search for life on Mars. The author's conclusion was that there may have been primitive life at some time in its history but since Mars no longer had a suitable atmosphere, life could not possibly exist on the planet. Good, I thought. That's how the Martians want it.

I spent the rest of the day looking at general books on the solar system, which I found interesting. Just before closing time, Sonia brought from the lending section a book called 'The Mars Mystery' which she said I could take home to read. I flipped though it casually, glancing at some of the photographs. There were some photos of the Cydonia monuments, some showing the face and the big pyramid. Then I noticed a slip of paper sticking out and I opened the book at that page. Something was written on the piece of paper. 'I'll come with you to Mars.' I glanced across at Sonia, who was putting on her coat and she smiled at me.

We went out into the busy street. We said goodnight and went our separate ways.

CHAPTER TWENTY-ONE
MACDONALD'S

The next morning I woke at 4 o'clock. It was still dark. I put on a sweater and, taking my pillow from the bed, I found a place by the wall and made myself comfortable. I think I really believed that I would make contact with Michu as soon as I closed my eyes. I sat for twenty minutes, trying to concentrate on her face but nothing came to me and I gave up and went back to bed, thinking I would have to borrow a book from the library on meditation techniques.

There was no more sleep for me that morning. I was curious to read the book Sonia had found for me. I sat up in bed and read the first two chapters, which considered the possibility of life on Mars, something on the first spacecraft sent there in the 1970's and early photos of Cydonia.

After breakfast I set off again for the library, carrying the rolled up photo of Michu under my arm, intending to have it framed in the photo framing shop. On the way I bumped into Ben and Tim and they invited me to MacDonald's for lunch. Sonia was already in the reference section as I came in the door. She gave me a bright smile. I noticed she had changed her hairstyle. Gone were the pigtails of the day before, replaced by what I can only describe as a 'piled-up' hairstyle. Also gone were the round glasses, the absence of which gave her eyes a cross-eyed effect. I decided she looked better with the glasses on.

'Do you notice anything different?' she asked as casually as she could.

'You painted the library during the night!' I said, in mock surprise, looking round at the walls.

'Silly! I mean about me!'

'You are wearing a different dress.'

'Forget it!' she said crossly and stomped off into the lending library.

I picked up the local newspaper from the centre table and, taking the same seat as the day before, I started flipping through the pages. Sonia came back into the room and I looked up. She gave me a scowl and busied herself at her desk. Poor girl, I thought. I have offended her. I crossed the room and went up to her desk.

'Look I'm sorry, Sonia. I didn't mean it: I was only joking. Of *course* I noticed and I like your hair the way you've done it.'

She looked at me with her blue eyes and flushed. 'It's okay. What book do you want to study today?'

'I want to read about the last ice age and the great meltdown,' I said dramatically, spreading my arms wide.

She gave me a sweet smile and hurried off to find the book. As I watched her go, swinging her hips, I thought to myself, take care, Bill, she really likes you. She really isn't your type and don't forget, Michu is waiting for you.

I went back to the table and began reading the local daily. After a while Sonia approached with two heavy books, which she placed on the table beside me. Then she lent over my shoulder and pointed with her finger at an article in the newspaper.

'My Dad wrote that,' she said proudly. 'He's a journalist.'

'Oh,' I said. 'What sort of stories does he write?'

'He can write about everything, but he likes a big story, the more exciting and dangerous the better.'

I read the first part of the article. It was about a meeting of the Women's League in the Town Hall the day before. I wanted to say to her that it was the most boring article I had ever read in my whole life, but I couldn't risk offending her twice in one morning.

'Cool!' I said, with as much enthusiasm as I could muster, which was not much.

'Dad's terribly ambitious,' she continued. 'He says one day he'll uncover a story that will shock the world and his name will be known in every newspaper office on Earth. Imagine! He'll get a job with the Times or even the New York Herald and editors all over the world will be crying for his services.' Sonia obviously thought a lot of her father.

'Let me see the books,' I said.

'Here you are. This is the best one, I think.' She pulled it across in front of me and opened it. Her face was over my left shoulder and her right cheek a bit too close for comfort.

'Thanks, Sonia, I can manage now.'

She took the hint and went back to her desk. I began to read. It was fascinating. Just imagine, this town was under many metres of ice 20,000 years ago! I remembered what the Similarian elder had told me about how the ice age suddenly ended with the impact of several enormous asteroids.

The book kept me entertained the whole morning and my eyes were sore by the time I was to meet Ben and Tim. As I was going out I said goodbye to Sonia.

'Are you coming back later?' she asked.

'Sure, but I have to meet some friends at MacDonald's.'

'Can I come?' she asked shyly. 'I can take my lunch now.'

'Er, if you want,' I said.

I waited for her while she went to the cloakroom. She was gone at least ten minutes. Typical, I thought. She was probably doing up he face, not for me, I hope!

We found a table for four in the bay window of MacDonald's. I watched the passersby and thought what an odd lot the English are, to be sure. Then I saw two familiar figures sauntering down the street. Ben, not very tall, short blonde hair, serious minded and Tim, stouter, tough looking, also with short blonde hair. They made faces at me through the window and then came to join us at the table.

'Meet Sonia,' I said. She works at the library. 'Sonia, meet Ben and Tim, friends of mine from school.'

Sonia smiled coyly and shook hands with the boys.

'So what mischief have you been getting up to?' Ben asked me, glancing at Sonia.

'Nothing at all, really. How about you?'

'Studying mostly,' he replied. 'A bit of tennis and of course the Tai-kwon-do three times a week.'

'Of course,' I said. Both boys were mad keen on Tai-kwon-do. I could never remember the order of the colours but the boys had gone far.

'Tim's been practicing hard with the school team, as you can imagine,' continued Ben. 'Mad keen on rugby and damn good!' The explanation was for Sonia's benefit.

Tim drew himself up to full height and puffed out his chest proudly. I couldn't help a chuckle but I could see Sonia was suitably impressed.

We were all seated now and were looking at the menu. Sonia was on my right, Ben opposite and Tim on my left. I put the photo down on the table next to my side plate.

'Hey, how's the spacecraft coming along?' said Tim rather loudly.

Sonia looked at me in surprise.

'Okay,' I said dismissively.

'We'll come round to your house later to have a look,' he said.

'I….er…I sold it,' I said quickly.

'Sold it!? What're going to go to Mars in then, if you've sold it?'

I looked sideways at Sonia and I noticed she was studying my face. I didn't know what to say to Tim.

'What do you want to eat, Sonia?' I asked, desperate to change the subject.

She looked again at the menu and was quiet.

'Why did you sell it?' Tim was not to be put off. 'All that work, three weeks, wasn't it?'

'I dunno,' I said, shrugging my shoulders.

'I can't believe it!'

'Don't then!' I said crossly. 'Sonia?'

'Veggieburger, please.'

'Tim, give it a rest. Can't you see he's upset,' said his brother.

We ordered our food and nothing was said for a while. People were passing along the street and I noticed some had put up umbrellas. The street was wet. My next thought was that I would have to take care to keep the photo from getting wet and I looked down to make sure it was still there. It had gone.

'Hey, this girl is something!' said Tim.

'Give it back!' I reached across to snatch the photo from him but he swung it swiftly to his left.

'What's wrong, Bill? You're so touchy today,' said Tim as he handed the photo back to me. 'Sorry, mate,' he said.

'It's okay.' I knew I was making too much fuss about it.

'Let me see,' said Ben.

I showed him the photo.

'So where did you meet this girl,' he asked.

'It's a long story,' I said.

'We've got the time for a long story,' said Ben.

'She's a long way away and I won't see her for ages.'
That was the truth.

'How far is a long way away?' said Tim. He never gives in, I thought.

'Millions of miles away,' I said, hoping that by making a joke of it, the subject would be dropped.

'Hey, maybe she's a Martian,' cried Tim, laughing.

The people on the next table all turned to see what the noise was about.

'Shush!' I whispered.

'Hey, wouldn't it be cool to have a Martian girlfriend!' he went on.

'Trouble is all those tentacles and aerials would get in the way,' suggested Ben.

'And her kisses would be slimy too,' said Tim.

They both laughed heartily.

While this was going on the blood was rushing to my face and I was silently fuming. Sonia looked very embarrassed.

'Stop! Stop it!' I cried. 'Michu doesn't have tentacles or aerials and her kisses are not sloppy or slimy! She's a beautiful girl and I love her and I won't hear you talking that way!'

Ben and Tim had both stopped laughing by this time. They looked at each other and I could see they were sorry.

'Sorry, mate,' said Tim. We had no idea.'

'Can't you see you've made him cry?' said Sonia, angrily, throwing her napkin on the table.

I hastily wiped away the tears that had inconveniently appeared in my eyes.

'Bill?' said Ben, slowly. 'Is she really a Martian? She doesn't look like she's from here.'

'I can't tell you,' I said. 'I have sworn to keep this a secret.'

'But we're friends and there should be no secrets between friends.'

'Friends or no friends, I can't tell you.'

Sonia pushed her chair back and got up from the table. She picked up her handbag which she had hung on the back of her chair.

'I've lost my appetite. Thanks for inviting me, Bill. I'll see you back at the library,' she said and walked out, without a look behind her. I watched as she tripped down the street on her high heels and disappeared into the Saturday lunchtime crowds.

Most of the rest of the meal was eaten in silence. Ben tried to make conversation but it was forced and in the end we kept quiet. Finally we all left MacDonald's. Both of my friends told me again they were sorry for upsetting me and I told them to forget it.

That afternoon, after going to the shop to leave the photo for framing, I sat at the table in the reference library and tried to concentrate on the great ice age, but it was difficult. I was worried that the secret I had promised to keep would one of these days leak out. Sonia brought me a cup of tea and did her best to cheer me up.

'She really *is* a Martian, isn't she,' she said gently, putting the cup of steaming tea down in front of me.

I said nothing. I looked at her, but I was thinking of Michu.

CHAPTER TWENTY-TWO
AN UNEXPECTED VISITOR

The next morning was Sunday and the library would not be open. I decided to get on with the book on Mars. But first I had to try to meditate again. I had a feeling that Michu was sending me thought waves that were going in one side of my head and out of the other, like water through a sieve. But I had no more success than I had had the day before.

Mum made delicious scrambled eggs on toast again. Dad always had a cooked breakfast on Sundays. We sat at the kitchen table and sipped tea out of brightly coloured mugs.

'Oh, I forgot to tell you, son,' said Dad, putting down his mug. 'Those two friends of yours from school came in the afternoon yesterday.'

I looked at my father in surprise.

'They were enquiring about your spaceship.'

'Ben and Tim,' I prompted.

'The very ones. I said you were not at home. They asked to see the spaceship, which I thought was a bit queer, seeing as you'd told your mum you'd sold it to them.' He looked at me intently and then went on. 'They went down the garden and looked in the shed. They asked me if you'd sold the thing and I said I had no idea. They examined the scorch marks for a bit. I left them to it. They stayed in the shed for ten minutes and then left.'

'I sold it, not to them, to someone else.' was all I could say.

Just then the doorbell rang and Mum went to answer it.

'Who can that be on a Sunday morning?' Dad said.

'Someone for you, Bill,' she said, coming back into the kitchen.

I went to the front door and found a small, thin man standing on the doorstep. He cannot have been more than one metre fifty. He reminded me of some of the men I had met in Similaria, but without the pale skin. He had dark eyes and dark brown hair and was clean shaven. He wore a well-cut dark grey suit and a blue tie. There was something about his face that reminded me of someone. He held a small parcel in front of him with two hands. I must have stood staring for too long because he shuffled his feet and cleared his throat.

'Hello Bill, may I come in?'

'Sorry Sir, of course. Come into the sitting room.' I led him into the front room and we sat down in the two armchairs facing each other. He passed the parcel to me.

'It's from Michu,' he said.

At the sound of her name, my heart missed a beat and I jumped.

'Open it,' he said.

I unwrapped the parcel, breaking the cello tape and removing the brown paper. There was nothing inside! The hairs on my neck stood out and my heart beat fast. I looked enquiringly at the small man opposite me.

He smiled at me. 'In case you should ever need to come to Mars.'

I was nonplussed. Then I understood. It was a bubble!

'Cool!' I breathed.

'You cannot see it but it is there. Just feel it.'

I felt the bubble. He was right. I could feel it but not see it.

'Keep it safe. One day you may need it.'

'And Michu? How is she?'

'She is well.'

'Do you live in Similaria then?'

'No. I am Michu's father and I live about 200 kilometres away.'

I realised then why I had found him familiar.

'Where shall I keep the bubble?' I asked.

'Somewhere you know where to find it quickly. Don't worry, no-one will ever know it is there. No-one but you can feel it. To all others it does not exist.'

'Wow!'

'It will only work for you, Bill,' continued the man. 'If one day you need to escape to Mars, just hold it with two hands and shake it gently. It will inflate itself. But make sure you are outside the house otherwise you will never get it through the door. Pass into it and you will be guided to Similaria. It is programmed and there is nothing more you need do.'

'Thank you Sir,' I said. I was completely overwhelmed.

'By the way, my name is Priam, P.R.I.A.M, Priam.'

'Can I offer you tea, Mr. Priam?'

'Martians don't care for tea, but thanks for the kind offer.' He paused. 'Now, I expect you would like a message to go to Michu.'

'Can I?' I exclaimed, delighted.

'Send an e-mail to this address,' he said, handing me a piece of paper with an e-mail address written on it in bold letters. After the address, write that code and only Michu will be able to read it.' He pointed to the letters which followed the address.

'I understand, Sir,' I said.

'Good, now I must be off.'

'If I want to contact you, how do I do it?' I asked him.

'Just think of me and I will know. I have to go to Russia tomorrow, but I will be back on Friday. Good luck!'

He stretched out his hand. I wondered again why his complexion was different from Martians I had met.

'We use a cream to make our skin look like yours, available from Boots, 3.99 a tube.' He smiled and pulled up his sleeve to reveal his natural colour.

He stretched out his hand once more. I was surprised because I had believed that Martians don't shake hands.

'When in Rome, my boy,' he said laughing

I shook his hand warmly and saw him to the door. I watched him as he disappeared down the street and round the corner, the little man called Priam. I nipped up to the bedroom and stashed the bubble into the top drawer of my cupboard and then went back down to the kitchen.

What did that funny little man want?' asked Mum, as I sat down again at the kitchen table.

'Oh, nothing much Mum,' I said nonchalantly.

'He stayed a long time considering he didn't want much.'

I said nothing but Dad looked at me with an anxious expression.

'Too many strange things are happening for my liking,' he said. 'Maybe one of these days you'll tell us what it's all about.'

'I met him in the library,' was the only thing I could think of to say.

I took up my mug and drained the rest of my tea, which had gone cold. I excused myself and went up to my room. I intended to write to Michu and I was excited about it. After that I would take a long walk. I had things to think about.

CHAPTER TWENTY-THREE
THE STONE BENCH

It was Monday morning and Dad had just left for work. For Mum it was washing day, 'come rain or come shine,' as the song goes. No matter what the weather, to my mother, Monday was the day one washed one's clothes, and that was all there was to it.

I was just about to get ready to go to the library when my mobile phone rang. I clicked the green button. The number was not one in my directory.

'Hello!' I said.

'Meet me at the stone bench opposite Barclays Bank at 10 o'clock sharp. Come alone. Is it clear?' It was a man's voice.

'Who are you?'

'Never mind who I am, just come, that's all.' The phone went dead as he disconnected.

'Who the hell....!' I looked at the phone and noted the number. I saved it under the name 'anonymous caller,' Then I decided I'd got the word wrong and I changed it. I sat on the edge of the bed and tried to figure it out. I didn't much like the sound of his voice. Should I go or just ignore it? It sounded like something important. If I didn't go, would he do something to me? At least if I went, I would know what it was about and I could decide what to do. There was nothing much he could do to me in the middle of the town. I decided to go. I looked at my mobile clock. It was just 9.30. It would take me ten minutes to get there.

I couldn't sit still, I was too nervous. I paced up and down the room, trying to work out who the mystery caller could be and what he wanted from me. I went to the cupboard drawer where I kept the bubble. It was there. It gave me some comfort to know that I could take it out, inflate it and be with Michu in no time at all. I closed the drawer and in doing so, my eye saw something odd. The clothes that normally sat neatly in a pile on the shelf were all in a messy heap. At first I couldn't see anything missing and then it hit me like a blow from a sledge hammer. My Martian tunic had gone! I searched the heap and then the other places where I may have put it, but it was nowhere to be seen. I called my mum and she came to look but the tunic had gone. Who could have taken it?

With these thoughts crowding my mind, I set off for my meeting with the anonymous caller.

It was cloudy and windy, one of those August days that normally coincide with the bank holiday weekend. I zipped up my windcheater and walked quickly into the centre of the town. Gusts of wind blew pieces of paper in circles like miniature hurricanes. The scene was like any other Monday morning, the shops preparing for a busy week, not that August was their best month of the year, with many people taking their holidays by the sea. I passed Marks & Spenser's and some girls setting up a window display waved to me. I lifted my hand in a half-hearted attempt at politeness. I had other things on my mind. Little did they know what I was going through. How could they?

The 15th Century stone courthouse stood in the centre of the market place. I passed between its columns and crossed the road. The clock above Barclays Bank told me I was five minutes late for my appointment. I crossed the street in the direction of the stone bench where I was to meet the stranger. As I drew near I could see a middle aged man in a raincoat sitting on the bench looking in my direction. He was a large man, with a big belly protruding from the open coat. He had longish brown hair which he had attempted to comb over the bald patch on top of his head. The wind tugged gaily at the hair. He held a mobile phone in his other hand. He straightened up as I came near to him and tried to smooth his hair back across his head. He gave me a stern look to let me know this was a serious business.

I came near the bench and as I did so he raised the phone and took my photograph. I stood in front of him expectantly.

'Sit down Bill,' he said in a gruff voice.

I sat beside him and waited for him to speak. How did he know my name? I looked across and saw a neighbour of ours go into the bank through the revolving door. Each of us has our own little slices of life, I thought.

'I'll get straight to the point, Bill. Do you want to be rich?'

It was the last question I could have expected.

'Well, I suppose everyone could do with some extra cash.' It was the first thing that came into my head and I was ashamed of saying it.

'Of course they could! And you and me could be filthy rich, just like that,' and he clicked his fingers. A thin smile crossed his lips.

I was trying to work out how I was going to become rich in partnership with this scruffy, middle aged man.

'Information, Bill, information!' he licked his lips and ran his hand through his long hair. 'In this modern world information is money and the more valuable the information is, the more it is worth and the more it is worth the richer we get.'

'What information? Why do you talk in riddles?'

'I will tell you. You are in possession of information that could make us both rich if we play our cards right, Get me?'

'No idea what you're talking about! Why don't you leave me alone?'

'Because, Bill, you want to be rich as much as I do, that's why.'

'Money is not everything,' I said.

'I agree with you there, but what money can buy is everything, nice big house, flashy car to run the girlfriend around in, holidays in Greece just soaking up the sun and sipping cocktails, following the team to the European Cup and so on.'

I was disgusted at the way in which he idolised all the material things in life.. But what information was he talking about? Then I began to see where he was leading and I didn't like it one bit. The neighbour came out of the bank and crossed the road. As she passed the stone bench, she gave a nod and a smile and went into the newsagent's.

The man was speaking again. 'One of the hottest questions of modern times is……. what?' He paused and turned sideways to face me. He looked straight at me with his brown eyes and I looked away.

'I'll tell you, Bill, the question that everyone wants to know. The one who has the answer to the question will be rich and famous overnight. Do you want to know?'

'I don't have a clue what you're talking about,' I said, but I knew exactly what the question was.

'Is there extraterrestrial life!? That's the question everyone is asking, Bill.'

'What's that got to do with me?' I asked hopelessly.

'Everything, Bill, everything!'

'Look, I don't know why you asked me to come here but I have many things to do. I can't waste my time here.' I was getting very frustrated.

'I am an ambitious man, but here I am, stuck here in this God-forsaken hole of a place, working my guts out for a second-class local rag, with no chance of promotion. I want to hit the big time, work for The Times for a bit, make my name and then retire in luxury. Not a bad dream, Bill, is it?'

This story rings a bell in my head, I thought. But he was speaking again.

'I know things about you that you don't know I know.' More riddles.

'What d'you know about me, then?'

'Shall I tell you?'

I wished he would get on with it and I could go off to the library and get some peace.

'Sonia has told me about you.' I stiffened and I turned to him.

'Sonia?' The penny dropped. 'Of course, you are her father, aren't you? The rat! She's told you about me.' I was angry. 'But its all lies! It's all nonsense!'

'Is it Bill? Are you sure?'

'Look Mr……Mr.'

'Smith, Albert Smith.'

'Look Mr. Smith, it's all a game, entertainment for the holidays.'

He smiled a wicked smile and straightened up, passing his hand across his head.

'Don't kid me, Bill.'

'So what did the rat tell you about me?'

'Sonia? Hey, that's my daughter you're talking about.'

'What did she tell you,' I repeated, more loudly this time.

'You'll know soon enough. The point is, even if you don't want to be rich, I do. I'm not getting any younger. My wife left me last year for another man. I live now with my daughter and she means everything to me. I want her to have the best in life, not to waste her days in that pit of a library, humping dusty books around. She's worth more than that.' He sounded bitter at the way life had treated him. At that moment I felt pity for the man, as much as he disgusted me.

'You see, Bill? I need a break and this is going to be it. I can't let it go: I may never have another chance.'

'I can't help you. I told you it's all a game.'

He reached into the left pocket of his grey, shabby trousers and pulled out a small object, which he held up in front of my face.

'Flash drive, Bill. It contains some explosive material.'

I was puzzled. What could the flash drive contain?

'Michu must be a prize girl, Bill.'

'I was stunned! I was completely speechless! How could he know about Michu? It wasn't possible. I never mentioned her name to Sonia.

'You should never leave personal letters on your computer, Bill. Always turn it off and use a password. That way, people like me can't read your love letters.'

I flushed red with anger.

'But, how did you get into my room?'

'On Friday, Sonia told me about you. She sounded as though she liked you. She said you had a passion for Mars and wanted to read as much as you could about it. She said you showed her the picture of your girlfriend and she thought she looked a bit odd, kind of ghostlike.'

'So what? What does that mean?' I said angrily.

'Sonia said you wanted to take her to Mars. She actually believed you. Sonia has always been a dreamer.'

'Just a joke!'

'Well, I got thinking and I thought to myself, this sounds interesting. Of course I also like to know the boys my daughter makes friends with, so I followed you on your way home from the library on Saturday. I found out where you lived.'

'Sneaky,' I said to him.

'Then on Saturday night Sonia told me you'd taken her to MacDonald's for lunch with some friends. She said you behaved very strangely when the boys started to make fun of your ghostly girlfriend. It was then she told me she had this funny feeling the girl was from Mars.'

'Nonsense, Michu is a normal girl.'

He held up the flash drive again. I went through in my mind the letter I had typed to Michu on Sunday morning. What had I said? I knew then that the man before me had information that directly linked me with Mars. I had said many things in that letter about my visit. But I could still deny it. I could still insist it was all a game. He was speaking again in that nasty, gruff voice.

'The grey clothes could end up being just the proof I need, if my hunch turns out to be right. I suppose they belong to your Martian girl and she left them behind when she went back home.' His mouth widened into a thin smile.

I stared at him in horror. 'You stole my things! I'll go straight to the police!'

'I don't think so, Bill,'

'How did you get in?'

'I was coming to that. I wanted to pay you a friendly visit on Sunday afternoon, you know, just to meet Sonia's friend. Your mother answered the door. I introduced myself as a Mr. Tomlinson. I said I knew her husband and her son,

Bill. She told me you were both out. That was the break I
needed. I said I had some news about a relation of hers. She
offered me some tea and while she went to the kitchen to
make it, I nipped upstairs and had a quick look in your
room. It was my lucky day. I never expected to strike it rich.
A letter to your Martian girlfriend and a suit that I had a
feeling was not made on this Earth. The only thing I didn't
find was the photograph. Where have you hidden it?'

'You're a crook and a thief!' I cried.

'No Bill, just smart. I'm a reporter and reporters need to
be smart. Only the smart ones get the stories, isn't that
right? I'm telling you, I'm not cut out to slave for a two bit
local newspaper that's not good enough to wrap your fish
and chips in,' he said bitterly. 'Anyway, back to the story,
so I was just coming down the stairs when your mother
came out of the kitchen carrying a tray of tea things. She
went into the sitting room. I waited at the top of the stairs.
She came out again and went back to the kitchen. I took the
chance and slipped out of the front door.

I put my head in my hands. Mum never told me about it,
probably because she felt foolish. It obviously never
occurred to her that he might have gone upstairs to my
room. She must have puzzled about his sudden
disappearance.

'Now Bill. The results of the forensic tests on the
material will be ready tomorrow. I'll give you till
Wednesday to make up your mind, if you want to be rich
with me or not. I am going for it and there's nothing going
to stop me. Understand?'

'What are you going to do?' I asked.

'That depends on you, my friend,' he said, pronouncing
the last word in an unfriendly way. He smiled again a sickly
smile. 'Do you want to see your letter to your girlfriend on
the front page on Thursday morning? Think of the scandal!'
He grinned.

'You can't do that!' I cried.

'I told you, Bill. It depends on you. Wednesday, same
time, same place. I'll bring the results of the tests.'

I understood.

He got up and walked slowly up the High Street, without a backward glance, the tails of his raincoat flapping in the wind. I watched him for some time and then I went off in the other direction. I had no stomach for the library that day. I would not be responsible for my actions if I were to meet Sonia, the RAT!

CHAPTER TWENTY-FOUR
A PROMISE

I heard my mother calling me from the bottom of the stairs. I was in my bedroom, pacing up and down, wondering what I was to do about Sonia's father's threat. It was 6.30 in the afternoon and since coming home from the meeting I had not left my room.

'Bill!' my mother called again.

I went to the door and shouted that I had heard her.

'Bill, there's a young lady at the door and she says she has to talk to you urgently.'

'Who is it Mum?'

After a pause she called out, 'she says her name is Sonia.'

'Tell her I don't want to see her.'

Another pause, then, 'she seems to be upset. I think you should come down and talk to her.'

I was debating what to do when Mum called up again.

'Bill! Did you hear?'

'I heard. I'll come down. Tell her to go into the sitting room and wait for me there.'

What could she want? I was still angry with her for telling her father about me. I decided there was no point in delaying. I would have to go and face her and tell her she was the biggest rat in the whole wide world.

I went downstairs and into the sitting room. She was sitting in the armchair where my Martian visitor had sat the day before. When she saw me she got up and came towards me. I noticed she was not wearing her glasses. She was crying.

'Bill, I'm so sorry! I didn't know!' she said between sobs.

I put up my hands and backed away from her. She stopped in the middle of the room. She held a small handkerchief to her face and dabbed her tears.

'Bill, don't be angry with me, it wasn't my fault.'

'Whose fault was it then?' I said, crossly. Sonia, you're a rat! How could you do this to me?'

This brought on a new fit of sobbing. She looked so desperate, I couldn't help feeling sorry for her. The girl was in a very bad state.

'Sit down in the chair, Sonia,' I said quietly. She obeyed.

I sat in the other chair and we were quiet for a couple of minutes. Then she recovered her composure a little.

'Bill, please forgive me!'

'I'm not sure I can ever do that, Sonia, after what you have done.'

'Then I will have to kill myself!'

'Sonia, don't be so melodramatic! Calm down and let's talk sensibly.

'Say you'll forgive me, please! I can't go on living with the shame!'

Women, I thought. Why do they always have to make you feel sorry for them?

'Sonia, what did you tell your father?'

She sniffed and then blew her nose noisily.

'I told him I'd met this nice boy who came to the library to read about the planets, especially Mars and the ice-age and all that. I told him you showed me the photo of your girlfriend. I only said she looked like someone from one of the planets you were reading about. I told him you had offered to take me to Mars with you. He laughed and we joked about it. I didn't think for a moment he would take it seriously.'

'Silly, silly girl!' I said.

'I know, Bill. I've been so foolish and naïve and I will understand if you say you can't forgive me and never want to see me again.' She looked at me with those big, blue eyes and I knew then that I would have to forgive her. Women!

'Sonia,' I said. 'What did you tell him about our lunch on Saturday?'

'Not much. I only said we had lunch at Mac's and you got upset because Tim made some rude comments about your girlfriend. I was angry at him. That's why I left.'

'I know. My pride and my love for Michu got the better of me. I should have ignored it and now I wouldn't be in this situation.'

'No, it's my fault and I am so, so sorry!'

I could tell she was genuinely sorry and I decided to forgive her.

'Sonia, if I forgive you, will you help me?'

She brightened up and smiled for the first time.

'I'll do anything for you, Bill! Anything you want.'

'Now, now, steady on girl!'

'What do you want me to do?' she said, wiping another set of tears from her eyes.

'First, Sonia, I want to know what your father has told you.'

'He said he had met you this morning. I can tell you, I was surprised. He showed me a printout of a letter he said you had written to your girlfriend. He also said he had a suit that belonged to her and that he was going to prove that it came from Mars. He never told me how he had got those things.'

'He stole them from my room.'

'What?' She looked shocked and the blood drained from her face.

'Yes, your father is a thief.'

She sat for a moment and then burst into tears. I went across to her and put my arm round her shoulders. I stayed like that for a minute or so until she had composed herself again.

'I told you my father was an ambitious man, but a thief! It's too horrible! He told me our troubles were over, that we were going to be rich. He said he had the ultimate news story that was going to make him famous. Bill, I was so sad at that moment. I have always thought my father a good man and when my mother left, saying she couldn't live another moment with him, I took his side. When he was telling me all this I knew that I had made a mistake. I know I said too much and I came straight here to say how sorry I am.'

'Sonia, I pity you. It must be so disappointing to learn that your father is not what you have always thought. Now listen. This is what you must do. He has given me until Wednesday to decide if I want to tell him my story. If I don't he threatens to splash my letter all over the front page. You must get back the letter and the tunic and if you can the flash drive.'

'I will do my best,' she replied. 'Of course he may already have copied the letter onto another hard drive.'

'Yes, it's likely, but the tunic is proof, according to him. This we must get back. Oh! I almost forgot. He took a photo of me this morning with his mobile. He may put that on the front page too. You must get hold of his phone and delete the photo. Will you do it?'

'Of course Bill. I will do all I can to help you.'

'I know you will, Sonia. And…I *do* forgive you. I know you didn't mean any harm.'

'I thought for a moment. If Sonia was going to help me I would have to take her into my confidence. I would tell her everything.

'Sonia, before I begin, I want you to make a solemn promise.'

'I will swear anything you like, Bill,' she said, smiling faintly.

'I am going to tell you everything and I want you to promise you'll never tell a soul what I have told you. Now promise.'

'I promise that I'll never tell a soul what you are going to tell me.'

She sat spellbound as I recounted my adventures on Mars. It took a full hour and she hardly moved a muscle the whole time I was speaking. At one point my father came home. He put his head through the door of the sitting room, said hello and went out again. I went on with the story.

'Well, Sonia, that's all of it, everything,' I said as soon as I had finished.

'Thank you. It's a wonderful story and I'm so honoured that you have shared it with me. I will never tell anyone as long as I live, cross my heart.' She placed her arms across her chest. Then she stretched out her arms and yawned.

'I'd better go. My father will wonder where I am.'

'I'll see you in the library tomorrow.'

I saw her to the door. She waved as she went out of the gate and turned in the direction of the town.

'Has she gone?' asked Mum from the kitchen door. 'What did the girl want? She was in a right state. You haven't put her in the family way, have you?

I didn't even answer. I went up to my room to figure out the next move.

CHAPTER TWENTY-FIVE
RAINY TUESDAY

The next morning I woke up to the sound of rain beating against the window panes. It was barely light. I took my pillow and settled myself in the place I had chosen for meditation. So far I had not managed to make contact with Michu and I was feeling a bit depressed. Would I ever be able to connect with her? In that frame of mind I doubted it. After thirty minutes I gave up. All I could think about was my meeting with Albert Smith and Sonia's distress. I would go to the library as soon as it opened to see if she had got back the things from her father.

I had breakfast in the kitchen with my mum. I sat most of the time in deep thought and she said I had changed ever since Friday and was it all to do with all those strange things that had happened that morning. I tried to make light of it, saying I had a lot of work and that's why I was quiet. She knew very well I never worried about my school work. Whether I worked hard or not, I always came top in exams. No, there had to be something else, she said. Was it that ginger-haired girl? Mum still believed I had got her into trouble, however much I tried to tell her it was nonsense.

The rain slanted down, blown by a strong South-Westerly wind, stinging the face. I put my head down and pulled the lapels of my raincoat as high as I could. I put my hands in the pockets and strode off in the direction of the library. I could feel my mobile phone vibrating in my pocket but I just let it ring. It crossed my mind that it could be Sonia's father, threatening me with death for stealing back my things but at that time I was too busy battling the strong wind to worry about that.

I reached the library, thankful for the refuge, and removed my raincoat, shaking it free of as much water as possible. I wiped my face with my handkerchief and entered the reference section. Sonia was at her desk, stamping the inside cover of a book.

'Hello Bill,' she said as she saw me come through the door. I could see from her expression that the news was not good.

'Well?' I said.

'No luck, I'm afraid. I'm sorry, I did try.' I could see she really meant it.

'Tell me what happened.'

She put down the stamp and closed the book, turning on her high stool to face me.

'The tunic is at the laboratory. He says he'll pick it up later. I hunted for the letter but he must have hidden it and the flash drive as well. I tried to open his computer to delete the letter in case he has copied it but he has a password and he's never told me it.' She shrugged her shoulders and screwed up her mouth.

'And my photo?'

'Nothing! He had the phone in his pocket all the time. There was no chance for me to take it. I slipped into his room in the middle of the night to see if he had left it out but I couldn't see it and I was scared in case he woke up.'

'Tonight, Sonia! You must get the tunic tonight! That reminds me, someone was ringing me when I was on my way here, but with that rain I couldn't answer it.'

It was Ben. I called him back. He said they were on their way to the library.

'Okay Sonia?'

'I will try.' She looked unhappy about it. 'I have never seen my father like this. He went on last night about being rich and famous and you were the key to his future. But he talked about you as if you were something to be used and then thrown away. I can't exactly describe it but it gave me a very bad feeling.'

'He intends to use me to get what he wants and then…dustbin. That settles it, Sonia. I won't agree to his plan, no matter what he does to me. He can sell my letter to the world and I'll just insist it's a fake.'

'I'll support you all I can,' she said, putting her hand on mine and squeezing it gently. 'It must be hard for you.'

'Very hard. If only I could make contact with Michu. She must know something is wrong: it's hard to keep thoughts from them.'

'You'll just have to make do with me, won't you?' said Sonia.

Sonia was jealous of Michu, I could tell.

Before I could tell her off, Ben and Tim walked through the door, shaking the water from their heads.

'What a day!' said Ben. 'It's all that global warming.'

'So let's go for coffee,' said Tim and get wet inside as well as out!'

'You three go,' said Sonia. 'Some people have to work for their living!'

'You call this work?' replied Tim, 'looking at books all day.'

'Tim is much more at home on the rugby pitch than in front of books,' I said.

'Well, I'll just ignore his stupid remark,' said Sonia crossly.

Tim laughed. Getting girls angry was his favourite pastime.

We left the library and battled our way to the nearest coffee shop. It was not as popular as MacDonald's but it was not so far. We took our seats and ordered our drinks. Tim ordered cocoa. He said it was better for athletes than coffee.

'Now, Bill,' began Ben. He wore his most serious look and I knew he had something on his mind. 'We came visiting on Saturday, after Tai-kwon-do.'

'I know, my father told me. So?'

'Why did you tell him you sold the spaceship to us?' asked Ben, searching my face for the answer.

'Because I had to say something quick,' I said. 'I had to explain somehow why it was in the shed on Thursday afternoon and Friday morning it was not.'

'So what happened to it?' Ben would make a good lawyer, I thought. He's a brilliant cross examiner.

'I sold it to someone else.'

'Who?'

'Ben! Why all these questions? Someone else, you don't know him.'

'Come on, Bill, it won't do. Tell us, where did the spaceship go?'

'To Mars, of course!' My attempt to make it sound like a joke was not going to work, I could see by the expressions on the two faces in front of me.

'To Mars! I thought so,' said Ben and he sat back in his chair with a triumphant look, as if he had won an important court case.

I made no attempt to deny it. What was the use?

'It's unbelievable but it's true! It's true, isn't it Bill? You really did go to Mars, didn't you?'

It was no good trying to pretend any more. 'Yes. It's true,' I said.

'And that girl in the photo, she really is from Mars.'

I nodded.

My friends could only sit and stare at me, as if I was from Mars myself. Tim kept shaking his head from side to side. The waitress brought the drinks but none of us was interested in such paltry earthly pleasures.

'So now you'd better tell us,' said Ben.

I sighed and sipped my coffee absentmindedly. Then I told them the story I had told Sonia the day before, but in less detail. I omitted the part about travelling back in time. It had been my idea since coming home to make a bet with them on the Test Match, to earn a few easy quid. I told them about my meeting with Sonia's father and his threat to expose my letter.

When I had finished we all sat quietly. Now three people knew my secret, the secret I had promised faithfully to keep from anyone. Where would it end? I promised myself I would tell no-one else, even under threat of torture.

'What are you going to do now?' asked Tim.

'Fight! That's what I am going to do, fight!'

'I can fight,' said Tim, clenching his fists and tightening his jaw muscles.

'It's brains that's needed for this, Tim,' said his brother.

'I've got those as well, mate,' said Tim hastily.

We laughed together. At least now I had my friends with me and I knew I could count on them in the hour of need.

'I have to meet Sonia's father tomorrow at ten. He says he will bring the results of the tests on the material. He is expecting me to tell him I will help him make us both rich. He's going to be disappointed because I'll not tell him anything.'

'Good for you!' said Ben. 'You can count on us. If you need us, just call.'

'Right!' Tim agreed.

'Thanks,' I said. 'By the way, the Test Match starts Thursday. Will you be watching?'

'Sure,' said both of them at once.

'I wouldn't miss one ball,' said Ben emphatically. 'That is, if it's not washed out.'

'Do you think England will win?' I asked.

'Of course, with Michael Vaughan in good form they can't lose.'

'Pietersen will get a century on the first day,' I said as casually as I could.

'No chance!' said Ben. 'He's all show. But Vaughan might.'

'Want to bet?' I said.

'Why not! Ben replied. 'My two quid says Vaughan will get a century.' He took from his pocket a two pound coin and tossed it onto the table. We all watched it as it rolled around in ever decreasing circles, quivered for a few seconds and then settled on the table.

'And my two quid says Pietersen will,' I said.

'Neither of them will,' said Tim. 'The four quid is mine.'

'It's a deal.' We all shook hands on it.

Ben paid the bill and we said goodbye. I walked back to the library, wondering how I would spend my winnings. The rain had stopped and the sun was shining weakly, but the wind was still gusty. The ground has time to dry out by Thursday, I thought.

I spent the rest of the day reading about the great ice age and the debate about its sudden end 10,000 or so years ago. Although Zeris had clearly told me it was caused by giant asteroids hitting the Earth, the book didn't even mention the possibility. The Martians knew a lot more about the history of our planet than we do, obviously.

I set about thinking of the chances of such a thing happening again. Would God allow such a thing? Human beings are his chosen race, after all, at least that's what we have been told to believe. But what about the other beings Michu told me about, the ones on Sonam for example? Were they not also chosen? There is much to learn and much to understand about our Universe, I decided.

At 4.30 I said goodnight to Sonia and I wished her luck with her dangerous mission. Would she succeed? I collected the framed photo of Michu from the shop on my way home and hung it on the wall above my writing desk.

In the evening I watched an interesting programme about our solar system. Sir Patrick Moore was explaining where in the sky to find the planets. He said that Mars would be overhead in the hour before dawn. I made a point to go into the garden and try to spot it before it was light.

That night I tossed and turned. I dreamt that Albert Smith had discovered Sonia in his room and had beaten her up. I had tried to stop him but I was somehow tied to the bed and couldn't move. I woke up in a pool of sweat.

CHAPTER TWENTY- SIX
DEADLOCK

It was Wednesday morning and my appointment with Albert Smith was at 10 o'clock. I was in defiant mood. I doubted if Sonia had managed to get hold of the evidence, otherwise she would have called me. Anyway, I knew what I had to say and was determined to spell it out plainly to him. I had a feeling he would turn nasty, because I was sure he was banking on my going along with him. Nothing was going to convince me to betray my Martian friends.

In this confident state of mind I walked into town. It was a cloudy morning but the wind had died down. There had been no chance of seeing Mars in the early morning sky. It would have to wait until better weather.

Before my meeting I decided to drop in at the library just on the off chance that Sonia had succeeded in some small way and I could face him prepared. But she had not been able to get anywhere, so I walked back into the centre.

I passed by the window of Marks & Spenser's and half expected the window-dressers to wave to me as they had done on Monday. The windows were attractively dressed but they had done their work and were probably stocking the shelves. I pushed on down the high street. The clock above the bank told me I was on time this morning.

Albert Smith was waiting on the stone bench, sitting with his raincoat open and his arms on his knees, bending forward and studying the ground. His hair hung down over the side of his head, clearly showing his bald patch.

As I crossed the road he gave a small cough and wiped his nose on a brown handkerchief that he held in his left hand. I approached the bench. When I was close enough for him to see my feet from the position he was sitting in, he looked up at me. Then he straightened up and, without saying a word, he waived his hand at the empty space beside him. I sat down and looked across the street at the revolving door of the bank, half expecting the same neighbour to come out. But that was Monday.

'Well?' he said finally.

'No deal.'

'Do you know what you're saying?'

'I know. The answer is still no.'

He sighed and gave a short, unpleasant laugh. He wiped his nose again and put the handkerchief in his trouser pocket.

'I'm sorry for you,' he said.

'I'm even *more* sorry for you.'

He grunted. 'You see, Bill, if you want anything in this life, you have to go for it. There'll always be people who'll want to stop you. They want it too, of course, but they haven't got the guts and so they'd rather you didn't get it either. I never had the chance before. My parents were always hard up. Dad was always out of work and what little money he had he drank. My mother didn't have much go in her so he ruled the house. They never took much notice of me or cared much about my education. I got where I got through my own hard work. Not very far, you might say. But now my chance has come to make the big time.'

'By becoming a criminal?' I said in disgust.

'Mark my words, I'll soon be up there with the Bill Gates' of this world.'

'At least he made his fortune through honest, hard work,' I said.

'Rot! He had the idea but others did the work for him. He's a smart man. He hired the wiz kids of the IT world, paid them well and made them work like slaves. He uses the cheap labour of developing countries and sits back in luxury, while the workers live in poverty. Smart man, Mr. Gates.'

'At least they earn something. And Bill Gates gives millions away to charity.'

'What's a few million to him! But me? I'll give nothing away. My house in St. Tropez will make Versace's look like a semi-detached council house. I can see it now, miles of deserted beach and waving palm trees, the white villa perched up on the cliff overlooking the deep blue sea, white coated servants standing with trays of cocktails waiting for me, and all mine.'

'And Sonia?'

'Sonia will never have to work again. I'll get her married off to some Italian Count with ten yachts in the Mediterranean.'

I thought of Sonia and knew she would never accept a life like that: she's far too down to earth for that.

'Want to change your mind, Bill? The offers still open.'

'No way!'

'Pity, 'cos I've got the proof I needed.' He put his left hand into the inside pocket of his raincoat and pulled out a piece of paper, folded in four. He passed it to me with a smug smile on his round face.

'Read it, Bill. You'll find it quite interesting.'

I unfolded the paper and read it carefully. It was typed on a sheet of headed paper belonging to a cloth manufacturing association. There was some information on the thickness of the cloth, the type of weave and other data, which I skipped. Then my eye settled on the paragraph at the foot of the page which said,

'The cloth is of natural origin and has no synthetic content. The plant from which the cloth was made resembles the Egyptian papyrus in structure but is courser and cannot be identified. It is unknown to us. The weave pattern is very unusual. We have never encountered this in our experience. We can only conclude that this cloth comes from a source yet unknown to any recognised cloth manufacturing industry in the world.'

I looked up at the man beside me. He was staring at me with a self-satisfied expression on his face.

'You see? That's the proof I hoped for.'

I screwed up the paper and threw it angrily into the street. He laughed.

'It's okay. There are plenty more copies and the original is safely locked up in my draw. That, together with your love letter to your beautiful Martian lady, is all I need.'

'You beast!' I cried.'

'There's still time to change your mind.'

'Never, never, never!'

'What will your parents say when they see your photo on the front page of the paper tomorrow morning?

'I'll solve that problem when the time comes,' I said defiantly.

''Bring her home to tea, dear and introduce her to us,' your mother will say when she reads the letter.' He was mimicking a woman's voice with an upper class accent.

I couldn't take this anymore. I got up from the bench and crossed the road, not even looking back to see if he was still there. I walked quickly along the high street towards the library.

Sonia was there and she looked glum. My face was still flushed with anger. She looked up at me and a pained expression spread over her face.

'What did he say, Bill?' she enquired in a worried tone.

'He's going to publish the letter and the results of the tests and he's going to plaster it all over the front page tomorrow, with my photo, that's what!'

'I *did* try last night, but he's too careful,' she said apologetically.

'I know.'

'So now what, Bill? Do you think he'll do it, put it on the front page, I mean?'

'There's still a chance he might not, Sonia.' I said hopefully. 'He is taking a big risk. It might backfire on him. What he needs is my story, with that he's home and dry.'

'Bill?' said Sonia cautiously. 'You don't suppose he would use force to get the story from you, do you?'

'You mean, torture me?'

''Yes,' she said slowly and shuddered.

We looked at each other and I could see then that Sonia really cared for me.

'Bill, be careful. I have never thought my father capable of such a thing but now I'm beginning to wonder if I really know him.'

'It must be tough for you, Sonia,' I said sympathetically.

'Yes, it's hard to believe. Just be careful though.'

'What am I supposed to do, get a bodyguard?'

'Why not?' Then she suddenly looked up. 'Tim!' she said, 'a perfect bodyguard!'

I laughed in spite of the situation facing me.

'I'll be careful, Sonia.' I smiled at her. 'Now I'll be going. I don't feel like reading today. I'll go for a walk in the park.'

'Take care, Bill,' she reminded me.

'I will,' I said, going out of the door into the entrance hall.

CHAPTER TWENTY-SEVEN
REPRIEVE

The alarm on my mobile phone told me it was time to get up. I turned it off and climbed out of bed. I went to the window and looked out. It was still dark and the street lamps were still burning but dawn was spreading its faint glow in the East. The nights are drawing in fast, I thought to myself. I remembered that Mars was visible in the sky at that time so I decided to take my binoculars into the garden and try to see it.

I went quietly out of the kitchen door and into the garden. The air was cool and the sky was clear. I looked up and almost immediately I saw it, small and red but glowing distinctly, rather than twinkling, like stars do. When I put the binoculars to my eyes, it was hard to hold them still, so I went inside the kitchen and took the blanket Mum used for ironing and spread it on the damp grass. I lay on my back and trained the binoculars on the tiny red ball above me. There it was, Mars! Somewhere there was Michu. What was she doing at that moment? Was it night or day? If I held the glasses very still I fancied I could see that Mars was not round but about three quarters full.

Suddenly I had the strong feeling that Michu was talking to me. I concentrated, removing the glasses from my eyes and closing them. Yes, I was sure! It was definitely her voice. What was she saying? I couldn't make it out. As I lay there, with my heart pounding in my chest, I heard her speak again. 'Bill, take care, you are in great danger. But don't fear, we are with you.' A lump came into my throat. I offered thanks to the Almighty at that moment. Here was the strength I needed. With Michu's support, I knew I could go through whatever it was I had to suffer.

There was silence. That was all I was to hear, but it was enough.

I went back to my bedroom and sat in meditation for about twenty minutes. My thoughts were all about Michu and I knew in my heart she could hear every one.

Dad was up and about, whistling a tune as he liked to do in the mornings. It reminded me that today was the day the front page of the local paper was going to shock the town. I shuddered at the thought, but after being in contact with Michu, it no longer spelt disaster for me.

Our newspaper was delivered every morning at around six thirty. I went to the top of the stairs and looked down at the front door. There it was, sticking out menacingly. I went back to the bedroom, lacking the courage to go down and look. I heard my father go down the stairs and I expected any minute to hear his voice roaring with rage. I went back to the top of the stairs and peeped down. The paper had gone and still no sound from Dad. Had he opened it? If so, why had he not hit the roof? I listened. I could hear him pottering about the kitchen, still whistling. There was no way he had not glanced at the headlines. He always did, as soon as he had the paper in his hands.

After ten minutes I came to the conclusion that Sonia's father had not carried out his threat. Strangely enough I felt a pang of disappointment. I had braced myself for the bombshell and now it had fizzled out. Why? He wants my story, that's why, I said to myself. He is not sure that publishing the evidence will work. He must have another plan. He is not going to give up, that I was sure of.

After breakfast I went straight to the library. The sun shone and I looked forward to hearing about Pietersen's great innings. Ben and Tim would never understand how I knew and I'd be four pounds better off. I might even buy Sonia a box of chocolates, I thought. She'll be over the moon.

But Sonia was not at the library. I asked the chief librarian if she knew why Sonia had not come to work but she said she had no idea, it was the first time it had ever happened. I became worried. I went out to the entrance hall and found her name in my phone directory. There was no answer. I realised then that I didn't even know where she lived. I was powerless. What if her father had found out she was helping me? There was no knowing what he might do.

I decided to go for a walk in the park in the sunshine. There were plenty of children playing on the grass and in the play park. I skirted the fence and wandered about. Some boys were playing cricket with a board propped up for the wicket. One boy bowled a tennis ball and it hit the board, knocking it over. 'That's not fair, said the batsman, the wind blew the wicket over. The bowler yelled at him and they started an argument, which was soon joined by all the fielders. I was afraid it might lead to a fight so I went over to them and gave them a lesson on sportsmanship. They listened intently but I had walked away only a few metres and they were already arguing again. Let them fight, I thought. They will learn someday.

I took a circular route which led me round the edge of the grassed area. I looked back at the cricketers. They were back into the game, the argument forgotten. It was then that I noticed two men about a hundred metres behind me. As I turned towards them they seemed to slow down. They were too far away for me to get a good look at them. I walked on and they followed. After a few minutes I turned round again. Once more they slowed down and this time they turned aside. I quickened my step and walked towards the exit. As I was going out of the park I quickly glanced round. They had closed the gap. It was then that I knew, without a shadow of doubt, that I was being followed.

With beating heart and clammy hands I hastened down the road in the direction of the town centre as fast as I could without looking suspicious. I didn't look round until I had reached the pub at the corner of West Street. I glanced back for a fraction of a second. They were still following me. I turned into West Street and once out of their sight I broke into a run. When I reached the first side road I turned into it and hurried down. At the next corner I stopped and peered round the wall. I waited and then peeped again. I had given them the slip. But I had no doubt they knew where I lived. Don't panic, Bill, I said to myself. Albert Smith is trying to frighten you into cooperating with him.

I went home and switched on the television. Play had started at the Oval. England had won the toss and Michael Vaughan had elected to bat.

CHAPTER TWENTY-EIGHT
A BURGLARY

At lunchtime I called Sonia's number again but still there was no answer. The chief librarian may know where she lives, I thought. With that idea in mind I told my mum I was going to the library for an hour but I would be back home before 4 o'clock. I was worried about Sonia but I also wanted to follow Pietersen's innings.

Before leaving the house I moved the curtain aside an inch and surveyed the street in case the house was being watched. I saw nothing unusual.

Mrs. Rogers, the chief librarian, a kindly, middle aged woman, gave me the directions to Sonia's house and asked me to let her know if Sonia was sick and if there was anything she could do to help.

I found Myrtle Road easily. The houses were small, brick-built semi-detached houses that I guessed were built soon after the end of First World War. The front gardens were small and the builders had not thought it worth building garages. Owners parked their cars in the gardens. I walked along on the side of the odd numbers. I passed No. 43 without stopping. The front garden was neglected, with tall weeds almost up to the front room window sill. There was no car parked outside. The upstairs curtains were drawn but otherwise I saw no sign nor heard any sign of life. I walked to the end of the road and down the other side. Then plucking up courage, I crossed the road, walked up the short, concrete drive of No. 43 and rang the bell.

Silence!

I waited. Then I rang the bell a second time. Again, no sound came from inside the house. There was a wooden door at the side of the house leading to the back garden. It was not locked so I went through. I tried the side door into the kitchen but it was locked. I was nervous in case Albert Smith should suddenly decide to come home but my anxiety about Sonia and my hope of recovering the stolen things was a more powerful force. Nothing ventured, nothing gained, I said to myself. I turned the corner into the back garden and surveyed the house. There was a small window open in what looked like the bathroom. Did I dare climb in there? A neighbour could easily see me and call the police. How would I explain that he had stolen a Martian outfit from me and I had come to get it back? The local cops would hardly believe that!

Then I had an idea. There was a ladder propped up against the small shed at the bottom of the garden. I found a bucket and a cloth in the shed. I slid the ladder up the wall of the house until it was next to the open window and, empty bucket and cloth in hand, I climbed the ladder and began cleaning the windows. A window cleaner is a common sight. With luck, no-one would bother to look twice.

After cleaning the window as best I could with a dry cloth and no water, I put my hand through the small window until I found the catch of the larger one. I opened it, looked round to see if I could see anybody watching, said a quick prayer and climbed carefully in. I tiptoed downstairs and went out of the back door of the kitchen to retrieve the ladder, which I replaced where I had found it. Then I went back into the house.

I had a good look round the ground floor. It was clean and tidy and I was sure Sonia must have done many hours of housework. I couldn't imagine Albert Smith to be very house-proud. Various family photos stood on mantle pieces and sideboards. I recognised Sonia in various stages of childhood. What must she have thought when her mother left home?

I looked in all the cupboards but found nothing interesting. Then I climbed the stairs as quietly as I could. I was sure there was nobody at home but I was not going to take any chances. There were three bedrooms. The first one, facing the back of the house, was Sonia's. It was neatly kept but empty. On a table in the corner she had left some writing materials and a novel. I scanned the open page of the writing pad. It was full of doodles. Among them was my name, written in various ways, interspersed with roughly drawn hearts. I didn't want to see any more. It was not the first evidence the girl was sweet on me.

The door to the front bedroom was closed. I opened it gingerly and peeped in. If there was an opposite of Sonia's room, this was it. The table was littered with papers and books. Over the back of the chair were several shirts and trousers. The bed was unmade.

I started looking in the cupboards in the remote chance that I would find something of mine, but there was nothing.

At that moment my phone rang and it made me jump. Ben's name was on the screen.

'Hey Bill! Are you watching?'

'Not exactly.'

'What do you mean, 'not exactly',' he said. 'You either are or you're not!'

'I'm not, actually. How is the game going?'

Ben laughed. 'Well, I've kissed goodbye to my two quid. Vaughan is out and England is in trouble.'

'Has Pietersen gone in yet?' I asked hopefully.

'Just now. I don't know how long he'll last though.'

'He'll put England right back on top, don't worry,' I said confidently.

'We shall see. So where are you? What's more important than the cricket?'

'Actually, I'm at Sonia's.'

'Aha! So that's what's more important.

'It's nothing like that, Ben. In fact Sonia's not here.'

If she's not there, what the hell are you doing in her house?'

Breaking and entering.'

'You're pulling my leg, right?'

'Straight up, Ben. I'm not joking. I came here to find Sonia. She didn't go to work today and she hasn't been in contact.'

Ben whistled. 'Careful, man!'

Suddenly I heard a key in the lock of the front door. My heart almost jumped into my mouth. I almost dropped the phone in my panic.

'Ben!' I whispered into the phone, 'I have to hide, there's someone coming!'

I switched off the mobile and stuffed it into my pocket. I looked frantically for somewhere to hide. I could hear heavy footsteps plodding up the stairs slowly. Those don't belong to Sonia, I thought. There's only one body that can make that sound, Albert Smith. I dived under the bed. It was not the best of places but I had no choice. I lay there, sweat pouring off my brow and my hands shaking. The steps had reached the landing. The next moment the bedroom door flew open and I saw his boots clump noisily round the bed to the side by the window. I turned over carefully to face the boots. One by one they were kicked off. Then I saw the trousers being lowered to the floor.

At that moment two pound coins dropped to the floor with a soft plop as they hit the threadbare carpet. One of them spun round a couple of time and then, horror of horrors, it rolled under the bed and came to rest a few inches from my nose. Then I saw a hand reach down. First it picked up the one that had landed near one of his boots and then the hand was groping under the bed for the other one. I lay there, petrified. The hand came nearer to my face, the fingers searching, first this side and then that. I prayed that it would retrieve the coin. What I should have done was to move the coin myself to within reach of the hand but there are things in life that you should do but somehow you don't and you spend the rest of your life wondering why you didn't. The hand was withdrawn and a round, red face took its place, the face of Albert Smith.

You could say that Albert Smith was surprised to see me under his bed and it would be the biggest understatement of the century. He lay there on the floor looking at me for a good ten seconds.

'Okay, out you come!' he said finally, getting to his knees and then to his feet. He was not a very agile man. He hoisted up his trousers and did up the belt.

I crawled out and stood up to face him.

'And would you mind telling me what the hell you are doing in my house?'

'I came to see Sonia,' I replied rudely.

'Sonia's not here. You probably won't see her again.'

I looked at his face with loathing. 'What have you done with her?'

'D'ye think I'd harm my own daughter? You must have a very low opinion of me.'

'I do, very low,' I said, anger building up in me.

My head was jolted sideways as he slapped my face hard. I put up my hand to feel my cheek. It began to smart.

'I wouldn't harm a hair of her head,' he said. 'She's all I've got. No, I've sent her away to her Aunt's for a month. When the money starts coming in I'll bring her back and we'll move from this place.'

'What about her job? I asked quietly, still holding my stinging cheek.

'Her job? She'll not need that job. I told you already, I've got great things lined up for her.'

'Like an Italian Count with ten yachts,' I said with as much sarcasm as I could muster. I smiled a thin bitter smile.

'You can make fun. Smile as much as you like, but soon you'll be smiling on the other side of your face.'

'Where does the Aunt live,' I asked, hoping that I might yet help her.

'Canada. My sister lives in Toronto. She called this morning. Sonia has already arrived there. I told her to take away her passport and her money. I don't want her running away before I've done what I have to do.'

Canada! I wondered how I could possibly help her, so far away.

'Now,' said Albert Smith, 'have you changed your mind yet?'

'No, and I never will!' I shouted.

'A pity,' he said softly. 'Well, I did warn you boy. We can still make the Saturday edition or even Friday. I've got till six o'clock.'

'Please yourself,' I said defiantly. 'Now let me go: my mum is expecting me.'

'You're not going anywhere,' he said flatly.

I stared at him. 'You won't get away with this.' I almost said that my friends knew that I was there but I stopped myself in time.

He just laughed his unpleasant laugh. He then frisked me, removing the contents of my pockets, money, keys and the mobile phone, all of which he put on top of his dressing table. Then twisting my right arm behind my back he pushed me in front of him, out of the room and down the stairs. He took a bunch of keys from his pocket and unlocked the door of a cupboard under the stairs. He tied my hands behind my back with some thin, red, plastic-coated wire, which he had stored in the cupboard and trust me inside, closing the door.

Inside the cupboard it was pitch black. I searched around with my feet and found what felt like a box. I sat down on it carefully and leant against the wall. A moment later the door opened and Albert Smith placed a large tin on the floor in front of me.

'Just in case you're caught short,' he said with a grin.

'And how am I to......' I indicated my tied hands.

'That's your problem. You'll not be drinking anything till tomorrow so maybe you won't need it,' and with that he shut the door.

My wrists were already beginning to hurt from the electric wire tied tightly around them and my hands felt as though they would drop off. My cheek still hurt from the blow he had given me with the flat of his hand. How was I going to survive until the next day, without light, food or water. I decided I had no choice and I would have to sit it out. I had read about people spending years in solitary confinement and coming out alive. But I was not to know how long Albert Smith was going to keep me there.

CHAPTER TWENTY-NINE
RESCUE

In that dark little cupboard under the stairs of No. 43 Myrtle Road, minute followed minute, hour followed hour and I sat on that box in agony. My shoulders ached, my back ached, my wrists ached, my head ached, my whole body was wracked with pain. In the darkness it was hard to keep track of time. I had left home at lunchtime, gone to the library and then straight to Sonia's house. I guessed it was about 3 o'clock when Albert Smith had discovered my hiding place. He had long since gone out. It must now be evening. What was my mother thinking? I had told her I would be home by 4 pm. She must be worried. Ben knows I came here, I remembered, and that gave me some hope.

At that moment I heard the front door slam and I guessed that Albert Smith had come home from work. Newspaper men often work late hours. It could be any time of the night. I expected him to open the door any moment but the next thing I heard were his heavy footsteps stumping up the stairs over my head. After that there were some noises from above and then everything was quiet. Albert Smith had retired for the night.

That night was the longest I had ever spent. I was dying to empty my bladder but had no idea how I was going to achieve it so I just put it off. I thought about Pietersen and wondered if he made the century that would earn me four pounds. I thought of Sonia in Canada and how she must be feeling. But most of all I thought of Michu. I tried hard to make contact with her. I knew that she must know that I was in trouble and I hoped something miraculous would happen. I tried to sleep and I suppose I must have dosed off now and again, but sleep is hard when pain invades your whole body.

Finally I heard the familiar sound of Albert Smith's shoes on the stairs and a few seconds later the door opened and his face appeared. The light almost blinded me and I closed my eyes.

'I hope you had a good night's sleep,' he said sarcastically.

I kept quiet.

'You'll want to go to the bathroom,' he said, taking hold of my arm and pulling me out of the cupboard. He untied the wire and I let my hands hang down in front of me. I looked down at them. They were blue from lack of oxygen and they hurt dreadfully.

'Go in there. I have to go to work and you're going back in there,' he said, indicating the cupboard which had been my prison since the day before.

I went to the toilet. The relief was wonderful but I hardly knew how to use my hands. I washed them and also my face and took a drink of water directly from the tap. He rapped on the door and called out, telling me to get out quickly. I came out.

'Back in there,' he ordered.

'How long are you going to keep me here with no food and no water?'

'That depends on you. When you want to talk, I'm here to listen: the sooner the better.'

I said nothing as he retied the wire around my wrists. He must have felt guilty seeing my swollen wrists because he was careful not to tie them so tightly. Finally, he pushed me back into the cupboard and shut the door with a bang. Soon after that I heard the front door close noisily and then silence.

The hours passed, I had no idea how many. I was desperately hungry and thirsty and my body ached all over. But I was determined not to give him my story, however long he kept me locked up.

All at once I heard a noise in the hallway, the sound of voices speaking in whispers.

I called out, 'hello, is anyone there?'

Then I heard a voice right outside the door.

'He's in here!' It was Tim's voice. 'Bill, is that you in there?'

'Tim, I'm here, in the cupboard!' I shouted. I had never been so happy to hear his voice.

'Wait! We'll soon get you out of there!' he called.

About a minute passed and then I heard Ben's voice. 'Okay, we have a screw-driver. Now let's get this door open.'

There were then some scratching sounds, some arguing about the best way of tackling the job, some splintering of wood and at last the door flew open, letting in the bright light of day. I put my hands over my eyes.

'Are you alright Bill?' asked Ben.

'Fine, apart from a sore face, hands that I can't feel, wrists that are just about cut open and a body that's black and blue, otherwise I'm in perfect health.'

'How long have you been in there?' asked Tim, untying the wire.

'About 24 hours, I should think, but it seems more like a week. I've been here since we talked yesterday afternoon. What a good thing you phoned and I was able to tell you I was here,' I said, shaking my head.

'Otherwise we would never have guessed,' said Ben.

'And my mother?' I asked.

'Don't worry about your parents. We went round to your house in the evening and told them you were staying the night with us.'

'That was a cool idea,' I said, gratefully.

'Look you two,' said Tim. 'We have to get out of here fast, in case your friend comes back.'

'Friend! He's no friend of mine, more like my worst enemy.'

On the way out of the kitchen I noticed the glass in the door had been broken.

'We had to do it, there was no window open,' Tim explained.

'I'd love to see Albert Smith's face when he comes home and sees the damage you've done to his house,' I said laughing.

'Nothing compared to the damage I'll do to him if I get my hands on him,' said Tim.

'Careful, Tim, he's a big man and strong,' I said, as we shut the wooden side door and went out into the street. Suddenly I remembered the things he had taken from me. I put my hand through the hole in the kitchen door and reentered the kitchen. I went quickly back up the stairs and into his bedroom. The things were still there where he had put them the day before. I put them into my pockets and rejoined the boys.

We went straight home to their house in Lilac Avenue. There they made me sit in a comfortable chair with my feet up and Mrs. Armstrong made tea and pancakes for us. I had never tasted anything so good in my entire life. I recounted the events of Thursday, including the news about Sonia being sent off to Canada.

I then remembered the Test Match. In the excitement I had completely forgotten to ask about Pietersen.

'Oh! By the way, did KP get his ton?

Both boys laughed and looked at each other.

'Well, did he?'

'He was on 98,' explained Tim. 'Kumble bowled and Pietersen came down the wicket. We could see that one going for six. But he can't quite have got hold of it in the middle, because the ball fell short of the boundary.' Tim paused.

'So it was a four, not a six!' I was relieved.

'No, it dropped straight into the hands of long off. He was caught out.'

I stared at the boys. It never occurred to me that Pietersen would not reach his hundred. There was my four pounds gone and Sonia's box of chocolates too.

'Ben has already paid me his two quid,' said Tim, holding out his hand towards me.

'You'll have to wait till Sunday when I get my pocket money,' I said.

'No problem.'

Never count your chickens before they've hatched was a favourite saying of my mother. I guess I learnt something that day.

CHAPTER THIRTY
THE LODGER

It was Saturday and I stayed home all day. I knew Albert Smith would be livid when he found out that I'd been rescued. He probably had his friends, the ones who had followed me from the park, watching the house, just waiting for the opportunity to kidnap me. Occasionally during the morning I peeped out of my bedroom window. People passed by on their way to the shops or whatever it was they had to do but I saw no suspicious characters hanging about. Once I saw a car drive down the road to the end, turn round and drive back but I decided it was someone looking for a particular house. I didn't see the car after that.

In the afternoon Dad decided to go to the football match at the local ground, where our home team was playing an important game against our rivals in a local derby. I made an excuse that I was feeling tired, which was the truth: I hadn't yet recovered from my ordeal. I was careful not to show my wrists, which were swollen and sore. Mum said she had some shopping to do and went out with her trolley that she always took shopping and gave me cause for shame. How can you have a mother who wheels a trolley to the shops? I asked her why she didn't take the car and she just said she had never been very confident in the traffic and anyway it was hard to park in town.

I stayed at home, reading the book on Mars that I hadn't got very far with, what with all the events of the past few days. The radio was on in the background so I could follow the Test Match. The rest of the England batsmen had failed miserably and India led the first innings by more than a hundred runs. England had just started their second innings and so far all their wickets were intact. I was engrossed in my book, sitting in the arm chair, reading about the so-called canals that Giovanni Schiaparelli had discovered on Mars in 1877, when there was a ring at the door. I jumped. My immediate thought was that Albert Smith had come to get me. He had seen my parents go out and had guessed that

I was alone. My heart started beating like a drum. I moved across to the window, being careful not to show my face, and peered through the lace. The figure standing on the doorstep was the very last person I expected to see. I rushed out of the room and headed for the front door, as if the caller might turn away and disappear in a few seconds.

I flung wide the door and greeted the figure with a huge smile of welcome.

'Sonia! How on Earth did you get here?'

She looked a bit bewildered and I was soon to learn why. I led her into the sitting room and she ploncked herself down in the armchair I had been sitting in. She was dressed in a white blouse and tartan skirt and her red hair was tied back in a single plait. She carried a small red handbag which she draped over the arm of the chair. She sat back in the chair and looked at me through her round glasses.

'A most curious thing.....' she began. 'You won't believe it Bill.'

'I'm ready to believe anything, dear,' I said. 'Go on, tell me.'

'My father put me on a plane to Canada late on Wednesday night.'

'That much I know. He told me himself.'

'Really? You know then that he wanted me out of the way for a month while he made big plans for our future.'

'Yes,' I said.

'I arrived at my Aunt's house in Toronto on Thursday morning. The first thing she did was to take away my passport and my money. She said that was my father's instructions. I can tell you, I was mad about it. She kept following me around as if I was likely to run away, as if I could without money and a passport. I was worried about my job. I knew my father was not going to tell Mrs. Rogers anything.'

She stopped and looked at me with a mixture of respect and gratitude.

'Early this morning the strangest thing happened. First I should tell you that last night I thought about Michu and I kind of asked for her help. Well, this morning someone called at my Aunt's house and asked to see me. My Aunt was *so* suspicious and at first she wouldn't invite the man in.'

'What did he look like?' I asked.

'He was very small and thin, and the odd thing was, he said he knew you.'

'Priam,' I said. 'He is Michu's father.'

'Wow!' said Sonia.

'And he gave you a parcel,' I said smiling.

'How do you know that? You're spoiling my story!'

'Sorry! Go on.'

'He gave me a parcel and told me to unwrap it. When I did, there was nothing inside. Then he made me feel it and it *was there* but invisible. He asked me if I wanted to go home and I said, 'yes and no.' Then he said, 'yes, you want to go to see Bill but not your father. I know.' Well, you can imagine how confused I was. He actually knew what I was thinking!'

'That is the gift that all Martians seem to have,' I said.

'He led me out into the garden, much to the annoyance of my Aunt. He told her calmly and sweetly that he only wanted to see the roses, they were so beautiful. So she went inside the house and watched through the window. Then he held out the invisible parcel, shook it and there appeared a big bubble, like the one you told me about. He said I need do nothing, that the bubble was programmed and would take me home. I hardly had time to think and I was whisked into the air, inside the bubble. It must have got here in only a few minutes. The next thing I knew, I was in the churchyard at the end of your road and the bubble was nowhere to be seen. And here I am!'

'I will believe anything after this Sonia. Michu is a marvel!'

'I will never be able to thank her enough, Bill. And Priam.'

'It's wonderful to see you. I was so worried about you, and so was Mrs. Rogers,' I said.

Sonia's face clouded over. 'Of course now I can't go home.'

'Your father would have a pink fit if he saw you were back.'

'What shall I do?'

'Stay here, Sonia. We have a spare room and Mum won't mind. We can tell her your father had to go away and you didn't want to stay in the house on your own.'

'If it's not too much of an imposition,' she said doubtfully.

'Of course not! But there are other problems.'

'Like what?' asked Sonia.

I then told her what had happened to me since we had last met on Wednesday morning after my meeting with her father. I told her of my concern for her and how I had gone to her house to look for her and had broken in. I could see the admiration in her eyes. When I got to the part where her father had discovered me under the bed and had hit me and then thrown me in the under-stairs cupboard, she showed great sympathy for my situation. I told her how I had talked to Ben on the phone and how they had rescued me and she clapped her hands with excitement.

When we both realised again what a mess we were both in we became serious.

'How can I go to work?' said Sonia gloomily.

'And how am I to leave this house?' I said in the same mood.

We sat for a while. I was desperately trying to think of a plan. We could leave the town for a while, I thought. Then I had a brainwave.

'We'll put on disguises!' I cried.

Sonia looked doubtful. 'If they see us leave the house, even in a disguise, they will know it is us.'

'Mmmm,' I mused.

'It could work though,' she said, brightening up.

'I acted an old man in the school play once,' I said. 'Everyone said how good I was.'

'I could wear a wig and stuff pillows in my clothes to make me look fat,' suggested Sonia. She was getting excited about my idea.

'There's a problem, Sonia. If there is someone watching the house, he will see two old people go out but won't have seen them go in. That will make him suspicious.'

'I've got it!' cried Sonia. 'We can escape through the back fence with our disguises in bags and then, calmly and slowly, we can walk down the street and knock on your door.'

'Sonia, you're brilliant! What a cool plan.' We can spread the word that my mum's long-lost aunt and uncle have come all the way from Australia to spend a week, or two weeks with her.'

'Mr. & Mrs. MacDonald from Sydney!' said Sonia dramatically, getting up from the chair and bowing.

'How's your Australian accent?'

'Terrible!' she said with a mock groan.

'It can't be as bad as mine sport.' I tried the accent with little success, which made us both laugh. It was good to laugh: it released some of our tension.

At that moment, Mum came back from shopping. She parked her trolley in the hall and came into the sitting room, finding Sonia and me bending over with laughter.

'What's the joke about?' she asked.

'Nothing Mum,' I said. 'Meet Sonia.

'We met the other day dear. Hello Sonia.'

'Hi, Mrs. Steadman,' said Sonia, holding out her hand.

'By the way Mum, do you by any chance have an aunt and uncle in Australia?'

'Not that I know of. I did have an Aunt in Canada but I haven't heard anything about her for years. She's probably dead by now.'

'I wouldn't bank on it. She might suddenly appear on the doorstep and tell you she has come to spend a month with you, and bring her old husband too!' I could hardly keep a straight face. Sonia had her hands over her face to hide the laughter.

'Heaven forbid!' cried my mother, looking horrified. That was too much. Both Sonia and I burst into laughter and we laughed until tears rolled down our cheeks.

Poor Mum, she tried to share the joke but could hardly know the reason why we thought it so funny.

'Mum, don't go. I want to ask you something,' I said, trying to be serious. Sonia was wiping her eyes on her handkerchief.

'Mum, can Sonia stay here? Her father is away and she gets scared in the house on her own. She can use the spare room. I'll move some of those old things into my room. Is it okay?'

'Of course,' she said. 'She's welcome.'

'Thanks Mum, it will only be a few days.'

She went to the kitchen to put her shopping away.

There was another ring on the front doorbell. Sonia and I looked at each other in alarm. I leapt up and peered through the lace curtain.

'It's Ben and Tim.' I was relieved.

I let them in. They were surprised to see Sonia and they were even more surprised when she told them how she had travelled from Canada.

'Put a call through to your Michu and ask her to send another bubble over. I fancy a weekend in the Bahamas,' joked Ben.

We sat round the small table in the bay window of the sitting room and went over the situation facing us. Albert Smith was too quiet: he had to have something up his sleeve, just what it was we could only guess. Tim said he had seen a car parked at the end of the road with two men inside, sitting smoking cigarettes. I told the boys of my idea of using disguises to go in and out. We had another good laugh but they both said it was a cool idea and agreed to find some good costumes for us, if the shop was open on Sunday morning. Until then, Sonia and I were advised to stay at home, but be careful not to get up to any mischief. Sonia and I beat both boys over the head for their cheek.

CHAPTER THIRTY-ONE
BREAKFAST NEWS

Sonia and I were sitting at the kitchen table enjoying a bowl of cereal, while my mum was pottering about the kitchen. Dad had gone for his usual Sunday morning walk in the park. It was a ritual he had followed for as many years as I could remember. He would stop at the newsagents and pick up the newspapers on the way back. He would always buy the local paper and one national paper, it could be the Telegraph or the Times or one of the tabloids, depending on the attractiveness of the front page. He was not one of those who would stand up and die for his favourite paper, not Dad! He was neither right nor left but somewhere in the middle when it came to politics. 'All tarred with the same brush,' he would say of politicians in general. Sometimes he would complain when the Telegraph got too patriotic and started beating the drums and waving the Union Jack. He was one of those who hailed Tony Blair's victory in 1997 but thought he had made the biggest mistake of his political career when he had followed his friend to Baghdad. Dad was an admirer of Winston Churchill and was fond of recounting his own father's exploits in the Second World War. He had some respect for Margaret Thatcher but disagreed strongly with her policies.

We heard the front door slam.

'There's your father now,' said Mum. 'I wish he wouldn't slam that door. Move along Sonia and make a space for him. He'll be hungry for his breakfast after his walk.'

Before she could move Dad appeared in the doorway. He was as white as a sheet. He just stood there, with the newspaper in his shaking hand, looking into space.

'What's up, Stan?' cried Mum. 'You look deathly.'

Dad threw the newspaper onto the table, knocking the spoon out of my cereal bowl and splattering milk over the table.

'That's what's up,' he said, pointing at the newspaper with a shaking hand. 'Read for yourself.'

Before I had even looked at the paper lying on the table in front of me I knew what had turned him pale. Albert Smith had carried out his threat!

There it was, a banner headline, the size normally reserved for the deaths of kings.

LOCAL BOY DATES MARTIAN GIRL

Underneath the headline was a picture of me, with Barclays Bank in the background and the clock on the wall above, the hands pointing at 10.05.

I looked up at Dad and then at Mum. She had approached the table and was peering over my shoulder. She said nothing, she just stared disbelievingly. Sonia had also gone a lighter shade of pale and her eyes were open wide.

'Do you mind telling me what this is all about?' said Dad menacingly.

'Dad, I can explain,' I said feebly.

'You'd better have a good story, my boy!' He almost shouted the words.

'Dad, I......'

'In all my life I have never had a shock like this,' he went on, waving his arms in the air.

'Stan! Let the boy speak,' Mum said, trying to calm him down. She turned to me.

'Bill, what is this all about? She said quietly.

Dad was still fuming but he stayed quiet.

'Can you let me read it?' I pleaded. 'How do you expect me to explain if I haven't even read it?'

'Go on, read it out loud,' said Mum.

I cleared my throat, which was suddenly clogged up. I glanced at Sonia. Bless her! The look she gave me helped me to go on. I started to read.

SCHOOL BOY ADMITS INTER-PLANETARY ROMANCE

'By Sunday Post Reporter-

A local boy, William Steadman, a senior student at Mill Road Secondary School, is corresponding with a Martian girlfriend by e-mail.

Steadman, whose photograph appears below .... writes to his alien friend in English. This newspaper has a letter written by Steadman to the girl, whose name is Michu. The letter is reproduced below.'

I looked down the page and there was my letter reproduced in full. My emotions were mixed. In one way I was disgusted at Albert Smith's claim that I had admitted having this relationship. I had never admitted anything. I also felt great sorrow for the feelings of my parents and I could imagine how they would feel when the full force of this revelation hit them. There were also other emotions. I was sad that Sonia had to see the father she had always loved and trusted turn into an avaricious liar and cheat. And there was the pride in me that surfaced for an instant, the pride that told me I had become famous overnight.

'Go on!' shouted my father.

'Steadman, who claims in his letters to have visited Mars recently, brought the extraterrestrial to his home in Dover Street. The girl left behind a tunic. Tests carried out on the cloth used to make the garment have proved that it was not made on Earth. The specialist who carried out the tests told this newspaper, 'We can only conclude that this cloth comes from a source yet unknown to any recognised cloth manufacturing industry in the world.'

'This astounding news is likely to shock the world. NASA, the US Space Agency, which has been in the forefront of the race to locate extraterrestrial life, is likely to step up its efforts to find the answer to the hottest question ever posed to the human race. The US Government is likely to increase funding for an early manned landing on Mars.'

There was more but I couldn't go on. I stopped reading and lifted my eyes. Mum had sat down on a chair and was sniffing loudly, dabbing her eyes with the corner of a tea cloth. Dad was still standing looking into space, his face creased up. Sonia, who understood everything, just sat and suffered for all of us.

'It's not true,' I said softly. 'That reporter is a liar. I have never admitted anything. Mum, you remember the day I couldn't find that outfit? You also came to my room to look, remember?'

She nodded.

'I admit I wrote a letter on my laptop to an imaginary girl called Michu. It was a game,' I lied. 'That reporter came here the other day and he copied the letter that was on my computer and took the outfit from my cupboard. Mum, you were the one who let him in.'

She just sniffed louder and wiped her eyes on her forearm.

'I'll go to the police and have the man locked up. How can he go round taking things from people's houses and making up stories about them?'

'Dad, don't!' I cried. 'It will just create more trouble. Please don't.'

'Alright, but there's one thing I don't understand,' said my father through the creases. 'How did that man know about the letter?'

I looked at Sonia and she smiled weakly at me.

'You know I have been going to the library. Sonia works there. I told her of my interest in Mars and we had a standing joke that one day I would take her there. She happened to share the joke one day with her father.' I paused and looked across at Sonia again. 'He took it seriously.'

'I still don't follow,' said Dad. 'That doesn't explain how the reporter knew about your letter.'

'He didn't, Dad. He came to our house to speak to me because he was curious about the story he'd heard. I was not at home but like a crazy idiot I left the letter open on my laptop.'

'But how did the reporter become interested in the story?'

'The reporter and Sonia's father….. they are the same person.'

Dad looked down at Sonia.

'It's true Mr. Steadman,' she said. 'My father is that reporter for the Post.' A sad expression came over her face. 'I hate to say it of my own father but I now believe he is insane.'

'Insane?' cried Dad.

'Yes Mr. Steadman, insane.'

'So the whole thing is in his imagination.'

'Sonia looked at me enquiringly.

'Yes Dad,' I said. I hated to lie to my parents but I honestly believed it was better than put them through the turmoil of knowing the truth.

'So you never brought that Martian to the house then?'

'No Dad, never.' At least that was something I didn't have to lie about. Albert Smith had made up that one.

'Do you know what this means, don't you son?'

'What?'

'It means we are going to be swamped by reporters from all the newspapers in the country. Can you imagine life in Dover Street?'

'Stan, you exaggerate,' said Mum.

'Not a bit of it, Doris. We may even have to move to another town.'

'No Dad, it will all blow over in a few days,' I said hopefully. 'And you won't call the police, will you Dad?'

'No. I hope you are right son,' he said. 'But I doubt if it will blow over that easily.'

'Trust me Dad, it will be forgotten in no time.'

How wrong I turned out to be!

CHAPTER THIRTY-TWO
ANOTHER SURPRISE VISITOR

That Sunday at number 16, Dover Street was like a mortuary on the day of a funeral. My mum and dad went around the house like mice, except that mice squeak sometimes. Occasionally they would look out of the window, expecting to see droves of journalists flocking to our front door. Nobody went out. Sonia and I sat reading, or at least trying to read. Ben rang to say how sorry they both were to read the local newspaper. I told them not to worry: everything would be back to normal after a day or two.

When in the afternoon the doorbell sounded, Mum and Dad were in the kitchen drinking tea and Sonia and I were in the sitting room. They both came in nervously and I was the one selected to look through the curtain.

'It's alright, it's Priam,' I said.

Dad asked, 'And who's Priam?'

'He's the man who called here last Sunday,' I said, turning to Mum for support.

'Is he alone?' He asked.

'He has someone with him, a strange looking man. But he's not a reporter, I'm sure of that.'

'What can they want?' said Mum. 'It's not really a time for visitors.'

'I'll have to ask them in,' I said. 'I will soon find out what they want. You go back to the kitchen and finish your tea. I'll handle it.'

My parents were glad to escape the stress of conversations with strangers at that time. They went back to the kitchen and closed the door behind them.

I let in the visitors and made them comfortable in the sitting room. When we were all seated, Priam spoke.

'I am happy you have made it home, young lady,' he said, bowing slightly. 'I hope the journey was not too frightening for you.'

'No. It was exciting Sir,' she replied. 'I'm grateful for your help. Did you fly over to Canada just to give me the bubble?'

'Think nothing of it,' said Priam warmly. 'We flit about like butterflies on a sunny afternoon. No distance is too great for us.'

Priam turned to me. 'Bill, I want you to meet Hermann.'

'Good afternoon, Sir,' I said politely to the strange man.

He did not reply and I had the chance to study him. He was a small man, plump, with a fringe of grey hair round his bald head. I could not see the colour of his eyes: they appeared to be like a mole's, almost closed. He wore thick glasses, through which he peered myopically. He wore a thick, grey moustache above a mouth that he screwed up. He wore a faded dark suit over a grey shirt with a blue bow tie. A more odd looking character I had never had the opportunity of meeting.

'Hermann was the one who actually wanted to meet you,' said Priam. 'Hermann and I have worked together on some scientific projects that our council of elders believes are beneficial to both Earth and Mars.'

'Why would he want to meet me?' I was nonplussed.

'He has read this morning's newspaper, or should I say, I read it to him.'

'So soon?' I was amazed.

'Of course,' said Priam with a laugh. 'I have a special responsibility here and that is to keep an eye on you. I report every day to the Council. As part of my job I read the newspapers. When I read the article this morning I got in my fastest bubble and came straight here.'

'How is it nobody sees you landing in the bubble?' I asked him.

'But surely you know the bubble can be made invisible.'

'Yes, I had forgotten,' I said.

'Very occasionally things go wrong but fortunately not too often,' he said, looking at Sonia.

Sonia had been studying Hermann and was not following the conversation. Now she looked at Priam.

'I have to say, young lady that your landing in the cemetery yesterday was not programmed and you and the bubble were clearly visible. I'm not quite sure how it happened: it must have been a programming error. We shall have to investigate it. These things should not happen.' He shook his head from side to side.

'How do you know the bubble was visible?' Sonia asked.

'Because I was right behind you.'

We both looked at Priam in surprise.

'Did anyone see me?' asked Sonia, with a worried expression.

'If there was anyone around at the time, it is possible, but I hope not.'

'And my Aunt?' she asked. 'Do you think she saw me getting into the bubble?'

Priam smiled and said to Sonia. 'You don't have to worry your head about your Aunt: she won't say a word to your father about your escape.'

Sonia and I looked confused. 'How is that?' she asked.

He gave a chuckle. 'Because I bundled her off after you left.'

'Bundled her off! Where to?'

'St. Helena. She won't bother anyone for a while.'

'St. Helena! That's where they sent Napoleon after his defeat at Waterloo!' I exclaimed. We had studied Napoleon at school. He had escaped from his first exile on the island of Elba and had returned triumphantly to Paris to the cheers of the French people. After his defeat at Waterloo Britain and Prussia decided to send him somewhere he couldn't escape from.

'Yes,' said Priam happily. 'A pleasant little island in the middle of the South Atlantic. She is bound to enjoy her holiday.'

Sonia and I looked at each other and tried not to laugh.

'Poor Aunt!' she said, hardly able to disguise her enjoyment at the prospect of her aunt, bewildered at finding herself on a far away island.

'But that's one problem less for us, Sonia,' I said. 'Your father will think you are safely hidden away in Toronto and won't come looking for you.'

'Now as I was saying, Hermann and I have been working together on some interesting projects, haven't we Hermann?'

Hermann looked over the top of his thick glasses, screwed up his nose and spoke for the first time.

'Ramjets and scramjets are old hat, mark my vords,' he said emphatically. 'Zhe future is electromagnetism, attraction and repulsion.'

Priam explained. 'Hermann is a brilliant man, but like most of his kind, he is totally focused on one set of ideas. He has no interest in money or comforts, only his ideas. He would gladly tell the world everything he knows and all sorts of people could cash in on his knowledge and inventions and it wouldn't bother him in the least. Fortunately everyone in the scientific community thinks he is completely cuckoo. He has only to speak and he is instantly ridiculed. No-one takes a blind bit of notice of what he has to say.'

I looked at Hermann and I could understand why.

'So how is magnetism going to help the problems faced by Similaria?' I asked.

'That's what we are working on, Bill,' said Priam excitedly. 'It's not only Similaria that's in trouble but all the peaceful clans on Mars.'

'So, just as you are helping us with our problems on Earth, we can also help you.'

'That's the beauty of inter-planetary cooperation, isn't it? But there is a long way to go, Bill. And time is running out.'

I remembered Zeris' face very well as he had explained the situation to me at that meeting before I left Mars. Time was short, for Mars and for Earth too.

Hermann sat up straight and peered at me. 'Zhey zhink I'm crackers, but I'll show zhem. You don't zhink I'm crackers, do you?'

'Of course not!' I said quickly, turning a little red in the face.

'Electromagnetism!' he repeated. 'Zhe most powerful force, it can be used for inter-planetary travel, defense, deflecting missiles and asteroids. It's all possible. I'm almost zhere!' Then he started mumbling to himself, reeling off a string of scientific jargon that no-one in the room could follow.

Priam continued, 'Hermann said he *had* to meet the boy who had just come from Mars. We have invited him to experience conditions on Mars, to help him solve the remaining problems. We have great hopes of frustrating the power-hungry Zeronerans and the Zoggs.'

'So he knows all about my trip to Mars,' I said.

'As much as he needs to know, yes,' said Priam.

'Electromagnetism is zhe answer,' repeated Hermann. He peered at me through his thick glasses. 'Believe me, young man, ve can do great zhings, but ve need access to sophisticated scientific apparatus.' He paused. 'No-vone believes in me. Zhey all say I'm stark-staring crazy, a raving lunatic, bonkers, round zhe bend, and.....' he stopped and looked from Priam to Sonia and then back to me.

'You don't zhink I'm a raving lunatic, do you young man?'

'Of course not Sir,' I said, a little less confidently this time.

'You see,' explained Priam,' those with the necessary facilities have no confidence in Hermann's theories. In a way that is good but in another way it makes it hard for him to finalise his work. We can hardly ask the Zoggs to help, can we?'

'I see the problem,' I said.

We sat talking for sometime and Sonia got to know the full extent of the dangers facing my Martian friends. Hermann didn't say much: he was in his own world of attraction and repulsion. But I was happy to have had the chance to meet one of the world's greatest scientists, even though he was extremely odd.

Finally they left. Sonia and I had another good laugh about her aunt holidaying in St. Helena and wondered, in the excitement of leaving in a bubble, whether she had thought of packing her swimsuit and sun cream!

CHAPTER THIRTY-THREE
DISGUISES

I was up very early the next morning. I meditated in the half-light of dawn, trying to feel the presence of Michu. Once or twice I thought I heard her voice in my head but I was not sure if it was wishful thinking or not. Success or not I was beginning to appreciate the benefits of sitting silently and going inside.

Once up and about I listened carefully for the sound of the local newspaper being stuffed through our small letter box. I wanted to see if there were any more stories following on from the big news in the Sunday Post. Maybe Albert Smith had thought up some more lies to add to the damage he'd already done.

About six-thirty, I heard Dad go down the stairs and I guessed he would beat me to it. He would *also* be anxious to see it for himself. He went into the kitchen and I heard him filling the kettle with water. This morning there was no sound of whistling and that was unusual. He's still in a bad mood today, I thought.

Then the sound came from the front door and I hurtled down the stairs two at a time. Dad came out of the kitchen at the same moment and we almost collided with each other. I was the more athletic and pounced on the newspaper. His hands closed over mine before I could get the paper out of the letter box. But the privilege of being the first to read the news was the father's not the son's, so I gave way. He carried it to the kitchen, walking slowly and scanning the front page as he went. I followed on behind, trying to look over his shoulder. At least it was not front page news today. Disagreements among Town Councilors was today's hot news.

Not finding anything to do with the story of Sunday in the first few pages he tossed the paper onto the kitchen table and continued with what he had been doing before the race to the front door. I sat down and carefully scanned through every single article on every single page, while he wordlessly made tea. I even skipped reading the sports news, which was normally what I would have done first. I just had time to note that England had made 398 in their second innings and had given India 288 to win on the last day.

Then my eye caught a single column article on page 2. It was headed 'I SAW AN ALIEN' I read on eagerly. 'A resident of the town reported yesterday that she had seen an alien land in the churchyard of St. Mark's Church in Cornwall Street on Saturday afternoon. Mrs. Sproggett, of 15 Dover Street had this to say, 'I was just going indoors when I 'appened to look round and what should I see? I saw this something coming out of the sky wrapped in cling film; leastways that's what it looked like to me. I can tell you I was flabbergasted. This thing just floats down in among the graves and runs off. My 'usband was at work at the time. I'm not making this up; I actually saw it 'appen. After that bit in the Sunday Post about hextraterrestrials in Dover Street, I can tell you I'm scared. I want to know what the Government is doing to protect ordinary, law-abiding citizens.'' I read on.

'This sighting so soon after the disturbing news of an alien visitor to the town is likely to pose awkward questions for the defence forces. So far, no-one else has come forward to corroborate Mrs. Sproggett's story.'

I decided not to share the article with my father. It would only annoy him more. I turned back to the sports news. Lewis Hamilton was still ahead of Alonso in the Formula One drivers' championship with a few races to go till the end of the season. The guy is amazing, I thought. Fancy, his first season and he could win the championship.

When Sonia came downstairs for breakfast, looking as if she hadn't slept, I showed her the article. Dad had already gone off to work. Despite her unsettled mood, she managed a smile at the thought of how she had given the lady the shock of her life.

Mum came down soon after that. She looked concerned. 'There's a BBC van outside our door, did you know?'

'Really?'

Sonia and I exchanged glances. We both got up from the table and rushed to the sitting room. Sure enough, there was the BBC van and on the pavement just outside our front gate, stood a woman holding a microphone in her hand. Beside the van stood a cameraman, his heavy camera resting on a stand and pointing at the woman, with our house behind her in the background. I pulled Sonia aside, in case we were seen looking through the window.

'Bill, the TV! Turn on the TV!' whispered Sonia excitedly.

I crossed the room and switched it on. There on the screen was the same scene. It was uncanny. I turned up the volume and heard the woman saying, '…in Dover Street which the girl from Mars is alleged to have visited. In this house lives the Steadman family, whose teenage son is said to have been corresponding with her by e-mail. Just an ordinary British family, you may think. Whether this story turns out to be true or a just hoax is yet to be seen. We will be bringing you further news on this incredible tale. In the meantime this is Janet Richards reporting live from Dover Street for BBC News.' The news programme announcer made some comment about aliens that I didn't pick up.

I turned down the volume on the television and Sonia and I sat on the floor of the sitting room, dazed by the new turn of events. Evidently the story was catching on. Next it would be the national dailies.

Sonia decided she had better telephone the library and tell Mrs. Rogers she was fine and would be coming into work tomorrow. She said she didn't want to say on the phone why she had been away since Wednesday but would explain in the morning. Mrs. Rogers said she was happy to hear her voice and what was all this about Bill Steadman and a Martian girl. She said she had been quite shocked when she had read the front page of the Sunday Post.

A little later, Ben and Tim turned up carrying a heavy suitcase, which Tim put down on the floor of the hall.

'Hey man!' he said. 'You've got half the world outside your door!'

'Yeh, and they all wanted to talk to us,' said Ben. 'Do you know Bill Steadman?' And 'are you friends of the boy Steadman?' So many questions!'

'Not only that!' I said. 'We've been on BBC TV too! Not us exactly but the house.'

'Fame at last!' said Tim, shaking my hand.

'I could do without it, thanks very much! By the way, did you read the bit in the morning paper about Sonia dropping in to have tea with the vicar?' I said facetiously.

Sonia frowned at me.

They hadn't seen it, so I read it out to them.

'The flying librarian!' exclaimed Tim.

Sonia aimed a kick at Tim's leg but he dodged cleverly.

'Beast!' she cried.

'Hey, you two! Okay, what have you got in that suitcase, the crown jewels?'

'Something much more exciting,' said Ben, going to get the case from the hall.

The case was opened and we were shown the contents.

'Wow! These things must've cost you a bomb,' I breathed.

'Not a penny, actually,' said Ben. 'I remembered our Uncle Arthur was on the stage, so I called him and told him I needed some costumes urgently to help out a friend and he said 'come over and see what I've got.''

'Hey, this is cool,' I said, taking out a wig of white hair complete with mustache and beard. Then I found a walking stick, some glasses and a fancy hat. Before long I was dressed as an old man and I hobbling around the sitting room with my stick, accompanied by the hoots from the others. My mum came in and joined in the fun, putting away her gloom of the morning.

Sonia was next. She made a stunning old lady, with her long skirt, half-length coat and white wig. Coming out of the dining room, where she had gone to change, she didn't resemble our Sonia at all. We all congratulated her on her theatrical performance.

'We're ready to face the world guys,' I said to the boys. 'Tomorrow we are going out through the back door with our costumes under our arms. When we come back, it will be through the front door wearing them. Sonia and I will be my mum's long-lost aunt and uncle from Australia.'

'A great idea of yours Bill,' said Tim.

'Sonia's idea actually,' I confessed, glancing at Sonia. She gave me a smile of thanks. 'Hey, thanks for all the trouble you've gone to to get these things!'

'Thanks to Uncle Arthur,' said Ben.

'Three cheers for Uncle Arthur!' I cried. The call was taken up by all, including my mum. This is becoming a real adventure, I thought.

CHAPTER THIRTY-FOUR
FACING THE WORLD

Never before had I known Dad to buy a national newspaper on a weekday. He would make the Sunday paper last the whole week, that way he would keep up to date with the world without spending his whole salary on papers he would never have the time to read. But that Tuesday morning he departed from his normal routine by walking down to the newsagents to see if the whole of the (and here he used a word that I could not possibly repeat) world was talking about us.

He was still not back home when the local daily was jammed into our letter box and I had a preview of the latest news. The headlines glared at me,

ALIEN SIGHTING CONFIRMED
RESIDENTS REPORT LANDING IN CHURCHYARD

I smiled to myself and read on eagerly,

'Since a resident of Dover Street came forward on Sunday to report having seen an alien descend from the sky in a clingfilm bag and land in the churchyard of St. Mark's Church in Cornwall Road, several other residents of the town have claimed to have seen the occurrence.

'The Vicar of St. Mark's, the Reverend John Thomas, told a Post reporter he was at the door of the church at the time. 'I was just going to the Vicarage to work on my sermon for Sunday Evensong,' said Rev. Thomas, 'when I saw this strange looking creature appear through the trees, in a kind of bubble. It is difficult to describe it. I withdrew into the porch so as not to be seen and I watched. My first thought was that it was the second coming but I soon realised it was a woman and could not have been the descent of our Lord on Earth. The bubble burst as the woman landed on the grass and disappeared behind the wall. I could see no more. I went to the altar and prayed for the safety of mankind.'

'Reverend Thomas, who has held the post at St. Mark's for over forty years, was at pains to point out that he did not suffer from poor eyesight nor did he have delusions.

'A teenage boy who was walking down Cornwall Road with his girlfriend told The Post that he clearly saw a bag drop from the sky and disappear behind the trees. 'We was on our way to my friend's place when I saw this great big plastic bag fall out of the sky. I could tell it was plastic because it kind of reflected the sun like plastic bags do, y'know. I pointed it out to Daphne but she was too busy arguing with her mum on the phone and she missed it. I swear it's the truth.'

'Several other people said they saw something like a being dropping out of the sky at the same time on Saturday afternoon, confirming Mrs. Sproggett's story. Some said they would be double-locking their doors and windows for fear of alien visits in the middle of the night. Others said they would stay at home until the authorities did something about the situation. One man told our reporter that he had once been attacked by an Alien and would never forget it.

'Since our lead story in the Sunday Post, the town has become the focus of attention for the whole country. Representatives of the national TV, radio and press have converged on the town and especially Dover Street, where the Martian girl is alleged to have stayed and from where the love letters were allegedly written.

'Asked to comment, His Worship the Mayor, Councillor Spratt, said the attention that was being given to the town would boost tourism and shopkeepers could expect increased business.

'The local Police boss, Chief Superintendent James Barlow CBE, said his men had been put on alert and would deal with any further incident. 'We are in complete control of the situation,' he said. Meanwhile he appealed for people to remain calm.'

I sighed as I left the newspaper on the kitchen table and went up to my room. Michu's face looked down at me from her place on the wall. I asked her for guidance. This whole thing is getting out of hand, I thought.

I went to the window and looked out. There were a few people in the street and some were looking towards the house. It was hard to tell if they were journalists or they were just curious onlookers. As yet there was no sign of any TV vans.

I knocked on Sonia's bedroom door. She was awake.

'Bill, I have to go to work,' she said sleepily.

'I know and I have to continue with my studying.'

'Let's try the disguises today, shall we?'

I smiled at her. 'I can't wait!'

'I have been thinking what to tell Mrs. Rogers,' she said slowly through a yawn. 'I'll have to be a new employee, the old woman.'

'Why? Who is going to link you with me?'

'We've been going around a lot together, Bill.'

'In that case you can tell her you can't afford to be recognised and see if she'll go along with the game,' I said.

'She's a good sort, but suppose the Council man comes and finds someone else working there. She might get into trouble.'

'Mmm.'

'It's not likely though,' she said after a moment's thought. 'He hardly ever bothers us and if he comes he usually says so in advance.'

'That's settled then,' I said cheerfully. 'Today is the day we become the long-lost aunt and uncle from Australia.'

Dad arrived back. He said he had been accosted by a group of reporters, who wanted to know if he was Bill Steadman's father and would he like to tell them if the story in the Sunday Post was true of not. He said he had told them to b…. off otherwise he would have to knock their teeth down their throats. I couldn't help a laugh. He glared at me menacingly and told me it was no laughing matter.

He sat at the kitchen table. He had not bought one national newspaper but three. All of them, The Sun, The Daily Telegraph and The Times, carried front-page stories. The Sun had a blown up version of Albert Smith's photograph of me almost filling the front page. The headline read-

SCHOOLBOY DATES MARTIAN GIRL

Beneath the photograph the following words:

WILLIAM STEADMAN, THE BOY AT THE CENTRE OF THE STORM

There was a short article, which didn't add much to the Post story. But I was sure that The Sun would have a reporter following me closely, hoping to get a story from me. Then I wondered how much The Sun had paid for Albert Smith's photograph.

The Telegraph and The Times were less sensational. The Telegraph printed parts of my letter to Michu and the results of the tests on the cloth. The report suggested that the whole story was probably a prank perpetrated by a bored schoolboy with nothing better to do in the long school holidays. Both newspapers mentioned the sightings of 'Aliens in the churchyard.'

After breakfast Sonia and I packed a bag each with our costumes. We told Mum the plans we had worked out and she agreed to be on hand when her Aunt Maud and Uncle Bert arrived. Dad reluctantly agreed to meet us in the next street and allow us to change into our costumes in the van and then drop us at the library door. He gave me three pounds for the taxi that would later bring the old couple from the station.

All went like clockwork. Our neighbour over the back fence was happy to help when we told her we had to escape the press. She said something rude about them which I didn't quite catch and told us we could use her house as a getaway whenever we liked. I decided not to tell her about the disguises until it was necessary. Dad was waiting by the van, walking up and down impatiently. When he saw us he opened the rear doors, complaining that he was very late for work and would probably lose his job and that would add to our problems. I told him his boss at the gas company would understand but he didn't sound convinced. In the back of the van we changed hurriedly into our costumes as Dad drove us to the library. He had to admit that we looked just like Mum's long-lost aunt and uncle from down under.

When we entered the library in our disguises Mrs. Rogers was completely fooled. She asked if we needed help. She could see we were hardly able to walk. When Sonia revealed her identity, Mrs. Rogers looked at her in astonishment but she soon understood the reason for the disguises. She kindly agreed to take on the new employee, subject to the approval of the Council, to replace the girl who had mysteriously disappeared. Mrs. Rogers was such a sport and so kind-hearted, Sonia and I could have hugged her.

I hobbled theatrically to the table where I normally sat and opened a book on the environment and endangered species by an eminent zoologist. I was so engrossed in the book I hardly noticed the entry of two middle aged men. It was when they walked round the back of my chair that I noticed them for the first time. They sat down at a nearby table and began reading news magazines.

The thin man who read the papers every day had not yet arrived but an old man with shaggy white hair and a light brown overcoat sat at the thin man's table, holding up a copy of the Daily Telegraph, over the top of which he surveyed the goings on in the room. He saw me staring in his direction and lifted the newspaper, hiding his eyes. Surely the press couldn't know I was there in the library!

The day passed uneventfully, except that Sonia sometimes forgot that she was an old lady and climbed the steps like a 10 year old, until I reminded her. Then she would insist on my hand to help her up and down the steps, much to the amusement of the old man. I prayed that he would not take a fancy to her and invite her for tea at his place! At one point my false moustache tickled my nose and I sneezed so violently that the moustache left my face and landed on the floor. Luckily the old man was slow in taking it in and I was able to replace the moustache in time. The other two men seemed to have no interest in what was going on.

At last it was time to leave. It was time to put our disguises to the test. We were both a bit nervous as we said goodnight to Mrs. Rogers and assured her we would be back the next day. The taxi that she had arranged for us sped off towards Dover Street. As we turned the corner from Cornwall Road I was shocked to see how many people were crowded into the street in front of the house.

'This is it, Sonia,' I said in my best Australian accent.

She squeezed my arm and looked nervously at me. 'Maud not Sonia,' she said.

'Oops! Sorry! Just act naturally and it will all go okay,' I reassured her.

'But I'm 18 not 80! How can I be natural?'

'Just say nothing. Leave the talking to me,' I said.

The taxi stopped two doors away because there was no room in front of the house. I got out first and held out my hand for my dear wife of fifty years! As we shuffled along the pavement on our sticks, the throng gave way to let us pass. Mum appeared from the front door and came to meet us. The reporters all crowded round her with their microphones thrust in her face. She waved them away, telling them to give her room to meet her aunt and uncle, who had come for a visit all the way from Australia. Mum was a star. Neither Sonia nor I had to say anything at all. After a minute or two we were safely inside the house.

'What I have to do for a bit of peace!' was all she said.

'Is that the way to welcome your folks who've come all the way from down under to see you? The least you can do is offer us a cup of tea.'

Mum went off to the kitchen dutifully and switched on the electric kettle.

CHAPTER THIRTY-FIVE
OUT OF THE FRYING PAN INTO THE FIRE

I woke the next morning wondering what Albert Smith was doing and why he was being so quiet. His newspaper article had set the whole country talking about me but I couldn't see how he was going to make his fortune, unless he had the whole story from me that he would then sell to the world. Albert Smith is going to make a move soon, I said to myself.

I had a call from Tim while Sonia and I were eating our toast and marmalade.

'Hey, how were the disguises? Did you try them out?'

'Yesterday,' I said, washing down a piece of toast with a gulp of tea.

'Were they good?'

'Terrific,' I assured him.

'Ben and I are going for lunch in town today. Want to join us?'

'If you can bear to sit with an ancient Australian.'

'That'd be cool. Why not? Did he ever play cricket for Australia, by any chance?

'I have a feeling he did …… but probably before Bradman was born.'

'That ancient!?' exclaimed Tim.

'Okay, what time and where?'

'Mac's at one o'clock.'

'Okay, I'll try to be there on time,' I said. 'But you know I don't get about as well as I used to when I was young.'

'Don't run or you'll have a heart attack in the middle of the High Street,' quipped Tim and he switched off.

After Dad had gone off to work, fighting his way through the hoards of reporters who were already besieging the house, and Mum had gone upstairs to hoover the bedrooms, Sonia and I took the same route as the day before. We climbed through the hole in the fence that Mrs. Fawcett had made and knocked on her back door.

'That's funny,' I said. 'She must be out.' I knocked again.

Suddenly the door flew open and there in the doorway to the kitchen stood none other than Albert Smith. Behind him was another man. He grabbed me by the shoulder and quickly pulled me inside before I could evade his grasp. The other man lunged at Sonia, taking hold of her by the hair and pulling her into the kitchen. We were both flung into wooden chairs. The bags with our disguises were abandoned outside the door.

'So, now I've got you William Steadman,' he growled, 'and this time you will not escape. And Sonia, what a surprise to see you!'

He stood back and stared at us. The other man moved back and leaned against the wall. He was of similar build to Albert Smith, but with a heavy moustache and a grey stubble on his face. Sonia and I were still too shocked to speak.

'Sonia, I never thought you'd ditch me like that. I thought I could count on your loyalty. I never thought I'd live to see the day when my own daughter ganged up against me, after all I've done.' He shook his head. 'I tried calling my sister in Toronto and for the life of me I couldn't figure out why she was not answering the phone. Tell me, how on earth did you get back here?' he looked at Sonia bitterly.

Sonia made no reply: she just stared at her father.

'Never mind, I will find out,' he said, turning to me. 'Well, I admired the way you escaped from my house. Of course there is the little matter of the damage to the doors.' He grinned. 'You were overconfident, my lad. One of my spies saw you leave this house yesterday and get into a van. I guessed correctly that you would use the same way again and so, as soon as the lady of the house left this morning we got in and waited for you.

'The lady will come back and you'll be in the soup,' I said.

'I don't think so,' was his reply.

'What did you do to her?' I asked anxiously.

'Nothing. But she got a cable this morning from her sister to say she should come to London urgently.'

'I suppose you sent the cable,' I suggested.

'Clever boy!'

'And the husband?'

'He'll come in the afternoon, by which time we'll be safely away from here.' Albert Smith creased up his face in an evil grin.

'Where are you going to take us?' I asked.

'That would be telling, wouldn't it? I don't want any of your friends finding you, until I've got my story.' He grinned again. 'How long that will be depends on you.'

Sonia looked into her father's face. 'Dad, let us go. You will get into terrible trouble! You'll end up in jail!'

'I'll risk that, my dear. I have waited too long for this chance and I'm not about to give up so easily.'

Has Dad come yet, I wondered. He had told me he would have to report for work that morning and then try to get away, so that we could repeat the routine of the previous day. There in the kitchen I had no way of knowing if he was waiting outside in the street with the Ford van.

I glanced at the other man, who was staring into space. Albert Smith intercepted my glance.

'Let me introduce you to Wally. He's an ex-policeman and a very good interrogator.'

The other man, on hearing his name, looked at me and the faintest smile flicked across his lips. 'Pleased to meet you, Steadman,' he said gruffly. I said nothing but I wondered what kind of techniques he used to extract information from his suspects.

'Now the introductions are over with,' said Albert Smith, 'it's time to get going! But before we go I am going to have to blindfold you. You won't know where you are when I take 'em off. And your mobiles: hand 'em over right now.'

With that he took both our mobile phones and frisked me roughly, just to make sure I didn't have another one stashed away in my pocket. Then he took two large handkerchiefs from his pocket and tied them tightly round our faces, first Sonia's then mine. Then I could feel my hands being tied behind my back. In the darkness I was led roughly out of the front door, down some steps and into a waiting car, which sped off down the road. Dad cannot have been there outside the house! He would not have stood by and watched his son manhandled like that!

I knew Sonia was there in the back seat of the car, because I could hear her sobbing quietly beside me. I would like to have reached out my hand to comfort her.

'Have faith, Sonia,' I said to her. 'We'll get out of this, you'll see.'

'Shut up!' came the voice of Albert Smith. 'No talking or I'll gag you as well.'

I kept quiet but my mind was desperately trying to get in contact with Michu. If anyone can help now, it is Michu.

Nothing more was said and after some time all that could be heard was the purr of the engine. I guessed that we had left the town behind and were heading for a place where we were not so well known. I began to feel very cut off from help and I my only consolation was that Sonia was with me in the car and Michu was with me in spirit.

Suddenly the car increased speed and there were mutterings from the front. Albert Smith was cursing something and then he said, 'faster Wally, that car behind is tailing us.' We reached a bend in the road. The sound of screeching tyres made me tense my whole body and I was thrown sideways against Sonia. But the driver, whoever he was, succeeded in gaining control of the car and it accelerated again. The squeal of brakes announced another bend. I was thrown forward onto the back of the seat in front and then against the door as the car took the right-hander, tyres screeching again. Not being able to see and only having a vague idea of what was happening was agony. I wondered what Sonia was feeling.

At that moment there was a sound of splintering glass and instantaneously a zinging sound as a bullet passed my ear by a very uncomfortable margin. I had seen enough films in which bullets fly around to know the sounds they make. I instinctively ducked my head and shouted to Sonia to do the same. I crouched as far down as I could, waiting for the next bullet to enter the back of my head. It never came.

All of a sudden there was a loud bang and the car swerved violently to the left and then to the right as the driver tried to control it. I guessed that those following had put a bullet into one of the rear tyres. I was rigid with fear. More curses came from the front. The car slowed to the sound of the remains of the tyre flapping madly and the smell of burning rubber attacked my nostrils. Then I was thrown into the air, hitting my head against the roof as the car left the road and leapt and dipped over rough ground. I heard Sonia cry out. Finally, after lurching and veering madly, the car came to rest and the engine died. The smell of burning rubber lingered in the air. There was the sound of doors opening and I could hear Albert Smith's panic-stricken voice telling Wally to run. Their voices quickly faded away and for a few moments all was quiet. I sat still, amazed that I was still alive. I called to Sonia but there was no answer. I feared she was hurt badly.

'Are you guys okay?' came a voice from the open passenger door.

I was too shocked to speak.

'Okay, let's get that blind off.'

The door beside me opened and I felt a pair of hands on the back of my neck and suddenly I could see again. Momentarily I was blinded by the light. I glanced quickly at the man beside me without taking in anything and then I turned the other way to see if Sonia was alright. She was lying still.

'Sonia!' I cried out. 'Sonia! Can you hear me?' There was no answer. At that moment I thought she was dead.

Another man appeared on the other side of the car and opened Sonia's door. He checked her pulse, removed her blindfold and lifted an eyelid. 'She's out cold but she'll be okay. It's probably just mild concussion,' he said.

I felt a knot in my throat. If Sonia dies I'll never forgive myself, I thought. I was the one who got her involved in my troubles.

I looked around me. After leaving the road, the car must have travelled a long way across a stretch of grass and through some thick bushes, stopping short of a line of trees. The road was hidden from view. The car that our captors had used, a BMW, was parked fifty metres behind, well screened from the road by bushes. There was a neat hole in the back window of our car where the bullet had passed through. A large jagged hole in the front windscreen showed where they had knocked out the shattered glass for the driver to see ahead.

The man who had taken off my blindfold went round the back of the car and the two men began a conversation, standing some few metres on the other side of the car. It was then I realised that they were Americans although I could not understand much of what they were saying. They were dressed in jeans, shirts and jackets. They were both medium height, one was dark haired and thin, the other was lighter and thickset.

I set about trying to work out why they had kidnapped us. It had to have something to do with the story in the newspaper but what in particular could they want from me. Were they journalists from The New York Times or Herald Tribune? Were they scientists interested in the secret of travel to Mars? Were they NASA men out to steal information, or were they CIA or FBI agents? To me they hardly looked like any of these, more like Texan ranchers straight from the prairie. They were certainly not stereotypes from Hollywood suspense films. One thing for sure was that they were serious. You don't go around shooting through the back windows of cars just for fun! And Albert Smith knew that too: he didn't hang around to ask them who they were and what did they want.

After a few minutes they turned towards the car. They light haired man took hold of Sonia and carried her, still unconscious, towards the BMW. The dark haired man motioned to me to get out of the car and follow him. Instead of putting Sonia into the car, the dark haired man placed her on the grass and untied her wrists. He slapped her face in an attempt to revive her. She moved slightly and was still. The wire that bound my wrists was removed and I was told to sit on the grass. I moved my hands and massaged them together to restore the circulation. One wrist was bleeding due to the violent movement of the car as it had bounded across the grass and through the bushes.

'Your name is Steadman, right?' said the thin man.

I nodded.

'And the girl is the daughter of the reporter who started this whole thing, right?'

I nodded again.

'Tell me Steadman, is the story in the newspaper true?'

'No. Why do you want to know?'

'I'm asking the questions, okay? He said impatiently.

I said nothing. I was beginning to dislike the man. He's as cold as a fish, I thought. The other man sat quietly on the grass, not appearing to take much notice of what his partner was saying. He absent mindedly picked a long stem of grass, which he put in his mouth and twirled it round. He then got to his feet and told his companion that was going to check out the road, to make sure they were alone. He walked off, still twirling the grass with his lips. The thin, dark man continued.

'Since you want to know why I want to know, I'll tell you, not that it'll be of much consequence. We work for the US Government, CIA.'

He paused and looked coldly at me with dark eyes. So they are CIA agents after all! Of all the possibilities, this was the most frightening. Fear began to spread through my body as I watched his expressionless face. My next thought was he could be Italian, why I should think of something so irrelevant I didn't know.

'What do you want from me?' I said and immediately I regretted having asked another question. He looked daggers at me.

'No more questions!' A pause and then, 'As a matter of fact, I want nothing from you.'

I was surprised at this. They practically killed us all but they didn't want anything.

'Smith is convinced the whole story is true, otherwise he would not have gone ahead and published it. We also believe it. You went to Mars, God knows how but you did. You brought back an outfit made of some yarn from another planet, not Mars maybe but some other planet somewhere out there. You have a Martian dame, who you write to. It's true, isn't it?'

'It's not true: it's just a game,' I repeated.

He grunted and then went on in his slow drawl.

'NASA has sent many unmanned spacecraft to Mars, some landed and some just took pictures. None of these has confirmed life exists on Mars. At least that is the official line. Unofficially we know for sure that there is life out there some place. How do we know? Because aliens have landed here in our own backyard! Maybe you remember reading about it. The military had to be called out to deal with them. They were taken to be analysed. We learned a lot from that. Officially nothing of the sort happened. Those who saw the bodies of the aliens being taken away were labeled as crazy and they were ridiculed. But the Government knew it was true. We never figured out where they came from. Their spaceship was examined, submitted to many tests and then demolished. The whole thing had to be hushed up, see? The President himself made the decision to exterminate them. We couldn't have the whole nation in fear of invasion, could we?'

I couldn't understand why he was telling me these things, if they were meant to be kept from the people, but I was to learn why soon enough.

'If there is life on Mars, we are going to find it sooner or later. Of course it will be kept strictly secret. Ordinary folk will never know, that is until the Government decides it's okay. For now, our job is to make sure the news of your little escapade don't get no further.'

'I swear I'll not tell a soul,' I said.

'Too right you won't!'

The way he said it sent a shiver running up my spine and the hairs on the back of my neck stand up.

'The girl, fortunately for her, will not feel a thing. She won't know anything about it. For you, Steadman, I'll try to make it as painless as possible.'

I was unable to speak. My throat knotted up and a cold sweat broke out on my forehead. There was nothing to say or to ask: his message was as clear as day. I thought of my parents and my friends. I thought of Sonia there on the grass and I thought of Michu. Michu, where are you? I need you now! Michu! I closed my eyes and prayed to God for an end to this nightmare. Michu, Michu, can you hear me? Michu!

The thin, dark man opened his jacket and put his hand inside, drawing out a hand gun, which was fitted with a silencer. He opened the breach, looked inside and then clicked it shut.

'Harry, the blind,' he called to his partner, who had just returned from his walk, announcing that there was nobody around and had sat down again, still twisting the grass stem around in his mouth. The thin man went on speaking slowly.

'The blind, Harry! We don't want him to see what's happening. We *are* human beings.'

Harry got up and came towards me with the handkerchief that Albert Smith had put on me earlier.

'Let me go! I won't breathe a word to anyone, I promise,' I pleaded.

'Sorry fella, It has to be this way.' He didn't sound a bit sorry. 'Your little secret must not go any further. You will die and your secret will die with you.'

'Michu is on her way here!' I yelled.

'Your Michu will have to get here pretty damn quick.' He grunted. 'Harry, put on the blind!'

I struggled for a while but was I only delaying the inevitable? I stopped struggling and allowed him to fix the blindfold. He then roughly retied my hands behind my back. I winced with the pain in my wrists. Harry stepped away from me. I waited with beating heart for the thud that was to put an early end to my life. The seconds ticked by. Is this man going to do it, I asked myself. What kind of human being is he, keeping me in suspense like this?

Suddenly a voice came from behind the thin man.

'Drop the gun! Now!'

CHAPTER THIRTY-SIX
FROM THE FIRE INTO THE FURNACE

My first thought on hearing the voice was that Michu had arranged for our rescue in the nick of time. But who was the owner of the voice? Not someone I knew. Inside my blindfold I was confused, relieved at the thought of delivery from the jaws of death and at the same time frightened by the sound of the strange voice. There was no time for more thoughts because a series of thuds and whizzing of bullets filled the air, then the sound of scuffling, muffled cries and heavy breathing burst out around me. I was powerless with my hands tied. I sat, trembling with fear, not knowing what was going to happen the next second. Another muffled shot sounded and immediately there was a cry and something almost crushed my legs beneath its weight. Then I heard more voices giving orders. It was pandemonium. I tried to move my legs but they were jammed underneath what I realised must be the body of a man. Then there was silence and the silence was more nerve-wracking than the noise. The smell of tobacco smoke caught my nostrils.

After what seemed like eternity, the weight was lifted from my legs and then I could feel hands untying the blindfold and then my hands. As soon as my eyes adjusted to the brightness of the day, this was the scene before me. Three men stood on the grass three metres in front of me. One held a gun in his hand, the other was smoking a cigarette, drawing the smoke deeply into his lungs. At his feet lay the inert body of the thin American The man who had untied me was kneeling beside the body that had fallen on my legs. Sonia lay in the same place as I had last seen her but with relief I saw that her blue eyes were open and she was looking around her vaguely. The man holding the gun was middle aged, tall and slim, with large angular features, steely, blue eyes and receding, blond hair. The other man was shorter but also slim, with light hair and a square face in which sat a pair of blue-grey eyes. The third man was small and dark and he wore dark glasses.

The man with the gun spoke to the other two in a language I didn't understand but I thought could be Russian. Immediately they set about preparing to leave. They sat the bodies of the two Americans in the front seats of their own BMW. Sonia and I were pushed into the back seat of a white Peugeot 605, which was standing some thirty metres away, behind thick bushes. The small man with dark glasses got in beside Sonia. The blond haired man climbed in behind the steering wheel and the engine burst into life. At the same time he was barking orders to the other man, who hurried to the boot of the car and removed something. I could not see what he was doing but after about three minutes he reappeared, leaping over the rough grass. As he slid into the passenger seat the car jerked into motion and began bouncing wildly over the ground.

As we neared the road the car slowed, then with a screech of tyres we hit the tarmac and accelerated away. At that moment there was a muffled explosion and turning my head and looking out of the rear window I saw a plume of flame and smoke rising into the air. The BMW was on fire. Before long nothing would be left to tell the tale but the burnt out shell of a car.

I looked sideways at Sonia. She turned to face me with a vacant look in her eyes. I hoped it was only a case of mild amnesia. I reached for her hand and held it tightly.

Who were these men, our new captors? If the Americans had been serious, these people, whoever they were, took their jobs just as seriously. What could they want with me? If they had the intention of disposing of us, they would have done it there and then and added us to the flames. No, they were interested in more than our silence. They must believe I have something of great value to them. They had not tied us up or covered our eyes like the others had done. I looked at each one in turn. Not one had addressed us since taking us over. How strange these people are, I thought.

There were few cars on the road. I surveyed the landscape around me. The little road wound through sparsely populated, hilly country. On either side lay sloping fields interspersed with patches of woodland. An occasional stone farmhouse nestled in the folds and sheep grazed in the fields. We passed through the odd sleepy village, mostly deserted in the heat of the August afternoon. I read the names but they didn't ring any bells. I had not the faintest idea where we were.

We travelled in silence. I held onto Sonia's hand and from time to time I turned to look at her. At least she knew who I was.

After about an hour's journey, the car turned left into another minor road, which led to more open, hilly country. A little later the road came to the crest of a hill and I saw the plain spread out below. We descended the hill and followed the road, which had now become straight. Another ten minutes passed and we came to what looked like a disused airfield on the right hand side of the road. The car slowed and then turned right, into an overgrown drive until we came up to a set of rusty metal gates, overgrown with climbing plants. A man in denims opened the gate in time for the car to pass through without slowing down. I looked at the man beside Sonia enquiringly but he offered no help to my questioning look. Ahead were a series of old buildings, beside which stood a small but sleek jet plane. The engines were whining as we approached.

Where are we going, I wondered, certain now that our captors were taking us out of the country? Which country could we be going to? East? Yes, there was no doubt in my mind.

As soon as we were aboard the plane it taxied out onto the rough runway. I felt myself being forced back in my seat as the plane accelerated, bouncing over the rough surface. Then the nose lifted into the air as the jet took off, climbing steeply into the blue sky.

The cabin was fitted with comfortable bench seats, arranged into two compartments, each with two sets of seats facing one another. Between the seats were low, bare tables. Sonia and I sat opposite each other and the three men sat on the other side of the plane. They lounged in a relaxed manner and chatted in what I now believed to be Russian. Still no-one spoke to us. They were in no hurry to let us know who they were or what they wanted with us.

The sun slid down the Western sky as the jet headed eastwards, carrying us further and further from home. What was going on there, back in my home town? Ben and Tim would have started to worry when I didn't turn up for lunch in town and would have gone to the library and then my house in the afternoon to check if I was there. That would have set my mother off and she would have rung Dad to tell him. Mrs. Rogers would have been concerned when 'the old lady' didn't report for work and more worried when Ben and Tim came enquiring if we had been there. By now, Dad would already have reported our disappearance to the police. How long would it be before the blazing BMW and the wrecked car were discovered in the bushes? Not long, judging by the size of the pall of smoke rising into the sky. A full-scale search was probably on country-wide. With those thoughts, I slipped into an uneasy sleep, exhausted by the traumatic events of the day.

CHAPTER THIRTY-SEVEN
IVAN'S DREAM

I awoke as the plane hit the runway. It bounced twice and then settled into a steady run, reducing speed slowly. I looked out of the window and saw that it was dark. Sonia was sleeping opposite me.

As soon as the plane came to a halt, the doors were opened and Sonia and I were shepherded down the steps into a waiting car, which sped away into the darkness. Only a minute later, the car came to a halt and we were led into a building near the airstrip. A door opened and we entered a square room, bare save for a desk and four upright chairs. A single bare bulb glared from the ceiling, instinctively causing my eyes to narrow. It was then that I was spoken to for the first time.

'Sit down in that chair,' said the blue-eyed, blond-haired man, turning to me. 'And you there,' he said to Sonia. He left the room, leaving only the short man, who stood up against the wall on one leg, with the other crossed over it, toe to the floor. He wore baggy dirty grey trousers and a thick, brown and yellow checked, long-sleeved shirt. Like that we waited for what seemed like ages. I turned to the man and told him that Sonia was not well and should be allowed to go to bed. He stared at me but didn't answer.

At last another man entered the room and behind him a woman. They pulled up chairs to the table and sat down facing Sonia and me. For a long time they didn't speak. The man was intently studying some papers that he had picked out of a folder on the desk. He was about forty, with a large, wrinkled and pitted face, wide mouth and grey eyes. His hair was fair and thin. He wore a blue-grey polo neck sweater. At last he put down the sheaf of papers, removed his glasses and stared at me. He gave me the faintest hint of a smile.

'I hope you had a comfortable journey,' he said in a thick accent, having difficulty with the word 'comfortable.'

'But my friend is not well and she needs to go to bed,' I repeated. 'And I am very tired.'

He turned and spoke to the woman, addressing her as Svetlana. She was tall, slim and good-looking. Immediately she got up and, taking Sonia by the arm, she led her out of the room.

'She will be taken care of,' said the man, scratching the side of his face.

I smiled a weak thank you and waited for him to speak again.

'My name is Ivan,' he said, 'and you are Bill.'

I said nothing. He must know a lot about me already, I thought.

'I know you are tired but we have some talking to do before you can sleep. It is good if we talk soon, then we can both sleep.'

I knew what he meant. He wanted information and he was not going to let me sleep until he got it. He cleared his throat and scratched the side of his face again before continuing.

'You are in Russia, my friend. You are here as a guest of the Russian Government. You will be treated well…….. that is………….if you agree to cooperate.'

Again I knew the meaning of his words. Fear gripped me again. I sent a plea for help into the night sky for Michu to intervene.

'We have time, so relax. I am a patient man. But even *my* patience has a limit. Do not exceed that limit, whatever you do.' He looked at me with his cold grey eyes and then went on in his halting English.

'You are familiar with Russian history, I hope? It was a question.

I nodded. I had learnt about the hundreds of years of Tsarist domination and the coming of the Bolshevik revolution in 1917, followed by more than thirty years of Stalin's dictatorship and the final collapse of communism.

'Under communism, the Soviet Union was ahead of the world in technology. The year 1961 was a great year for our country, the year cosmonaut Gagarin was the first man in space.' Ivan sighed. 'The Americans got to the moon first, I know, but we were having some small problems. After 1990, when the Soviet Union broke up into many small states, Russia was weakened and the United States of America,' he almost spat out the words, 'went far ahead. Russia will again be strong.' Ivan spoke with conviction, his eyes blazing with patriotism.

'My friend, Russia will soon again be great, under the powerful leadership of the P.M. Putin. America has had its day. In the future our rival for world leadership will be China. But Russia will take its rightful place on the world stage, not to dominate but to lead. We want to live in peace with our neighbours. War is no good for us or the world.

'I am just a small cog in the wheel of progress. And you are also a cog but smaller still. But take out one cog and the machine stops, No?'

I looked at Ivan's pitted face and his fair bushy eyebrows. He put on his glasses again and took up a sheet of paper, reading through it quietly. He scratched the side of his face as he read. I wondered when this nightmare was going to end. To Ivan I was to be a cog in the machine of Russian leadership of the world. I didn't like the role he had cast for me. Finally he put down the sheet of paper, removed his glasses and spoke again.

'I have seen that you are a brilliant student and will one day become a scientist and help to save the planet,' he said, looking intently at me. 'Russia needs brains like yours and Russia rewards those who contribute to its greatness.'

I wondered how he knew about that and then I remembered I had mentioned it in my e-mail to Michu.

At that moment, Svetlana entered the room and spoke briefly to Ivan, before going out again.

'Sonia has been checked by our doctor. You will be pleased to know that she is recovering from her concussion well. She is eating now and then we will see that she sleeps until the morning.'

I was thankful for the information. At least these people have some compassion, I thought. Don't let him lull you into a false sense of security, Bill, my more cautious side was telling me. Ivan continued.

'We know a lot about you, my young friend,' he said. 'Ever since your local newspaper printed the story on Sunday, our agents have been watching you and finding out all about you.'

I thought about the two men who had followed me in the park but that was before the story came out. My mind saw the two men who had come into the library, when was it? Yesterday morning! It was hardly possible, so much had happened since then.

'The disguises were good, my friend, but they would have to be much better than that to fool our secret service. Yes, you are right, the men who watched you in the library were Russian agents.' He smiled a thin smile.

I remembered the time I had sneezed in the library and the false moustache had flown off and landed on the floor. I had thought they had not noticed but trained agents don't miss a thing but at the same time they don't let on.

'MI5 was also interested in your story. But they don't have a James Bond these days.' He smiled at his own sense of humour. 'The early bird catches the maggot, I think you say.'

I didn't correct him.

'Let us get back to business, shall we?' he said. 'You have a story to tell, a story that is very important to us. The Americans are short-sighted. They would have exterminated you, like they exterminated those aliens that time. If only they had sent an ambassador with them back to their planet, just think what they could have learnt. But the American Government is paranoid about anything that might disturb their world. We need the information you have and you are going to give it to us. Our Government believes you have the key to the door to Russia regaining her rightful place as the leader in space exploration.'

'How are you sure I will cooperate?' I asked bravely.

'We have our ways of making people cooperate, my friend. In your case I think those ways will not be necessary.' His voice carried a good deal of confidence.

'How do you know I wouldn't rather die?'

'For two reasons, first, because there are many ways of dying, some quickly and painlessly and the other kind of death.'

'And the second reason?'

'Secondly, because you also need help.'

'What help is that?'

'Your Martian friends are in trouble, I think. Your letter to your Martian friend was very revealing. You will expand on it, of course, because there are some gaps. You see, you help us and we help you. I scratch your stomach and you scratch mine.'

I couldn't resist a smile at his attempts at English proverbs. Then I thought of my meeting with Zeris and his warnings of a Zogg invasion of Mars. I wondered then if Russia really could help Similaria combat their enemies. Again my cautious side warned me not to weaken in the face of either threats or promises of help. Let the Martians decide that, not you Bill.

He took up another sheet of paper and put on his glasses to read it. When he had finished he leant back in his chair and closed his eyes. I waited for him to continue. I felt myself nodding off in my chair. A nudge on my shoulder brought me back to my senses. It was the man who had been leaning on the wall behind me. He was there to ensure I didn't sleep. At last Ivan opened his eyes and sat forward in his chair.

'Russia will again be strong,' he said with passion. 'America is following a dangerous path and they will become weak. They have a leader who allows his personal feelings to cloud his reason. As a world leader that is very dangerous. America is involved in Iraq and Afghanistan, like they got involved in Vietnam. Who will be next, Syria? Or Iran? Russia learnt her lesson in Afghanistan and will not repeat the mistake. Russia must follow the path of scientific development. We lost fifteen years but we will catch up.' Ivan was passionate in his love for his country, that was clear.

'Shall we start? The best place to start is at the beginning, so start at the beginning, my friend.'

I moved in my chair. Shall I tell him or not, I thought, torn between the wish to sleep and the fear of betraying my friends. I had no idea if Ivan would honour his promise to help Similaria.

'I need time to think about it,' I said.

He looked at me and I guessed he also had a decision to make. After some time he must have concluded that there was the possibility that I may willingly tell him my story and decided to allow me to sleep.

'Very well my friend,' he said. 'Tomorrow we will continue.'

I was led out of the room by the other man who had stood against the wall. He led me into another room nearby. On one side stood a bed and on the other side by the wall, a basin and water jug stood on a wooden table. Another door next to the table led to a small toilet.

The man, who said his name was Alexei, went out and locked the door behind him. I pulled aside the brown curtains that covered the window and saw that it was heavily barred. Beyond the bars lay the blackness of the night.

After visiting the toilet I lay on the bed, exhausted, and was soon lost in a deep sleep.

CHAPTER THIRTY-EIGHT
INTERROGATION

When I woke up the sun was already above the horizon, shining dimly through the curtains. I parted one side and looked out over a patch of waste ground to a tall wire fence. Further off I could see a distant range of mountains, blue-grey in the early morning light. There were only a few stunted trees. Where can I be, I wondered. What is today going to bring? Why is Michu so quiet?

I went to the toilet and then rinsed my face and hands in the bowl on the table. At that moment, the key turned in the lock and Alexei entered. He was wearing the same clothes as the night before. His face was expressionless. He beckoned to me to follow him. He led me down a corridor into the dining room, where there were three rectangular tables surrounded by hard, wooden chairs. I was surprised to see Sonia sitting at one of the tables with Svetlana. Sonia looked up as I entered the room and she smiled. She looked happy to see me but she was clearly troubled. Her face was pale and her red hair was roughly combed back. I attempted to cross over to where she was sitting but Alexei pulled me to one side and sat me on a chair at another table, so that I was facing away from Sonia. I desperately wanted to talk to her and I was angry at him for not letting me.

After a breakfast of coarse bread and tea, Alexei took me back to the room where Ivan had been the night before. I sat on the same chair and waited. Soon Ivan came into the room and sat opposite me. He was wearing a blue jacket over a cream shirt.

'Good morning, I hope you had a good sleep. Now you are fresh we can get on with the business.' He shifted a few papers around the table and then, arms on the desk in front of him, he looked straight at me.

'Begin!'

I looked down at my hands and wondered what I should say.

'Please begin,' repeated Ivan, softly but with a sharp edge to his voice.

I glanced quickly at his face and then away. I still said nothing.

'I let you sleep: that was kind of me. Now it is your turn.'

I was in turmoil inside. How much longer before he loses his patience?

'I am a patient man, but I am human,' he said quietly.

'There's nothing to tell. It was all a game.' I knew he wouldn't believe me.

'That will not do, my friend. So who is the girl in the picture?'

I looked at his face. How did he know I had a photo of Michu?

'Do not deny the picture! It will not do!' he said louder. He flipped through the file on his desk and drew out a sheet, which he turned to face me.

I was stunned. I looked blankly at the photo of Michu that he held up in front of me.

'Our people searched your room, my friend. They found nothing much of interest except......' he tapped the top of the paper with one finger, '......this picture hanging on your wall. Who is she? Where does she come from?

'She's just a friend,' I said.

'Your Martian friend; the one you wrote the letter to.'

'No! That letter was made up. It's from my head.'

'Michu, Michu is her name, is it not?'

'Michu only exists in my imagination,' I said hopelessly.

'No, Michu is as real as you and me.

I said nothing.

'How did the reporter get your letter?' he asked.

'He searched my room.'

'And he found the strange clothes that belonged to Michu, I suppose,' Ivan said.

I nodded.

'So they *did* belong to Michu?' He smiled.

I realised I had said the wrong thing. I had admitted the tunic was Michu's.

'And he had the material analysed. He is sharp, that one! Of course, if you look at the picture carefully you can see that she is wearing the same clothes. That settles the matter, does it not, my friend?'

I knew there was no point in denying it.

'Our people are at this moment searching for the clothes. We will have them analysed by our own methods.'

I wondered if they had found Albert Smith and what they would do to him to get him to hand over the tunic to them.

'You said in your letter to your Martian girl that you hoped you would soon go back to Mars.'

I remembered saying so. I waited for the next question.

'How did you travel to Mars?'

'I made a spaceship in the shed in the back garden.'

The put his head back and laughed. 'You did what?'

'I made a spaceship in the shed.'

'And you went to Mars in it?'

'It's true.'

'And what kind of fuel did you use?'

'Petrol.'

'Petrol! Come on my friend! Pull the other arm!' Ivan suddenly became serious. He leant forward with his arms folded on the table and put his face as close to mine as he could.

'You are wasting my time,' he said through clenched teeth.

I squirmed in my chair but said nothing.

'We have other methods, as I told you last night,' he said threateningly.

'I won't tell you anything!' I cried, the anger building up in me. 'You can do what you like to me!'

'I intend to do nothing to you.' He paused. 'But your young friend, you do not want anything to happen to her, do you?'

I stared at him in horror. 'Don't touch Sonia!' I cried.

'Then talk!' he said angrily.

'I made a promise not to tell,' I said.

'Tch. Never make promises you cannot keep, my friend.'

'Stop calling me 'my friend!' I'm no friend of yours!' I was really angry now.

'Okay,' he said, stretching out his hands with the palms facing me.

He went to the door and called out for Svetlana. He stepped outside and I could hear him talking to her in Russian. Then he came back inside, closed the door and sat down again.

'I have asked for the girl to be brought here. Maybe your tongue will become loose.'

We waited a few moments and then Svetlana appeared at the door, pushing Sonia before her. They crossed to the other side of the table and sat on hard chairs. I looked at Sonia and ventured a smile through my inner rage. She looked anxiously around her. I was sorry that I had involved her in all this.

Ivan turned to face Sonia. 'Tell your friend what Svetlana has told you.'

Sonia spoke hesitantly. 'Bill, they will not let us eat or sleep until you tell them.'

'Sonia, I'm sorry I got you into this mess.'

'I am glad I am here with you,' she said softly and a tear ran down her cheek.

'Enough!' shouted Ivan, thumping the table with his fist. I jumped and Sonia let out a sharp cry.

'Start talking,' he said, controlling himself.

'If I tell you, will you let us go?' I asked.

'I make no promises I may not keep. We shall see.'

'At least you must release Sonia,' I said hopefully.

'We shall see,' was all he would say.

I began to tell him of my trip to Mars, omitting the part about my homemade spaceship. He was not ready to listen to miracles. I tried to give away as little as possible but when there was something he didn't understand he would stop me and put a question to me. I managed to avoid describing the bubble and its capabilities but he was clearly mystified how the Martians breathed and coped with the iciness and thinness of the Martian atmosphere. I told him I didn't know about those things. He listened intently as I told him how the people had been exiled from Earth all those thousands of years ago. He appeared to believe everything I said. When I came to tell him about their fear of invasion from another planet he shook his head and made tutting sounds.

'The Zoggs you call them?'

'Yes, they say that the Zoggs are not really interested in Mars but actually in the Earth. They say that Mars has nothing to offer them that they don't have already, but Earth would be a planet worth conquering.'

Ivan looked momentarily worried. 'Mmm. Mars may not be their final prize but what a good jumping-off place. If they control Mars they can launch attacks on the Earth from there. That must be their plan, and a very good one too.' Ivan paused and his face became animated. 'Russia must become strong to prepare for this threat. You must find out more about these Zoggs! That is your task,' Ivan banged the table with the flat of his hand.

He was quiet for a moment. I looked again at Sonia, who was following every word Ivan said.

'Where to find the technology?' he pondered.

I thought of Hermann. Should I reveal his name? Would I be sentencing him to permanent slavery in the hands of the Russians? I had a strange feeling that Russia might just help Similaria fight the Zoggs, with Hermann's brilliant ideas in exchange for the technology to lead the world. I would be taking a huge risk, which, if it backfired, may cause endless misery to millions, on Earth and on Mars. This may be the most difficult decision I will ever have to make, I said to myself. But it might just work. I looked across at Sonia, as if to find inspiration in her face. Yes, it might work. I suddenly had a question for Ivan.

'What is your Government's attitude to the environment? Do you believe our world is in danger of being poisoned, you know, by how we are abusing it?

He didn't answer the question immediately, but searched my face for a few moments before lifting his eyes to the ceiling and saying, 'The Soviet Union under communism totally neglected the environment. Pollution was allowed to go on unchecked.' He levelled his eyes at me again. 'We believe it is vital to preserve the environment for our own survival. Does that answer your question?' He smiled at me.

I nodded. 'Martians want to help us with that,' I told him.

'How will they do that?'

I hesitated to tell him that there were Martians on Earth at that moment. 'I'm not sure,' I said vaguely, 'but I believe they mean what they say.'

'Your Martians are *very* interested in the Earth.'

'Being neighbours, they believe it is in their interest as well as ours,' I said.

'That is very sensible of them and they are right. In a hundred years or so Mars and Earth will be like London and Moscow are today.'

I decided to mention Hermann.

'Have you heard of a scientist called Hermann?' I said.

'Hermann who?' he asked.

I felt foolish. I didn't even know his second name or where he was from.

'The name sounds German,' he said.

He got up from his chair and went to the door. 'Alexei!'

Alexei appeared and Ivan spoke to him briefly. Ivan returned to his seat and Alexei went off down the corridor.

'We will find out just now who this Hermann is,' said Ivan. 'How do you know this scientist?'

'He came to my house,' I replied.

'Why did he do that?' His eyes narrowed and he looked at me suspiciously.

'He said he read the newspaper and wanted to meet me.'

'Because you had been to Mars? And what did he tell you?'

'Nothing much. But he had a theory he was working on, something to do with electromagnetism.'

'Interesting!' said Ivan, scratching his face. 'And you believe in him?'

'It's hard to say, but my Martian friends do.'

A young woman brought in a tray with mugs of steaming tea and set it down on the table. Ivan said something to her in Russian and she gave each one of us a mug. We sat sipping the hot tea for five minutes.

There were footsteps in the corridor and the door opened. It was Alexei with a piece of paper in his hand. He handed it to Ivan and stood waiting to be dismissed. Ivan read the paper, smiling occasionally to himself. Then he translated it for us.

'Hermann Winke, German born scientist, born 13th July 1939, now living in the UK, naturalised British citizen, known for his research into electromagnetism. Works on the edge of the scientific, you say 'establishment?' he looked at me and I nodded. '….establishment. His ideas are not taken seriously by the main body of scientists. There is more but well, so what is he like?''

'He's very odd but I'd like to believe he's a brilliant man,' I said.

'And how would you know?' he asked.

I had to admit I didn't. I just had a crazy idea Hermann could have hit on something.

'Anyway, if my superiors agree, we will have the man brought in and our scientists can question him. We will assume that he is genuine. We have nothing to lose.'

'How will you find him?' I asked.

He laughed. 'The Russian Secret Service will not take long. We have a lot of experience with these things.'

Ivan turned to Alexei and gave him some orders. Alexei went out and I heard his footsteps fade away down the corridor.

'I have something else to say,' I told him.

'Go on.'

'The Martians are very concerned that comets, asteroids might one day destroy or damage the Earth. They say we must start watching all bodies that cross the Earth's path and develop the technology to deflect them before they strike.'

Ivan leaned forward in his chair. 'You may not know this but we have started a programme to do just that, to put a satellite into orbit with a powerful telescope to do nothing but catalogue all Earth-crossing asteroids. What we do not have and what we are a long way from having, is the technology to deal with them.' He scratched his face.

'What about Hermann's theories of attraction and repulsion?' I ventured.

'Perhaps, but let the technical people look into that one,' he said. 'Now I think we have had a good morning. I am beginning to see a great future for our motherland, not forgetting, of course all the people on Earth and let us not forget Mars. I begin to see how valuable Mars is to us. Let us not forget them.'

Ivan smiled and put out his hand.

'Especially Mars,' I said.

CHAPTER THIRTY-NINE
IN THE SHADE OF A TREE

Sonia and I were allowed to sit together at the table for lunch. Svetlana sat on the next table and left us alone. We ate a large bowl of mixed vegetables and potatoes with the same course bread we had eaten for breakfast. We felt that our captors wanted to treat us well in return for my cooperation. We talked little. Sonia was almost her normal self again and I was confident that she would be completely well in a day or two.

When we had finished eating, I asked Svetlana if we could take a walk. She went to ask and came back to tell us it was possible, as long as we didn't go outside the compound. Someone would go with us to make sure we didn't get lost. Run away, I thought more likely.

The August sun was hot and the earth under our feet baked hard. We walked for some time and then found a tree where there was at least a bit of shade. We sat on tufts of course grass. Svetlana sat under another tree, far enough away for her not to hear our conversation.

'Sonia?' I said.

She looked at me with her big blue eyes and waited for me to continue.

'They are looking for your father, the Russians I mean.'

'What for?'

'They want the tunic, to do tests for themselves.'

She looked worried. 'I hope my father isn't stubborn and decides to refuse them. You know how fixed he is on getting rich on your story. What might they do to him?'

'Who knows,' I said. 'He might strike a deal with them, you know, the tunic in exchange for money.'

'My father is not interested in peanuts, Bill.'

'Right, and the Russians are not going to give much. They have other methods.'

Sonia shivered. 'I know my father has turned bad but he is still my father and I love him.'

'Of course. I will talk to Ivan. I will ask him to let you go and you can find your father and put some sense into him.'

'Do you think they will agree?'

'It's me they want. There's nothing you can give them. I am sure they will agree.'

We got up and walked back towards the main building. Ivan was standing outside, smoking a cigarette in the hot afternoon sun. We walked up to him and we shook hands.

'Can Sonia go home?' I asked.

He drew heavily on the cigarette and blew a thin column of smoke into the air. As he considered the question the gentle breeze took away the smoke. He took another draw and another puff of smoke followed the first.

'It is not possible now,' he said at last.

'Why?' I asked, frowning at him.

'Because, because she will talk, that is why,' he said a little testily. 'We are not yet ready for that.' He flicked the cigarette end onto the ground and turned to go into the building.

I decided not to pursue the question any more. I didn't want to make him angry. Sonia and I walked off again and found the same tree as before. We sat for a few minutes in silence. Then I turned to Sonia and looked into her eyes.

'Sonia, let's run away!' I whispered excitedly.

She smiled. "Do you know where we are Bill?'

'Well, not exactly,' I admitted.

'Not exactly?' she laughed. 'We have *no* idea at all. We could be anywhere between Moscow and Vladivostok!'

'I think we are not far from the border with, what would it be, Poland?'

'That's your guess,' said Sonia.

'The plane journey was not *that* long, maybe four hours.' Then I remembered I had slept. I was so tired I might have slept for at least four hours.'

'You're right Sonia, it's hard to know for sure where we are, but don't let's give up!'

'I'm not ready to trudge for a thousand miles across Europe Bill! Don't you think it would be easy for them to see we are foreigners?'

'Shhh! Keep your voice down. Svetlana might hear.'

She continued more quietly. 'With no money and we don't speak Russian, or Polish and we don't know how friendly the people are.'

'We could try to cross into Poland and find the nearest British Consulate.' I was still convinced it was a good idea. 'Just think what an adventure it would be, Sonia!'

'But Bill, you have made friends with that Russian and he says they will help your Martian friends fight the Zoggs.

'Ivan may be genuine, but who can tell. They may have their own agenda and we are just the pawns.'

'That's true, but if we escape and even if we make it home, which is doubtful, they will only come looking for you again and who knows what they might do next time.'

'Yes,' I agreed. 'But Sonia, there's another thing that bothers me.'

'What's that?'

'Should we not try to warn the British authorities? I mean, I am British and here I am, giving secrets to a foreign power. They shoot people for that, you know.'

'What secrets? What you have told him the British don't know anything about. They are not British secrets: they are Martian.'

'True Sonia, but somehow I feel like a traitor, helping the Russians to become powerful.'

'Bill, it's not the time to be patriotic. You have to see yourself as a citizen of the world. Your mission is to help save the world, not just your own country.'

I looked at her in admiration. I had no idea she was so wise.

'Sonia, you are talking sense. I feel humbled in your presence.'

'Bill, don't joke!'

'But I'm not: I'm deadly serious, Sonia. You are *so* wise.'

She blushed and looked down at her hands. I stretched out my hand and placed it on top of hers, squeezing them slightly. She looked up at me and smiled.

'Sonia, having you here is a great source of strength to me, do you know that?'

'I'm happy to be of service, kind sir,' she said.

We sat for a few more minutes and then continued our walk in silence, in an atmosphere of peace. Sonia's right, I thought. It is time to widen our vision. We must not work for the good of one country only but for the good of humanity. We are citizens of the world. No, not just citizens of the world, we are citizens of the Solar System: not even that, we are citizens of the Universe!

CHAPTER FORTY
A VODKA TOAST

The next morning I woke before dawn. Getting out of bed, I peered out from between the curtains at the Russian darkness. A dim light on the wall of the building threw a pale glow on the immediate vicinity but further off nothing was visible. I climbed back into bed, shivering in the chill of the early morning, and sat with my back to the wall. I concentrated my mind on Michu, hoping to make contact with her. I was anxious to know whether she had any idea of my present situation and if she did, what the Similarians thought of my divulging the secrets. I had made a promise to Zeris not to mention my trip to Mars to anyone on Earth and I had not kept my promise. Would they understand?

I had the vision of Michu in my mind and I started to talk to her. I told her my hopes for some help from Earth to meet the threat for the Zoggs. I said I was sorry for giving them away but that it may turn out to be in the interests of all of us. Then I sat still and tried to empty my mind of thoughts, so that I would be able to hear her response. Suddenly I heard her voice as clear as day. She told me the Almighty was guiding me and she wished me strength, courage and wisdom to make the right choices. And that was all. But that was all I needed to hear.

I got out of bed and went to the bathroom, turning on the shower. A thin stream of cold water fell on my hands. I stripped off and stood under the meagre shower, gasping as the cold jets struck my back. After drying myself on the small, thin towel that I found on a peg on the back of the door, I dressed and sat back on the bed and waited for the door to be unlocked.

The time passed and dawn turned into day, but no-one came. I was beginning to feel very hungry. Finally, Alexei unlocked the door and I followed him to the dining room. Sonia was not there. I ate in silence. Alexei sat opposite me and said nothing. I came to the conclusion that he knew no

English at all. I finished eating but Sonia had still not appeared and I was getting anxious about her.

'Sonia,' I said to Alexei, 'where's Sonia?'

He just shrugged his shoulders and said nothing.

Just as I was beginning to think something had happened to her, she walked in the door of the dining room, accompanied by Svetlana.

'I overslept,' she said, smiling.

'I am relieved to see you,' I told her.

I sat while she ate her breakfast in silence. When she had finished, I asked Svetlana what we would be doing today. She said in her broken English that Ivan had been called away to Moscow and wouldn't be back before the evening. We would have the day free. I asked her if she could give us something to read. At first she said they only had things to read in Russian but then she said she would see. She was gone for about thirty minutes but when she returned she was carrying a sheaf of papers, which she handed to me. I looked at the page on top. My heart started beating fast as I began to read, wide-eyed. It was the day's news from the website of one of the English daily newspapers. Sonia could see my expression and wanted to know what I was reading so I read it out to her.

'Police were this afternoon still searching for the two lost teenagers who went missing from their homes on Wednesday. William Steadman, aged 16 and Sonia Smith, 18, were last seen on Wednesday morning. A police spokesman said that the search was being conducted country-wide and that all airports were being watched.

'William Steadman is the boy at the centre of the storm about the visit of extraterrestrials from Mars. His companion, Sonia Smith, is the daughter of the newspaper reporter who first uncovered the earth-shattering story on Sunday last week. There is anxiety that the two may have been kidnapped by Martian invaders. The world's infrared astronomical satellites are being used to search the sky for fleeing spacecraft.

'So far, according to the police, the main lead is the discovery of two abandoned cars in the Welsh borders. One car, a Toyota Corolla, has been traced and is known to belong to Albert Smith, the father of Sonia Smith, the missing girl. The other car, which was found nearby, was completely gutted by fire. It was thought to be the remains of a BMW saloon. Forensic experts are working at the scene, hoping to unearth more clues.

'At a press conference this afternoon, the Senior Superintendent in charge of the investigation said that detectives had found bullets at the scene and these were being studied. He said that police had also found traces of blood on the back seat of the Toyota and police pathologists were trying to identify them.

'The Senior Superintendent said that the search for Albert Smith had not produced any results so far and that police stations throughout the country had been told to look out for him, as he was wanted for questioning in connection with the case. A photograph had been shown on all television stations in the country.

'He said that as soon as more information became available, the press would be informed. Meanwhile he appealed to the public to remain calm.'

There were other news items and I read them out to Sonia. One item quoted friends of mine as telling the press, ''Bill had agreed to meet us for lunch in town and when he didn't show up we became worried. Bill is normally so reliable,' said Timothy Armstrong. His brother Benjamin said he feared their friend had been abducted by secret service agents.'

There were a few items of sports news but nothing about the England vs. India Test Match. Of course it had finished four days before and I realised that, with all the excitement, I had missed the last day and didn't know how it had ended.

Sonia and I spent the day together, sitting in the shade of trees or sitting in the dining room. Svetlana was never far away but she never imposed herself and we felt free to talk. She supplied us with tea and drinks whenever we asked.

Sonia and I discussed the situation we had found ourselves in and argued about how the drama would unfold and where destiny would lead us. I told her the mess was mine and I had to solve it myself but she insisted that the Almighty had thrown us together and she was as much part of the drama as I was. But we both agreed on one thing: whatever we could do for the good of Earth and Mars we would do it.

Towards evening, while we were sitting on a fallen tree stump, enjoying the sunset, we heard a plane approaching from the direction of the sun. We first saw it as it skimmed over a few trees and lowered itself onto the airstrip, with a roar as the air brakes were applied. It came to a halt in front of the main building and we saw the door opened and Ivan descend the steps. With him were a man and a woman. They walked slowly towards the building, Ivan explaining something to them. They disappeared inside.

After supper that evening, while we were still sitting in the dining room, Svetlana came to tell us Ivan wanted to talk to us. She led us to the room which we had come to refer to as the 'interview room.'

'I would like to introduce you to two of Russia's top scientists, Dr, George Kaznikov and Professor Emilia Resichenko. I have already told them who you are. Please sit down.'

We all sat round the table, the guests on padded chairs especially brought in for them, with Ivan in his usual place behind. Ivan continued.

'These are some of the fortunate ones who have the power to make Russia strong again,' he said, stretching out his left hand as if to sweep his guests onto pedestals in the sky and at the same time, bowing his head almost to the table in reverence. 'Dr. Kaznikov specialises in the development of hydrogen fuel and our lady professor is a nuclear physicist.'

Dr. Kaznikov bowed his head in acknowledgement. He was a large man, with reddish complexion, thick, black hair and bushy eyebrows. He wore heavy glasses and carried a pipe in his hand. He was dressed in a blue blazer and grey trousers. Professor Resichenko was a heavy woman, with greying hair and large, pale features. She wore round glasses and a tweed suit.

'Mr. Steadman is a young man who has travelled widely,' said Ivan with a smile. 'Although he is still not out of school he has knowledge and has contacts with those who can help us in our journey to greatness. That is why he is here.'

I looked across at Sonia and our eyes met. I wondered if she was thinking along the same lines as I was, that Ivan had one goal in mind and that was Russia's greatness. What of his words of the day before about not forgetting the world and Mars?

Ivan addressed me. 'This morning I attended a top level meeting chaired by the Russian leader himself. I briefed him on our little meeting and he appointed me the coordinator of what will be called The Mars Programme. He has instructed me to work closely with you and your Martian friends and to use our top scientific brains to evaluate your friend Hermann's theories. I now have the hope that they will give us the technology to smash the Zogg threat to our planet and at the same time to give us the weapon to destroy Earth-bound comets and asteroids before they destroy us.'

'Long live the Russian people,' cried Professor Resichenko. 'One day Russia will be hailed as the saviour of the world.'

'Ivan Ivanovich is right, we are the fortunate ones who will make it happen,' said Dr. Kaznikov.

'And Mars?' I said. 'Let us not forget Mars!'

'Of course,' said Ivan brusquely. 'We will soon be in the race again.'

'The race for what?' I asked.

'The Americans were the first to land on the Moon. *We* will be first on Mars!'

'Hold on, I was the first on Mars and I am not Russian!' I said indignantly.

'That does not count,' said Ivan dismissively, waving my objection away with his hand.

I got the feeling he was being carried away by his own sense of importance. I also began to fear he would forget about the wellbeing of the Similarians and my involvement in the story, once he had got the information he needed. I looked at Sonia. She seemed to share my concern because her forehead was creased into a deep frown.

'We shall meet tomorrow,' declared Ivan. 'We have had a long day. In the morning I should have the first report on Hermann Winke and we shall decide if he is to be brought here. I think if he sees you here he will have more confidence to share his knowledge with us, without the need for other methods.' He looked pointedly at me. 'What do you think?'

'Do you have Hermann already?'

Ivan nodded and smiled. 'So what do you think?'

'It is my guess that Hermann will work with anyone who will listen to him and not send him off to the Lunatic Asylum and who will give him the material support to develop his theory.' That was my honest opinion.

'I was hoping you would say that. I believe it too,' said Ivan. 'Now to rest, but before we do, let us drink a toast to the glory of the new Russia.'

He went over to a cupboard at the back of the room and came back with a tray of tiny glasses and a decanter of clear liquid. I had read about the huge amounts of vodka drunk in Russia and I was surprised I had not seen the bottle on the table before then.

Five glasses were filled with the clear spirit and handed to each one. Sonia screwed up her face and was about to refuse the glass offered to her but I shook my head at her. It was better to play the part and drink with them than to appear rude by not supporting the toast. The three Russians held up their glasses, spoke some words in Russian and downed the liquid in one swift gulp.

I sipped my vodka gingerly at first and then I emptied the rest into my mouth. It trickled slowly down my throat and I could feel it burning all the way to my stomach. I was not used to spirits and I barely managed to avoid coughing and spluttering. Sonia had a harder time with hers. She sipped the fiery liquid slowly, never losing the contorted face, much to the amusement of the others. Halfway through the ordeal she gave up and held the half full glass in her hands until it was taken away from her.

Three glasses were knocked back by each of the Russians before the meeting was declared closed. After saying goodnight, we were escorted back to our rooms, Sonia by Svetlana and I by Alexei.

The vodka ensured a swift fall into deep sleep.

CHAPTER FORTY-ONE
A PLAN MISFIRES

The next morning, after a cold night, the sun shone fiercely as it had done each day of our stay in Russia. We had breakfast in the dining room, the sun pouring in at the windows. We sat and waited for a call from Ivan, but no call came. Ivan and his two guests were locked in discussion in the interview room and Svetlana didn't know how long the meeting would go on. I began to get frustrated at the lack of action and I said so to Sonia.

'Sonia, I'm getting impatient. By now, if the blood stains in the car, you know, from my cut wrists, if they have been identified as mine, my parents will be frantic with worry, thinking the worst has happened. We are sitting here as prisoners in the middle of Russia, God knows where, with no hope of escape and no idea how long they will keep us locked up here. We have to do something.'

'Bill, relax. What are you going to do, pinch the jet and fly off into the sunset?'

'If only I could fly a plane Sonia!'

'Well, be realistic, you can't. They can't keep us here forever.'

'Still, I wish I could get a message home,' I said, pulling on my left ear.

'And how are you going to do that?'

'I don't know. But wait! If only I could get on the computer, I could send an e-mail to Ben and Tim.'

'The keyboard will be in Russian,' said Sonia.

'I expect so, but if only I could change the language to English.'

'Do you think they will be on e-mail, Bill? They are a secret service after all.'

'I know but they will have some kind of security system and they probably write coded messages.'

'It's risky Bill. Suppose you were caught? It might ruin everything.'

'Why? Ivan knows he can't do much without me. He has no idea how to contact my Martian friends and I never told him about the bubble. He still isn't sure exactly how I went to Mars.'

'Yes, that's very odd, isn't it? She paused for a few moments. 'But those scientists will want to know and they are switched on enough not to be fobbed off with vague stories. They are going to want to know everything. And if you try to lie, they will know. Don't forget the other methods Ivan threatened you with.'

'I had forgotten about that,' I admitted.

'Anytime now Ivan could call us into the interview room and the questions would start to come your way.'

'Sonia, I *have* to get a message out. I will *have* to take the risk.'

'Do you know where the computer is?'

'No but it must be in one of the offices near the interview room. Your room is on the other side, Sonia. How many doors do you pass on your way to your room?'

'Let's see, I think only three, and one is a bathroom. That leaves two.'

'Good,' I said. 'I have a plan. Tell Svetlana you want to go to your room. On the way, ask her casually what is in those rooms. Then we meet back here and decide on the next phase of the plan.'

She then turned to Svetlana, who was sitting at the far end of the dining room, talking to one of the kitchen staff. Svetlana came over and Sonia told her she needed to get something from her room. They went out and left me sitting there, going over in my mind how I was going to manage with a Russian keyboard. It was not long before they returned. Sonia looked pleased. She sat down and acted as if she had nothing to tell me, but I knew she was dying to tell me something. About two minutes went by and then she leaned forward and spoke in her best conspiratorial voice.

'It's the first door after the interview room. She told me that's where all the computer equipment is kept.'

'Sonia, you're a gem!' I said, full of admiration. "I wonder if it is kept locked.'

'Sure to be.'

'Let us not rush into it,' I said slowly. 'We'll bide our time until the right moment comes, then we'll strike.'

'You sound just like the Zogg invaders,' said Sonia laughing, her bright eyes shining.

We left the dining room, Svetlana trailing us faithfully. How to get away from her, I thought, as we went out into the bright sunshine.

Lunchtime came and still there was no call from Ivan. We ate a good lunch and felt sleepy. Suddenly the thought of sleeping gave me a brilliant idea.

'Sonia, listen, I have a cool plan. After your lunch do you feel sleepy?'

'A bit, why?'

'With a couple of headache pills you would sleep in the shade of our tree like a log, wouldn't you?'

'I would, but why do I need tablets? I don't have a headache.'

'You could fain one though, we both could.'

'Okay, I don't get it, Bill.'

'Go and ask Svetlana for some. Tell her we both have bad headaches.'

She went off to the end of the dining room where Svetlana was sitting and spoke to her. Svetlana got up and went into the kitchen, returning with four tablets, which she gave to Sonia.

'Don't take them,' I said, as soon as Svetlana was out of earshot.

'Why not? What's your game, Bill?' she said with a puzzled expression.

'Because they are not for us, Idiot!'

'Who are they for then?' Then her face lit up. 'I get it now. It's a brilliant idea! Now who's the genius?

'It's nothing really,' I said with mock modesty. 'Just pretend to take them,' I said, pouring water from a jug into Sonia's glass and offering it to her.

We both pretended to swallow the tablets. Then, shielded by Sonia's body from Svetlana's view, I put the four tablets into a paper serviette and crushed them with a knife. I screwed up the serviette and held it my hand.

It was normal for tea to be made after lunch. We could either take it in the dining room or outside.

'When the girl comes out of the kitchen with the tray,' I told Sonia, 'ask Svetlana if you can help her carry it outside. As soon as you get outside the door into the sunlight I will slip the powder into her tea.'

The plan worked even better than I had thought it would. Svetlana took her cup of tea with the bowl of sugar and sat under a tree while we found our usual spot in the shade. We drank our tea and watched Svetlana closely out of the corners of our eyes. We saw her put three teaspoons of sugar into the tea and stir it well. She drank it slowly, showing no signs of anything wrong with it. It is just as well she likes her tea sweet, I thought. Sure enough, after ten minutes, her head dropped onto her chest and she fell into a deep sleep. We waited for a further ten minutes.

'It's now or never,' I said to Sonia. 'You stay here, so that if she wakes up you can make up some story about my having gone for a sleep.'

'Good luck Bill. Take care,' she said, taking my hand and putting it to her lips.

I went across to Svetlana and untied the bunch of keys from her belt, hoping that one of them would unlock the computer room. I sauntered as casually as I could into the building and down the corridor to the first door past the interview room. I tried the door: it was locked. With trembling hands, I fumbled though the keys until I found some that I thought would fit. I tried one, then another and yet another. There was only one more. I looked left and right down the corridor, expecting someone to appear at any moment. I tried the last key with shaking hands and a beating heart.

It fitted! The door swung open and I slipped quickly inside, closing the door quietly behind me. There on the table stood a desktop computer and it was switched on. It's my lucky day, I thought. I stared at the keyboard. It could have been Greek, Japanese, Chinese or Arabic for all I could understand it. The fact that it was Russian didn't help me one bit.

My eyes scanned the shelves of the room. There on a shelf about two and a half metres above the floor I spied another keyboard. I reached for it and brought it down, being careful not to disturb anything else that would create a noise. The thing had a layer of dust on it and I blew strongly to remove it. I felt a sneeze coming on. My Dad always complained that my sneezes were enough to wake the dead. If they could wake the dead, they could certainly attract the attention of Ivan in the room next door. I put down the keyboard and buried my face in my shirt to muffle the sound. I waited with bated breath for the sound of footsteps but none came.

The keyboard was in English! I couldn't believe my luck. I quickly unplugged the Russian one and replaced it with the one from the shelf. Then I clicked on what looked to me like the e-mail icon and waited for the inbox to appear. So far so good! Although I didn't understand the commands I recognised the symbols. I clicked on the new message symbol and when the page opened I typed out the following message, as quickly as I could, with my heart thumping in my ribs like a pneumatic drill.

'This is Bill. We are in the hands of the Secret Service somewhere in Russia. We are well and they are good to us. Try to get a message to Priam or Michu. Whatever you do, don't tell anyone except Mum and Dad where we are. You understand why. See you soon. By the way, who won the Test Match? For God's sake don't reply! From Russia with love.'

I entered Ben's e-mail address and clicked the 'send' symbol. I waited, trembling and sweating for what seemed like a century. Would it go or was there some codeword I needed to enter? Then I saw that it had gone. I deleted it from the 'sent items.'

I had succeeded! I sat back in the chair and heaved a big sigh of relief.

At that moment the door opened and in walked Alexei.

CHAPTER FORTY-TWO
IN SOLITARY

'Who gave you permission to use the computer?' yelled Ivan. 'And who have you been communicating with? You have taken advantage of our hospitality! You have abused the freedom we have given you here! This is the payment we get for our kindness!'

Ivan strode up and down the interview room, waving his arms in the air and shouting in my face each time he passed my chair. I sat still, nursing my aching head and bruised face.

I relived the last ten minutes of my life a dozen times while sitting there in the chair, cowering under the fiery blast of Ivan's anger. I had been so relieved, having despatched the e-mail to Ben that I forgot the danger I was in. When I heard the door open I had swung round violently to find Alexei in the doorway. He had advanced towards me and had given me a blow to the head that brought stars to my eyes and made me cry out in pain. Then I had been frog-marched into Ivan's room. I had stood there while Alexei shouted abuse at me in Russian and Ivan had grown more and more red in the face.

Now I nursed my aching head, wishing Ivan would calm down and go back to his chair behind the desk. I expected another blow every time he passed my chair. Alexei stood by the door and he looked to me as though he might suddenly attack me.

'You will tell me who you have sent a message to!' he shouted again.

'I can explain,' I said with difficulty.

'Explain!'

'It is hard when you are walking up and down,' I said.

'Impudent boy!'

I didn't reply, but I kept my eye on Alexei, ready to dodge if he were to move an inch. He stood stock still with his arms folded across his chest. After another few lengths of the room Ivan sat down in his chair.

'Explain then!' he bawled.

'I was worried about my parents. I wanted to get a message to them to tell them I am well and not badly treated.'

'When they read the message they will know it comes from Russia,' said Ivan more calmly. 'Fortunately they will not know where.'

'I sent the message to my friend. My parents don't have e-mail.'

'Do you know what this might lead to?'

'I didn't think about it,' I said honestly.

'You didn't think?' roared Ivan, rising from his chair and leaning across the desk towards me.

'I didn't mean any harm.'

'You want Russia to help your Martians but you are not going to get it like that!' he shouted.

I decided it was better to be humble and apologise, even though he needed me even more than I needed him.

'I'm sorry,' I said.

Ivan sat back in his chair and spoke to Alexei, who went out of the door.

'I will have to move you from here,' said Ivan.

'And Sonia?' I asked anxiously.

'You will not see the girl for some time and maybe you will not see her again.'

My stomach turned over and with the throbbing of my head I felt like vomiting.

'I need to go to the bathroom,' I said.

Ivan got up and called for Alexei, who came in and escorted me to the bathroom. I sat there until I felt better and then was taken back to the interview room. Ivan busied himself with some papers until another man, whom I had not met before entered the room. Ivan spoke some words to him and the man gesticulated to me to get up and follow him. As I left the room I looked at Ivan but he didn't even look up from his papers.

Outside the main door stood a four-wheel-drive vehicle, with a driver already at the wheel. Before loading me into the car, the man fixed a blindfold around my eyes and handcuffed my hands behind my back. I was made to lie in the back seat. The car drove off, bouncing along the rough track. I could feel the heat of the late afternoon sun beating through the side window of the car.

I lay there thinking of Sonia and wondering what they were going to do with her. Would they also move her? When would I see her again? I realised then how much Sonia meant to me. How long had I known her? Barely two weeks, I decided. But it was so hard to keep track of time.

I tried to concentrate on Michu, Michu, the only one who could help me out of this desperate situation. Why does she not communicate with me? But she probably is all the time: it is just that I am too dumb to hear her.

The journey by car over those rough roads seemed interminable. My head ached and the bruise on my face throbbed angrily. The metal handcuffs cut into my already sore wrists. The driver said nothing but he whistled softly what sounded like a Russian folk tune. I had seen the film Dr. Zhivago and had always thought Russian music so appealing. I could never listen to Russian music again without remembering that journey.

At last the car slowed down and stopped. I heard the sound of voices as the driver's door creaked and then clunked shut. Then the door beside me opened and I was roughly pulled out and made to march across some stony ground. A metal door squeaked in front of me and I was pushed inside. The blindfold was removed but the handcuffs were not. I looked round to see a man disappearing through the door, which groaned and then shut with a clang. There was the sound of a heavy key being turned in the lock. I was alone.

I surveyed the interior of the room. It was a round hut made entirely of metal, with one small window in the roof and a concrete floor. On one side stood a wooden bed with a small table beside it. The bed had a single course blanket and a dirty pillow. There was no other furniture in the room.

Apart from its sparseness the most unpleasant aspect of the room was the heat. Because of its metal construction it had become like an oven in the blazing sun, even though the sun was now low on the horizon. I sat on the bed and I could have cried. How long am I going to be kept here, I wondered. Ivan had not said a word and I had not had a chance to say anything to Sonia. Where was she and what could she be thinking? The situation was desperate and the future seemed bleak.

I lay down on my side on the hard bed, trying to find a comfortable position, hampered as I was by the handcuffs. I pushed aside the filthy pillow, which smelt vile. As I lay there, looking up at the tiny window, the daylight faded and night drew on. The temperature in the room dropped slowly but surely. Soon the room became dark, the only light coming from the dim square in the sloping roof. The room was becoming cool but I knew that by dawn I would be cold, with only a thin shirt and trousers and one blanket.

I called for Michu more intensely than I had ever done.

'Michu, why don't you hear me?'

CHAPTER FORTY-THREE
RESCUE

That night was the longest I had ever spent in my life. As the night wore on it became colder and colder. I lay on the bed and shivered under the thin blanket. From time to time I would get up from the bed and walk up and down the room to keep warm. Then I would return to the bed and try to sleep. Hunger gripped me but thirst was my worst enemy. I had had nothing to drink since the tea after lunch and I had lost a lot of body liquid during the dusty car journey. Sleep wouldn't come, no matter how much I tried to calm my mind. My head ached from dehydration and the blow from Alexei's fist.

At last, when I was beginning to think that the night would never end, the square above my head became lighter and I knew that dawn was on its way. Slowly the black of night turned to grey of early morning. I decided to try to see out of the window. I got up and shifted the small table, using my legs to push it along. It was not heavy. I positioned it underneath the window and with difficulty I clambered onto the table, getting to my feet and wobbling. One of the table legs was too short, which made it see-saw up and down. Stretching up on my toes I was able to see out. I could see nothing but grass as far as the eye could see. A wire fence crossed about two hundred metres away and that was all. Whatever buildings there were must be on the other side, I thought.

I slowly climbed down from the table. As I was about to put one foot on the ground, I lost my balance and fell over backwards onto the floor. The handcuffs cut deeply into my wrists and I felt a searing pain in my left shoulder. I lay on the floor in pain and regretted having had the crazy notion to look out of the window, which had revealed absolutely nothing.

I lay there for what seemed like hours. First, the sky turned blue and the hut filled with light. Then a shaft of sunlight touched the ceiling of the hut and slowly spread downwards as the sun moved higher in the sky. I continued to lie on the floor, the pain still strong but easier. Hunger gnored at my stomach and thirst caused my mouth to dry until it was like sandpaper. And there I lay.

I decided to try to return the table to its original position and get back onto the bed but when I moved the pain in my shoulder returned and made me cry out. I gave up. The oblong of sunlight passed slowly across the floor towards me and as it did so the temperature in the hut rose. The patch of sunlight reached my face and I glanced up, squinting in the glare. I moved to avoid the direct sunlight. It was hot in the hut now. My mouth was as dry as dust and my head throbbed with pain, so much so that I couldn't decide whether the pain in my shoulder was worse than the pain in my head.

The day wore on and it became hotter. The rectangle of sunlight became thinner as it advanced across the floor until it disappeared altogether. But the hut was still an oven and my pain continued to haunt me. I fell into a fitful sleep, lying there on the floor.

The next time I opened my eyes, it was evening and the sky through the skylight was purple. My body ached and I moved to find some relief, but my shoulder hurt so much I had to give up.

Night came and with it the cold. With no blanket and lying on the concrete floor, I felt the cold even more than the night before. No-one visited the hut to see me. I thought then that I would die there and later someone would come and find my body and they would take it and bury it under the rough sandy ground of the Russian steppe. With that thought I fell into a shallow sleep full of strange visions. Ivan was there, shouting at me and Alexei was standing over me with his arms crossed over his chest. Then he suddenly became Ben and he was telling me that England had lost the Test Match by eight wickets and Hermann had scored a century for Germany. Sonia was there in a bubble telling me I needed to do nothing because it was programmed in advance.

The next thing I remembered was having water poured into my mouth and then being picked up and carried outside. It was night and the air was cold. How many days and nights I had lain there on the floor of the hut I couldn't say. I no longer felt hungry, just weak and my body ached from head to toe.

'Don't worry Bill, we'll soon have you out of here,' said a voice, a strangely familiar voice.

'Careful!' I cried out in pain. 'My shoulder, I think it's dislocated.'

I opened my eyes but saw nothing. Another wretched dream, I thought. When is this nightmare going to end?

'The nightmare is finished Bill,' said the familiar voice.

I opened my eyes again but still saw nothing. I closed them and tried to sleep. It was hard to sleep when you are being carried and you have so much pain.

'Steady,' I said, 'the pain in my shoulder...'

'Sorry about the pain, Bill. It won't be long now.'

Suddenly it dawned on me that the people around me were not Russian. Then I knew who the voice belonged to, that familiar voice. She had read my thought about the never ending nightmare. But was it a dream? Surely it had to be!

'Michu?' I said quietly.

'Yes Bill. I'm here.'

'Is it really you, Michu?'

'None other, Bill' she said tenderly.

'And Sonia? Where is Sonia?'

'I am here Bill. You just sleep: you'll be fine.'

It was then that I passed out again, safe in the knowledge that I was in good hands.

THE END

EPILOGUE
A TASTE OF WHAT IS TO COME

Bill and Sonia's challenges are by no means over with their rescue by Michu from the heart of the Russian steppe. Bill's silent plea to his Martian friend has led to their being snatched from the clutches of the vengeful Ivan Ivanovich and whisked off by bubble to temporary safety on the Red Planet.

But no sooner do they reach the surface of Mars than the two friends find themselves at the centre of a battle for survival of the Martian people after millennia of peace. Zeris, the Chief Elder of Similaria has already warned Bill of the very real threat to their civilisation ... and that of the Earth too ... from the power-hungry Zoggs and their Martian allies, the Zeronerans, led by the cruel dictator, Zigismo.

And that is not all! If that challenge were not enough, a monster asteroid, dark and dreadful, is identified by the Russians and will almost certainly collide with the Earth several months in the future, spelling doom to all life on the planet Hermann Winke, the brilliant scientist with his incredible invention may be the only way to save our planet from annihilation. But the Russians may be the only ones able to provide the support to achieve that almost impossible goal. Which way will Ivan go....and how are the Martian people going to meet the threat to their existence?

There are plenty of surprises in store for the reader of *Operation Stargazer,* the second book in The Mars Series and no end of nail-biting suspense as the date on which the Zoggs are due to arrive and the giant asteroid, *Attila* hurtles ever closer to its fateful meeting with the Earth.

Lightning Source UK Ltd.
Milton Keynes UK

171944UK00001B/31/P